Diamonds
in the
Dust

Jean Debney

ISBN;9781980948049

Typeface set in Apple Baskerville

Prologue

Convergence

The sky was a gunmetal grey reflected in the tarmac and fractured pavement and, along with a fine persistent drizzle, gave this particular Monday morning the feeling of the beginning of a very long week ahead. It was not her first research visit to the jewellery quarter, but that day had started slowly; appointments not being kept, or changed, and what had been a full interview schedule had shrunk to one thirty-minute discussion much later in the afternoon. She had decided to take her camera around the quarter and try and capture some of the images and old grand buildings that illustrated the heart of this thriving Victorian industry. Unfortunately, the weather and the light were not forgiving to a keen amateur photographer, who had hoped for sunny blue skies.

She wandered along the length of Vyse Street away from the larger factories towards the terraced Victorian houses, many of which would have been small workshop enterprises in times gone by, now cleaned up and reinstated as residential places with shops and offices along the frontages. Most of these jewellery shops were interlopers – as she had learnt on a previous visit – small trading businesses that had moved in, taking advantage of the prime location and title of the area. Rather than buying from the local manufacturers and workshops, their owners were acquiring products from other parts of the world to sell at lower prices, so much so that many of the fine craftsmen and women could no longer compete. Every now and then, there would be the remnants of what used to be: an older more established shop with an air of permanence, and signage from times gone by. These windows held her interest far more than the others, as much of what was on display was

1

second-hand and antique, possessing character and craftsmanship, just like these fine old retail establishments.

As she browsed one window, a ring stood out from the many assembled pieces of gold and semi-precious antiquity. The colours attracted her attention – very unusual, very modern – a lime green and a deep purple, the fashion colours of that season. The aged quality of the stones and the yellow gold gave away its more distant heritage, the stones slightly marked, the gold not as bright a polish as modern gold might be. She checked her watch – it was eleven-thirty, she had plenty of time, and the drizzle had become a little more incessant. Now would be a good time to step inside just to look and admire.

The bell tinkled as she opened the door. The shop was very small in the interior and abandoned, the smell of beeswax and tobacco pervaded the air. She looked over her shoulder into the window to see the ring, and just as she did so an old gentleman entered from a backroom, smoking a pipe.

'Can I help you, dear?' He enquired in a soft non-demanding tone.

'Yes, could I look at that ring, please?'

She pointed into the depths of the display in the window.

'Ahh, a discerning eye I can see… it's a nice piece… from round these parts.'

Obligingly, the old gentleman reached into the window and brought out an old ring box and offered her the ring. She examined it critically; it was even more beautiful in the light of the shop than it had appeared through the window. It was a yellow gold band, not too thin, but not too heavy. The stones were mounted in a rose formation, the four large, almond-shaped, purple stones, interspersed with four smaller, similarly-shaped, green stones.

'It is amethyst and peridot, very popular in its day, it was probably a small commission for some local lady, maybe

2

part of a collection… it has the anchor and date mark, it is Birmingham, around 1860s.'

She looked inside for the now familiar assay mark of the anchor; she had discovered the significance of Matthew Boulton and his fight to secure an assay office for the town. When the victory was secured, Birmingham took the anchor and Sheffield the crown, with reference to the public house of the same name where those with vested interests from the two towns had met to discuss their plan of campaign to persuade the Select Committee. There was the anchor, and gold stamp and date, but there was another set of rougher stamps inside the ring. She could just make out the figure 'two', the letters 'Nov.' and part of a figure… 'eighteen', but the rest she could not see with the naked eye.

'What are these other marks?' she enquired quizzically.

'Let me look… sometimes the maker would put an individual engraving inside, or once their mark had been registered with the assay office, their makers stamp could be applied. Ah, yes, it looks like a date, I think it is twenty… twenty-one, could be twenty-seven, November, and the rest would be the year, eighteen sixty… err… I think that is three… yes, eighteen sixty-three!'

'Are you sure? That is amazing. That is a hundred years from my date of birth, especially if it is twenty-one; I was born on the twenty-first of November, nineteen sixty-three, not far from here actually… in Loveday Street. What a coincidence!'

'It certainly looks like it could be a twenty-one. Obviously this ring has chosen you, my dear… maybe you need to have it?'

'Well I didn't really come into to buy it…'

She looked at the tag, presuming something totally unaffordable. She was pleasantly surprised, the price was very moderate; to be expected of course, this was the quarter, where prices were the value of that which the local market would stand, and thus highly competitive. She mused, if an antique dealer from the Home Counties possessed this piece the price would be double, or even triple, the handwritten figure on the paper tag. It was certainly good value, very unusual and very modern.

'Is there any way of finding out more about this ring and who made it?'

'Unfortunately, no, there is no registered maker mark; it was probably a local jeweller working from his own bench. It was presented for assay though... they may hold a record, but millions of objects have passed through their hands. It is a bit like looking for a needle in a haystack.'

She fondled the smoothness of the gold, she felt connected, strangely, the date was too much to ignore, and impulsive madness grabbed her.

'I will have it!'

Half an hour later she was sitting in Warstone Cemetery, out of sight of the occasional walker that had braved the drizzle. She opened the old box and took the ring out, she had not even tried it on, it probably would not fit any finger, many of these period rings had been made for much finer fingers than hers. She tried it on the third finger of her right hand. But no, it was not going to go, but it would be a very nice pinky ring. She slipped it onto her little finger, holding her hand out, stretching her fingers out and upwards; it was a beautiful purchase, and it seemed to have found an owner.

As she mused about its provenance, she wondered who it might have been made for, and why was it stamped with that specific date? She would never know. All that was lost, like much history gone from living memory, but it did not matter; it was a fabulous artefact, of beautiful colours, and it was enough to know that it had a future that was not in a shop window, but on the hand of someone who appreciated its beauty and fine workmanship.

It was time to resume her research, to walk the streets and talk to people. The drizzle had subsided, and a watery sun was breaking through the dark sky, gilding the edges of the clouds. The sooner she got to work, the sooner it would be done. She grabbed her bag and her camera and walked off towards the street.

Chapter 1

The hearth and home

Streams of golden light cascaded through the mottled windowpane; the glass, old and smeared with decades of grime, rippled with the distortions of liquid history. The rays caught the delicately crafted piece that he lovingly clutched between his forefinger and thumb. He rotated it again and again, examining every mount and every join. He checked for imperfection and doubted in his own skill, yet all he could see was the perfect symmetry and balance; his insecurity led him to closer scrutiny. The amethysts blazed in perfect splendour as they basked in the sunlight, a purple and red fire lighting their inner hearts as if alive. The peridots like cats eyes, fixed his gaze. The gold glistened with the perfect polish; no scratches, scars or scabs... all was good. He verified the size once more and scrutinised the order; it was right, it had to be right. This piece was the most important jewel that he had yet made, and it mattered more than anything.

Just then, he checked his pocket watch; time had caught him out again. He had been so determined to finish that he had not noticed the hours disappear. The sun had mocked him in its evening glory; it was late, he had to go, he wanted to get home, he must get away and hurry; he did not want to be caught in the clamouring crowds. His mother was waiting – he had said he would be home before six o'clock, and it was now gone past seven.

He wrapped the ring in a cloth and concealed it in his leather skin with his tools and rolled all, before securing with the straps. Now he must rush! He grabbed his remaining things frantically, and leapt for the door, shutting it quickly and turning the great key in the lock. He descended the two flights of rickety stairs and out into the June evening. The sky was a deepening orange as the sun was beginning to sink over the buildings. All was a bustle in the square, as others busied themselves leaving their places of work, or sat near the church passing the evening in the glorious sunshine.

A familiar face caught his attention as he dashed across the square and a quiet acknowledgement, a grunted 'Evening,' passed between the two: caps jerked, heads nodded. As he entered Graham Street, he was eased by the lack of physical presence. The street was quiet apart from the few others who hurried along with an urgent need to get away, get by, quickly. He marched purposefully on, head down, clutching his rolled skin under his arm for security. His boots clicked on the cobbles from the steels that saved their soles from damage.

He made it to the end of the street not looking right or left. As he passed the monumental building that stood domineering and imposing, he could hear the rising clamour that was coming from within. Voices, many voices, of women and girls chattering and laughing, screeching and caterwauling, occasionally interspersed with octaves of much lower speech as the few men interjected their humour into the melee. He had made it, one two, one two more and he was in Legge Lane. He turned briefly to witness the surge as the tide of human life swarmed into the empty streets, tens, fifties, hundreds, the noise ever-rising. Don't look back, keep moving and then, one two, one two more; faster. The last hundred yards he was practically running as he scurried down Camden Street and into the court, slipping into the first corner doorway and avoiding the assembled females and offspring venting forth at one another over their washing.

The back kitchen was cold and smelt damp. There was little warmth in the range, no kettle boiling, nor the smells of scraps and scrag-ends – a welcome feast when there has been so little. The remains of yesterday's stew sat in a large pot on the table, waiting expectantly for attention. He opened the range and filled the still-glowing embers with wood ends and placed the pot on the hob. He knew that today had not been a good day, and his urgency led him into the back parlour.

That room, with no window and no air, was dark and musty, walls and ceiling blackened from the soot and tar of years of many fires in the grate. A few sticks of furniture and two makeshift curtains filled the emptiness, punctuated by chipped pieces of china and a few jumbled mementoes. A crucifix dominated the wall above the hearth, a crafted wooden cross, with a passive Christ in rapture towards his glory beautifully crafted in silver. Among, the ramshackle detritus of life, this piece seemed surreal and out of place: a devotion to God, who overlooked the poverty of living. The curtains crossing the room at ninety degrees to one another concealed two brass bedsteads – bedrooms of sorts. A small fireplace lay cold and unmanaged from its last use. Two wooden chairs sat either side of the hearth. Odours of rot and mould intermingled with sweet and sickly medications and vapours. A small paraffin lamp sat on the mantle, barely alight, and added to the mixture of putrefaction and decay. As his eyes adjusted from the bright sunlight of the evening, he surveyed the bundle of cloth and blankets that half sat, half lay on the chair in front of him.

He was gripped with sudden apprehension. He held his breath and moved cautiously towards the mantle and turned the lamp to illuminate the bundle. As he did so, it began to move and stir, rising upright before breaking into explosive coughing.

'Oh…' (more coughing)

'I… am… sor…' (more coughing)

'I must have… fallen asleep…'

He bent over her carefully.

'It's alright, Ma, I have put the stew on the range. Let me light the fire…'

He felt her withered hand which now reached up for him.

'You're cold Ma, you should have lit the fire.'

'I did not want to waste the wood and it has been warm today. I am sorry… I only sat down for a moment… and…' Her voiced trailed off in fatigue.

'It's alright, I told you, I am sorry that I am so late, I meant to come home hours ago, but I had to get it done.'

The scrawny face lit up and her smile beamed at him.

'Have you finished it then?'

'Yes, Ma, if Mr Jennings is pleased we will make a few shillings this week and I will get the doctor to you.'

'There is no need to waste the money on doctors, I will be right as rain in a day or so… let me look, I want to see.' Her eagerness showed in her face and upwardly held hands.

John unwrapped the skin, taking the felt bag carefully out and unwrapping the gold ring. His mother held it in the palm of her shaking hand and admired the fine work.

'Ooh, it is glorious, Johnny boy, truly glorious… what beautiful stones, amethysts and small peridots, truly beautiful… some fine lady will wear that soon and everyone will admire it and my fine son has made it.'

'I don't care who wears it, Ma, I just need to make a few shillings, maybe our luck will change and things will get better again and I can move you out of this hell, back to decent rooms.'

The old lady shifted slightly in the chair and offered a reassurance in her voice.

'Oh, Johnny, I know things will get better, they always do. We have been through much worse than this, we always come good. And it's not so bad here, there are many fine folk, and they all look after one another; we will get by. And my clever lad will make sure of that.'

'Ma, this place is not fit for man nor beast, and as soon as I can make things right we will move back to the square and have decent rooms again. I just need a few more jobs like this to make a bit clear, then we can make a good start again, and once the silver picks up we will be in the money. But first we get a doctor to you.'

His mother said nothing, she knew by the edge of his voice that it was best not to contradict, besides which she had neither the energy nor the strength to argue. She felt much older than her years, and this illness seemed to drag on and no matter what she had tried she could not seem to get on top of it. Perhaps he was right, after all he needed her; she had to keep going, she was all that he had left in the world. She nodded her head appreciatively.

'I will go and get something warm for you to eat and you just sit here. First let's get this fire going. It may be summer but these rooms are so cold and damp, we don't want you getting worse now do we?'

Again, she nodded, and accepted her son's care. He set to building the fire and before long the wood roared and crackled, the room was brighter, and she gazed at the furious heat. John got up to go to the kitchen; he looked back at his mother who was unaware of his attentions.

How she had aged, he thought, and now she seemed skin and bones, not that he had not seen that before. May Donnelly, once the prettiest colleen in the village, and the one that all the young men wanted to marry, now sat like some shrivelled old hag of seventy or more, yet she had only just passed her fifty-second year. Her hair still dark, now sprinkled with pepper and salt; her blue eyes had not lost their sapphire lustre. Her skin, drawn and pale, appeared to take on the glow of the fire. He watched her for a moment as she lost herself, basking in the growing illumination of the blaze with the warmth of her memories; memories from times long, long ago, before they all lost everything that mattered in their lives, even their dignity.

He made a turn into the kitchen, just in time, for in his haste to seek his mother he had left open the fire door to the range and smoke now filled the kitchen. He rushed for the backdoor to the yard, not wanting the noxious cloud, now wafting through, to worsen his mother's condition. His stomach retched at the stench as opened the door a crack and was met with the strong stink of the closets across the court mixed in with rotten fish and the reek of decaying flesh. The last few days had been very warm, and the whole warren of human existence of this place had made use of the less-than-adequate facilities as normal, but without the rain to wash away the vile stagnation of excrement and foulness. Others seemed unaffected; the two crows that he had witnessed earlier still cackled over their shabby washing lines, one with a small child nagging, attached to her skirts.

'Mummy I want a piecey… mummy I want a piecey.'

The small boy seemed to go completely unheeded, but still he persisted, and occasionally he was met with a swipe of an impatient hand as if a fly were being swatted away.

John looked over at the tap on the far wall, dripping and leaking, a scraggy dog trying to lick what it could in its desperate search for water. He looked back at the large pail in the kitchen, which he knew was all but empty. He dreaded the thought of negotiating the court to get water; it would be needed tonight and tomorrow and he knew his mother was unable to lift herself, never mind a heavy pail of water. He reluctantly stepped back from the open door and, with the pail firm in his hand, he put his head down he strode across the court, praying for invisibility with every step. He was not lucky this time.

'Awe, there 'ee goes,' one crow cackled to the other. "Ee can look at me drawers any time.' With that comment, both broke into raucous laughter. The other crow retorted:

'What? Look at yer drawers? Are yer sure yer got any on today?'

'That's enuf of yer sauce, missus! I let you know I washed 'em yesterday. But 'ee is tall and dark and I would tomorra, like.'

Both fell about, the small boy nearly lost in the voluminous swirls of his mother's skirts as they twisted with her contorted laughter. John felt the redness rise from his neck and throat. He wished he had not heard their dialogue, and was gripped by excruciating embarrassment. It was bad enough when the young factory girls jibed him, but old women with no shame? He felt unclean. He felt violated and longed to run. He got to the tap and tried to ignore the banter which had now focused upon him.

'Oi! Paddy! Yer too good to talk to us then...? See, 'ee thinks him better than us. It's all the same when the tally man comes.'

Just then, a softer voice spoke in low tones to him.

'Don't let them get you, lad, they don't mean no harm. You just bring a bit of cheer to their day, you and your looks.'

Standing next to him was a woman in her mid-forties, quite well built and with a kindly face; she was Mrs Morris, their neighbour. John acknowledged her with a smile.

'How's your mum? I have not seen 'er about for a day or so, but I've heard her coughin'... real bad, so it is. You'd best get a doctor to her, son. I will pop in with some beef tea and bread tomorrow and see for meself.'

John was grateful for the kind concern, his mother was right: they may be rough, but their hearts were in the right place. He hung his head and spoke with the anxiety that he kept contained most of the time.

'I know, Mrs Morris, I am worried, but I am getting the doctor to her, and I am trying to get her well, but she will insist on not keeping a fire. I am really worried that the damp and cold will enter her bones and she will never shake this off. Could you check that she has a fire when you pass by? I wouldn't ask but I have to wait for the factor tomorrow. I must, or I'll have no money for the doctor… it would help so much…'

He didn't have to implore, a smile beamed back at him with compassion.

'Course, dearie… it's no trouble. I like yer ma and I now she's 'ad it hard, like. I'll look out for her… don't you worry.'

John felt most reassured as he made his way back across the foul-smelling yard, slopping his over-full pail. Even the cackling crows seemed more palatable, and he even managed to acknowledge them with a smile, which caused the one with the clean draws to feign a swoon as he did. He passed the stinking midden of rubbish with its collection of scavenging cats and dogs and back into the relative safety of the kitchen. He leant on the door with his back to close it tight, to shut the mayhem and foulness out. The pot on the stove had now begun boiling, the warmth of the parlour had crept through to the kitchen, and his mother was humming a tune softly from where she still gazed at the glory in the hearth.

All was right with the world now, or at least felt like it could be. The only thing that he longed to do was turn around and open the door upon the view of the green hills again, to hear his da in the back shed chopping wood, and the voices of the others all about their chores. He wished it was all those years ago, he wished it was Cork, not the back streets of Birmingham, at least not these back streets of Birmingham.

Chapter 2

The violets that bloom

In another court, not far away from where John now stirred the scrappy stew, two girls passed a brief goodbye.

'I gotta go, Vi. Can't trust our Kitty these days, she has taken up with a rather shaky lot from the other side of town. I told her to get the food and start the tea for the young 'uns, but she took off after work, I doubt she's bothered. And I haven't seen me dad in weeks, since he got his wages for that building work he done. Thank God I nicked a few bob outta his jacket before he took off.'

'I don't know how you are managing, I find it hard with all the jobs I have to do at home – but at least me mum does her best, and my dad always helps when he's home, and there is only three of us since Bill left. You have six to look after!'

'Five with me dad gone, and no bruises on Suie. And flighty madam won't be seen tonight so it is not too bad, but it is a struggle trying to get them to go to school, especially the little lad. Really gotta go, see you tomorrow.' Fanny spun round on her heels and headed off into a neighbouring court with her hair unravelling as she pulled her pins out to give her some relief from the closeness of the evening.

Violet stood and lingered for a moment facing her court, gazing skyward at the disappearing evening sun, her thoughts following the rays of light over the eaves of the roofed terraces. As she stared into the evening sky, she tried to imagine what life might be like beyond the red brick blocks and red-tiled roofs that flanked her world. A world composed of foul-smelling stench, and people living cheek by jowl in overcrowded houses, where bugs climbed the walls all year and water ran down these same walls during winters; where nobody knew what being private meant, because privacy was a luxury out of reach to those who inhabited the back-to-back houses which created the rat-infested courts. She was lucky, she thought, at least her family was small, and she slept in her own bed. Many did not, in fact some shared shoes and clothes because there was not enough of anything to go around.

Her mum would be waiting with a meal that she had managed to transform out of very little, her dad, home after a hard day's work cleaning the streets, sitting with his boots off, his feet soaking in a pail, but at least it was just the three now. The last rays caught her flaming auburn hair and illuminated her deep blue eyes, before the sun dipped behind the roof and the cool shade swept over her. She strode purposefully forward into the court, leaving her 'life' behind.

Fanny caught young Teddy with a gang of other young boys tormenting a dying cat with a stick in the court. She grabbed him firmly by the ear. He let out a high-pitched shriek as she yanked him round and began to direct him towards their open door.

'What you doing, my lad? And look at the state of you, you've not been to school today have ya?'

Teddy, caught in the vice-like grip of his elder sister's strong fingers, had his head angled at forty-five degrees. His feet were bare, and from his toes to his tip he was covered in the black grime of a day being spent in activities other than learning.

'B-but... b-but...' he stuttered, as she let fly with words.

'What have I told ya? How are you ever goin' to learn if ya don't go?'

By now Teddy was scuttling behind Fanny, his head to one side and half-turned to the rear. She continued to hold his ear tightly as she marched for the front door which was slightly ajar. She had a purpose in mind: to give her younger brother a good talking to, as well as a good wash, but more awaited her behind the misleadingly calm frontage.

'Gawd blimey!' she exclaimed, as her eyes met the disaster that was the kitchen. 'What the 'ells been goin' on 'ere?'

In front of her stood two guilty looking waifs, one about twelve, though from her size she could have been easily mistaken for a younger eleven, and the other, an emaciated ten. Both girls were barefoot, wearing discoloured pinafores over their dresses that had seen better days; these garments, normally just grey with years of over-washing, were decorated with black handprints and soot marks. The girls' faces and hands were smudged with the blackness, as was most of the kitchen floor, which was also covered by layers of ash from the range that some attempt had been made to sweep away. The kitchen table held a collection of jumbled implements for peeling and scraping, and a few pots. A large pot sat on the range, bubbling with a strange smell of rotten warmth. The older of the two girls, sensing her elder sister's displeasure, attempted a speedy reply.

'Me and Mouse tried to put the tea on, but the fire was out, then we 'ad to clean out the range, and we got it on the floor, sorry... Then we 'ad to get some coal from the wharf, coz we 'ad no wood, but we 'ad nuffing to carry it in, so we used our pinnies. But we managed to find some spuds and carrots, so we peeled um and put um on. Sorry 'bout the mess, Fanny, but we really did try...'

Fanny stood dazed. In her shock she had still retained hold of Teddy's ear, who had given up struggling, but rather whimpered with the pain and humiliation of being stood in front of his sisters at a contorted angle. The littlest girl began to cry and tears streaked her coal-marked face, leaving white rivulets as the hot liquid made its trail down her cheeks. Fanny was suddenly overcome with remorse for being harsh at her younger siblings. She released Teddy, who collapsed to the floor rubbing his ear in relief.

'Oh, Mouse, don't cry, and I know that you and Suie were only trying to 'elp, we'll sort it all out, but where is Kitty?'

'We ain't seen Kitty, she dain't come home,' Suie replied forcefully. 'She dain't even bother to get us any food today, so we 'ad to do sumfink. We knew you'd be tired, but all we could get was old tatties an' carrots, they're a bit stinky and I dain't think they'll taste nice, but that was all we could find, at the back of 'em big houses in Vyse Street.'

'I'll swing for our Kitty when I get hold of 'er. I told 'er and told 'er to get the food and get home. I don't like the smell of that though... I will ask the neighbours for a bit of food to see us through till tomorra and we will get you all fed... But you are all goin' in the bath before we eat. Suie, get the tub from the yard... Mouse get that pot off, and you and Teddy carry it out and empty it on the midden, it is not even fit for the rats! I will get the brush and clean up the mess 'ere.'

Fanny set about clearing the well-meant disaster that her youngest charges had caused in their efforts to satiate their hunger and help her. She was exhausted and famished from her long day in the factory, but she was used to this role she had played for eight years since her mother had died; at least she had not got to battle her father as well. Proficiently, she cleared the table and laid it out with an assortment of chipped crockery and mismatched spoons and forks. The mess was cleaned quickly, after a fashion; the black soot still edged the quarry tiles which were set in the dirt floor. Large pots were set to boil and grimy water brought in from the washhouse, where the day's laundry had been conducted by those women in the court who had done their weekly wash. It was soapy and dirty but at least it was still warm, it could be topped up quickly with some fresh hot water from the range.

Soon, three miserable children were passed through the murky contents of the tin bath: Suie first, being the eldest, then Mouse, and finally Teddy, who complained bitterly about having to have a second bath in so many days. As Fanny scrubbed his battle-scarred red knees he let out a yelp.

'Well if you'd gone to school, like you were told, you wouldn't be filthy and I wouldn't be having to scrub ya!'

Teddy knew not to protest further, and passively accepted his fate.

The three were sitting at the table, old blankets draped over their shivering forms as their clothes soaked in the grimy tepid remnants of their undignified scrubbings. The weak broth begged from a neighbour and a hunk of stale bread was divided between them, a little saved back for two more mouths. Fanny sat at her place, and waited for the others to eat.

'You can't keep doin' this, Teddy, you have to go to school.'

The little boy snivelled as he slurped at his soup.

'But… but… I can't do it, I can't… I 'ate it.'

Suie piped up.

'Mr Cartwright says 'ee'll be round for ya with the tickler if you dain't come, 'ee thinks you're a bad boy.'

Teddy scowled and looked down into his now empty bowl, as Mouse chimed in.

'You'll be at the front with the dunces wiv a 'at on, yes you will!'

Teddy dissolved into sobs.

'But… bu-but… I can't do it… I can't… the numbers …the reading… it-it's… it's too hard!'

Fanny's voice softened as she regarded the snivelling, stuttering child and tried an attempt to reason with him.

'Now look, Teddy, you don't wanna be like Dad do ya…? You are never going to learn if you don't go… and it's really important to get some learning… you will never get anywhere without it—'

'Why? Didn't do me much bloody good!'

Fanny was interrupted as a large young man strode through the door from the court. He was tall in stature, dark and swarthy. He was too grown to be a child, but his face was still soft and boyish and not yet hardened from efforts to shave.

'Now, Tommy, you wouldn't have your apprenticeship unless you could read and do your numbers, you know that!'

'What, to sweep up? Oh, I see Kitty has let us down again... no food... that would be right. I work my backside off sweeping and clearing up shit all day and I come home to nothing. Bloody marvellous!'

'So do I, Tommy! But at least you haven't got to clear up all the mess 'ere. We are going to have to put our pennies together, I am getting short, and these young 'uns need some boots... and Dad's not—'

Tommy interrupted sharply.

'It is not my job to pay for them's shoes, it's our dad's. And where is 'ee? I know, drunk in some whorehouse somewhere! He'll come back when the money runs out and 'ee's got a hole in his belly!'

'Shush! Not in front of them, what have I told ya?'

Teddy looked at his elder brother quizzically.

'Tom... wha... wha... what's a haw 'ouse?'

Tom was silenced by the stern reproach of his sister, and acknowledged her fixed stare.

'I'm sorry... I'm just fed up with this all the time... why can't Kitty do as she's told? Why do we have to do it all? It's not fair on any of us.'

Fanny motioned to him to take his place at the table and ladled the remnants of the broth into his bowl.

'I have done it a lot longer than you, Tom... and who else will do it if we don't? At least you remember Mum; poor Mouse never 'ad a chance, she was too young... and

Teddy… well we're all 'ee's got left… we owe it to Mum to take care of him.'

Three younger siblings sat in embarrassed silence, while their elders dispatched the paltry offering quickly. Fanny rose, and collected the bowls, Suie was sent forth with the empty pail to the yard for another collection of water, as she and Mouse set to cleaning the dishes. Fanny wrung out the clothes in the black, grimy bathtub, while Tom and Teddy bailed out the now cold putrid-smelling liquid to the yard sewer.

A little later, the girls and Teddy were settled to bed in the one room upstairs, while Tom and Fanny sat in the back parlour; damp clothes hung on a raised rail over the range, steaming.

'Listen, Tom, I have a hard enough job trying to get Teddy to go to school, 'ee isn't finding it to his liking. I don't need you saying things like that, especially in front of him.'

'I know, Fan, but it is true. What good has learning done me? Yes, I am sweeping up at Vaughton's every day, and putting pitch on all the time, but that is all I do, and have done for a year!'

'You are on an apprenticeship, Tom. You couldn't have got it without your reading and writing, they wouldn't have taken you, you know that. It won't be forever, but you got to start at the bottom, then they'll move you up… you know they are going to train you up as a chaser, maybe an engraver. At least you'll be in the money one day. I mean, look at me… what hope do I have? Thousands of pens a day, an' all I do is punch patterns all bloody day. I mean, most girls my age have met a young man by now… may be thinking of marriage… of an home of their own… but I can't do it, can I? I have to take care of the others. There is only me an Vi left at the factory of our age, we are nearly old maids… the only reason she doesn't meet anyone is her mum and dad won't let 'er out anywhere.'

Tom sat in the chair staring at his boots, his arms crossed across his chest, refusing to look at his sister and accede to her reasoning. She continued.

'I mean, don't get me wrong, I am glad of the money, and many girls my age haven't the 'ope of the wages I get. And Mr Gillott's a good boss… and I am so used to being 'ere and lookin' after you all – I mean, I have 'ad to since I was twelve – but I am jus' saying your life really ain't that bad. At least you got prospects, and that's cos you did your learnin', and that's what Mum wanted for us all… remember?'

He nodded slightly, but his eyes remained downcast as he mumbled into his chest.

'It's just not right, we shouldn't have to do everything, with Dad an' all… an' Kitty not bothering.'

'Don't you worry about Kitty, I will deal with 'er when I see 'er. She is not goin' to keep getting away with not pulling her weight. We just have to make the best of it for now, it will come good eventually… and at least if Dad's not here there ain't no trouble for anyone. Let's just hope 'ee don't come back too soon. But you got to 'elp me keep the others at school, otherwise they ain't got no hope, you know that.'

He raised his head and looked into her eyes. Sensible Fanny, they would all have been lost without her, she was always so cool-headed. It did not matter what life threw at her, she just got on, as stoic and as optimistic as she always had been. He knew she was right, and he knew that he was the man of the house and she depended on him. Any thoughts he had of leaving and getting out would have to wait; Jenny would have to wait.

'Yeah, I know, we have to stick together. I will have a word with Teddy, see if I can get him to go to school and stay there!'

Two courts away, the evening was drawing in and the back parlour of another hovel had darkened considerably. Three adults sat in silence as the embers of their small warmth had begun to die. Father sat, his feet relieved after his soak. Mother had her darning mushroom with an old stocking that had long seen better days, carefully darning in the dimming light. Daughter leafed through an old school book, a prized possession, for that is exactly what it was: a prize for a clever girl who loved words, who loved how words could make beautiful phrases that coalesced with rhythm, wit, and rhyme. Father admired his beautiful, red-haired daughter as she lovingly turned another page, mouthing the words that she knew so well to herself, imprinting each piece of prose to her memory.

'There is a beautiful Violet, Mother, she is always learning, always whispering, she's a good girl. Our Violet is a good girl... I always knew we had a good 'un in her... with her violet eyes... even when she was a dot... you could see it in 'er eyes the day she was born.'

Mother nodded appreciatively and, smiling, returned to her sewing task. Violet did not raise her head from her book, but pretended to passively read and memorise; her mind had been diverted. She loved her parents dearly, she knew they loved her too and they needed her, her wage, her help, even more so since Bill took off. She was the only one who could provide for them, and Mother was struggling more and more with simple things, even just remembering things. But what about her? what about poor Vi, seventeen nearly eighteen, never been kissed or admired, working in a factory every day where the girls went out and had some fun; what was her life? Well she did not have one, really. What did she have apart from this precious book? She could not afford anything else, she gave all to her parents. How would things ever change for her caught in this homely prison? She had no future and no prospects of ever having a future. Her thoughts settled from their anxious race. Well, at least she could work, and not have to leave her job because she married. At least there were some benefits to her life. Her job granted her some independence from her role caring for her parents and relief from her mundane existence, and while she worked she had friends like Fanny to talk to. She had calmed herself, her focus returned to her page once more in full contemplation.

Two figures huddled in a darkened alleyway, the smell of the sewers and stray cats perfuming their night-time tryst with a reeking stench. An onlooker might confuse them for lovers meeting after dark, making plans, deciding their future together. Every now and then he would grab for her skirts and try to pull her closer, and she would resist with playful discouragement. He seemed unsteady on his feet, the worse for wear after a night spent in some public house, she seemed in control and determined to resist.

'Now I've told you I ain't doin' that. I'm a good girl, I don't do things like that.' She said with a coquettish tone.

'I know you're good, Kitty,' he slurred. 'Everyone says you're good, now just let me have a bit.' He lunged again for her skirts trying to pull up the layers of dress and petticoat to reach for what he wanted. She slapped his hand down with force.

'Now I'll have none of that I told you, I don't do that. I don't care what you've been told, I don't do that.'

'Oh, come on, Kitty, you're the prettiest girl I know, and I know you want me, so let me have a bit?' he persisted.

'That's for the man I marry and it ain't going to be you.' She pushed him away and patted her dress down. Footsteps in the passing street dampened his ardour somewhat and he grumbled.

'But I took you for beer and I've fed ya, you could at least give me something in return, it's no trouble for ya.'

She retorted forcefully, while trying to regain her composure and adjusting her hair.

'You dain't have to buy me anything, I didn't ask ya, did I? I just said I'd meet you after work that was all. Anyway, I know you're married, so why don't you just clear off back to 'em wife and kids of yours!'

'Well you are just a little trollop, everyone's right about you, Kitty Tulloch. You're just trouble, jailbait, and you are begging for it... I only thought I'd try you out coz everyone has.' Angrily, he adjusted his trousers.

'I am just friendly that's all, and I decided that I would be friendly to you today because I felt sorry for you, you didn't have to buy me anything! I wouldn't waste my time on you otherwise!'

She spun round on her heels to head for the closest public road, and as she did he caught her arm aggressively, sobered by her humiliations.

'I've told you, little madam! You're asking for it! And one day you'll get it, you just see if you don't, and then what you going to do, pretty Miss Kitty, when you got a bab' an' no man? You'll work the streets like the whore that you are, an' you'll be a claptrap and no decent bloke in his right mind will touch you. You'll be sorry for knocking me back when I could have treated you right, you'll be sorry.' He did not stop for her reply, releasing her quickly and heading down the darkened passage.

Kitty stood, somewhat stunned by his aggression. She could not understand it, what had she done? All she did was meet up with him for a drink. After all, loads of the girls from work did it, they all had a good time, why shouldn't she? She pulled herself together, raised her head arrogantly and flounced into the dimly lit street, to walk the half a mile to her home.

Her head was full of her anger and the impertinence she had left behind. She had not made any promises, she had not made any offers. Yes, sure, she had flirted a little and may have been playful, but all the men like that, don't they? That's how she had always got her own way, with the boys in the courts, with her dad. She had always got her own way! Yes, she had done some touching and been touched, but that was all, she never let any of them put it up her, she knew not to do that.

My God, she grown up in a family where her mum had popped a baby out every year or so, and what had it done to her? Killed her, that's what! Teddy had seen her off with a bad birth; Kitty had been seven at the time. She had seen her mother screaming her guts out on the kitchen floor, and the pool of blood! The blood was everywhere – she had haemorrhaged. And then the midwife came, too late, and got the baby out, but she had lost too much blood, too much! And as her mother had lain there dying over the next day, her skin sheet-white, dark circles round her eyes, Kitty had made up her mind there and then she was not going to have babies. She was far too pretty, after all, and thin. And all the boys wanted her, so she would touch and play a little, she would let them touch and play a little, but that was all, even with her father when he was drunk. But she knew she was safe there because he was always too drunk to do anything, and she would always get a bob to spend on herself out of him the next morning, when she asked nicely of course.

She hurried quickly through the streets avoiding any more darkened passageways just in case she got more than she bargained for. They would all be in bed now, she would not have to face Fanny's wrath; she did not need that, too, this evening. As she entered the court, she could hear indistinct shouting from one of the rooms, a couple arguing while a baby screamed inconsolably. No, she definitely was not going to have that! A cat screeched and darted past her feet, unnerving her. She crept into the dark kitchen, and through into the parlour. Tom was snoring on his bed in the curtained corner, she stepped as lightly as she could so as not waken him. She removed her shoes and stole up the darkened stairs, and into her and Fanny's room. No light burned, she removed her clothes quickly and raised the blanket on her side of the bed, in an attempt to get in without detection.

'Where the 'ell have you been?'

Fanny had wakened from her disturbed sleep.

'God! You smell like a brewery!' She sat bolt upright, as Kitty proceeded to get into bed without discussion.

'You can't just ignore me! I was depending on you, you know that! You promised to get the young 'uns their tea. I came home to a mess and you nowhere in sight, while you have been out cavorting with your rough friends. What you got to say for yerself?'

Kitty turned her back to her sister and laughed.

'I am too tired for this, Fanny. If you want to have a go, let's do it in the morning, you'll wake the whole bloody court with your ranting. Home sweet home! Goodnight Francis!'

Chapter 3

Labours of love

A disturbed night gave way to a thundery day, a steel-grey sky threatened rain and the air hung heavy. Fanny's mood was reflected in the oppressive weather. She felt the weight of the world on her shoulders as she dragged her tired body out of the bed, as Kitty lay dead to the world. Half of her wanted to waken her sister and demand that she help with the morning chores, but the thought of more recalcitrance when she was feeling so weary and barely able to keep herself going meant that she simply washed with a flannel, dressed speedily and crept out of their tiny room.

The younger ones were already up to greet her. Tom had woken them so that he could have a chance to speak to Teddy before he left for work. Teddy was sitting at the kitchen table, his arms folded and his chin down, shoulders hunched up, sulking. The girls were busying themselves playing with some pots and cutlery, pretending to be making food. The pathos of the situation hit Fanny hard, as she knew there was very little in to give them any sort of breakfast. She had some oats and water, an unseasoned porridge without milk was the best that she could do.

After the grumbles had subsided and the makeshift breakfast had been cleaned away, a reluctant Teddy was dispatched with his older sisters to school. He still protested up until the last moment that he really did not want to go, but the force of opinion from three others finally wore him down and, scuffing his bare feet on the floor, he trailed after the other two as they chatted nineteen to the dozen on their way. Fanny grabbed her coin purse and secured it in her bodice by force of habit; it was the only money that they had to keep the wolf from the door, and experience had taught her that there too many light-fingered individuals around, even in her own family. She ventured out of the court to find Vi standing waiting for her.

'I just seen the little 'uns go. Teddy seems none too happy.'

'Yeah. He doesn't like school and won't go. Tom's had a word this morning so hopefully he will stick the day out. But he is not my biggest problem. Our Kitty is becoming a right handful, and she is too big to clip round the ear now, not that it would have done any good. Dad always showed her more favouritism than the rest of us. She has always got away with murder. She dain't 'elp or nothing, not even any food yesterday. I'm goin' to have to do all that today too. I really am getting sick an'—'

Fanny was cut off in mid-sentence as Kitty raced through the middle of the two chatting girls without stopping or acknowledging either of them. Fanny was incensed at her sister's rudeness and shouted after her.

'S'cuse me!'

Kitty spun round and threw an accusatory look back at both.

'What?'

As she did so, and having paid absolutely no attention to the direction she was racing in or anybody else that was using the road, she barged into a tall man clutching a bundle and knocking him flying, and snapped:

'Get outta my way, you!' before racing on without concern.

Witnessing the unfortunate collision, and very embarrassed by her sister's uncouth brashness, Fanny raced to help the young man regain his composure, as he had sprawled over the ground with the contents of his precious bundle spilling and clattering all over the cobbles. Vi followed at a quick pace.

'I am so sorry, are you alright?' Fanny tried to appeal to the very flustered and concerned man on all fours, who was desperately scrabbling for some tools and papers

28

that had spilled out of his skin; he was mumbling under his breath with indistinct curses. He did not make eye contact, just continued to grab for the things he had lost and throw them into his skin without checking. He began to rise to his feet.

'Look, I really am sorry, I am apologising for me sister, she was very rude.'

Still he would not look at her, rather his mind was lost elsewhere as he searched the floor just in case he had missed something. Vi bent down and reached for a small felt bag which lay near her feet, and as she lifted it a small gold object rolled out and clattered in the gutter. She reached for it quickly and, lifting her hand to her face, observed the most beautiful thing that she had ever seen in her life. It was the most fantastically polished yellow gold, with a glistening of purple and green from several clear stones; she was truly in awe. She turned to the two, one trying to engage the other in dialogue, the other refusing to acknowledge her presence, lost in his concerns.

'Is this what you are looking for?' she asked, offering her palm out to him. He grabbed at it quickly, barely looking at her, his eyes downcast, and grumbled:

'Where's the bag?'

'Ooh! I'm sorry, I have it here.' Vi offered it to him with her other hand, and this time as he reached for it he looked at her face, and the blueness shot back at him. Instantly, he averted his gaze downwards.

'Thank you, I'll be on my way.'

Fanny was troubled by what had transpired, or rather, what had not transpired. Yes, her sister had caused this through her extremely bad behaviour, but Fanny had done her best to make amends – he could have said thank you to her.

'Well!' she remarked. 'Well not in all my life! I don't know who is ruder, that bloody sister of mine, or him and his ignorance. He could have at least said thanks.'

'He did to me, Fanny, but not exactly charming I grant you. Did you see that ring? Have you ever seen anything more beautiful in your life?'

'Yeah, and the likes of you and me are never likely to see anything like it again that close up, except in a window. They're all the same them bloody jewellers, think they're something special. He could have said thank you, that's all. Come on, girl, we'll be late for work and I can't afford to be locked out until lunch, let's get a move on.'

The morning passed slowly for Fanny and Vi as they worked their presses hour after hour, Vi stamping in images and emblems onto the punched pens, Fanny cutting the slits – hundreds, then thousands through the morning. Vi was lost somewhere and barely paying any attention to what she was about.

'Hey you, where are you? You haven't said a word all mornin'. You best be careful, you'll mash your fingers.'

'I am sorry, Fanny, but I keep thinking about that beautiful ring; he must be extremely clever to make something like that, don't you think?'

'I don't know about clever, 'ee's extremely bloody ignorant. But yes, it was beautiful. He was lucky our Kitty didn't see it, she'd have made off with it and he would have never seen it again. No doubt 'ee's getting a pretty penny for it now? I'm sure he won't be struggling to put food on the table tonight.'

John stood stunned in his attic workshop, a tall thin man in a brown herringbone suit and matching bowler facing him, holding the ring.

'I am sorry, lad, that is all I can offer you for it. It's the market you see.'

'But Mr Jennings, you were offering me double that two months ago, and I have to get the money. My ma, she's sick, I have to get the doctor to her.'

'I am sorry, lad, it's like I teld you, there is no market, I can't shift this stuff any more. I am offering over the odds anyway, because I like you, and I promised Old Zac that I would take care of you.'

'But it doesn't even cover the cost of the gold and the gems, never mind the weeks work, can't you see your way clear to giving me a bit more, sir, it's for my ma?'

'Listen, sonny, no one's buying. Since Prince Albert snuffed it and the Queen went into mourning, it has gone out of fashion. Because she ain't wearing jewellery no more, no one is. Yes, I could have shifted it just a few a week ago, but not now, I am sorry.'

'But what am I going to do? I have very little left, and if I can't sell this I don't know how we are going to get by.'

'John, you are a damn good silversmith. I've seen your work and at least there is still a market in silver, especially since all the municipals are putting big orders in for mayoral chains of office and such like. You ought to get yourself back into that game, you and Zac had good connections at Hardman's – if nothing else you can do the ecclesiastical stuff for them. My advice, is get yourself up to Newhall Hill and put your face in there, you are bound to get some work. I know they are all after the same work, but you are good and they know you.'

'But what am I going to do now? I need to get a doctor, I need to buy food. It will take me weeks to produce something that I can sell in silver. Can't you give me a little more? I can't sell it to you for what you are offering and I really need the money.'

'Well I can't buy it then, laddie, you'd best hang on to it until the market picks up.'

Mr Jennings surveyed John's crestfallen face, and turned to leave; as he did, he reached into his coat pocket for some loose change.

'Look, I know it's not much, but it will keep some food on the table for a week or so, and you'll just have to avoid the rent man like they all do. And there's always poor relief.'

'Not entitled… I'm Irish,' he mumbled, staring at the floor.

'Oh yes, of course. Sorry, lad, I have got to go.' And with that, the factor closed the door and descended the rickety staircase.

John stood frozen to spot, looking at the ring in his hand. He had had high hopes for this work, really believed he would be fetching the doctor to his mother that day, even taking her a bunch of flowers and some medicines. Now all he had was a couple of bits of loose change of charity, and a few shillings of savings. He knew in his heart that Mr Jennings was right, the market had been dropping for a year or so, but like everyone else he had assumed that it would not, could not, go on forever; the Queen had to resume normal life soon, surely? He realised that he had no other options but seek silver work. It would mean working harder and longer for a lot less. Mind you, when working as hard as he had the last week all for nought, the prospect of any return for his efforts would be desperately welcomed.

John turned to his bench and slouched in his chair, peering through the grimy window to his left, which barely gave a view above the rooftops. From his vantage point he could just about catch a glimpse of the red and grey spires of St Chad's Cathedral and his conscience was pricked, he had not attended Mass in a while, and he had not stayed in contact with those that mattered. Everything had overtaken him in recent months, the business declining, losing the decent lodgings which had granted them some respectability, and now the severity of his mother's condition. He had been hoping for a break in the bad fortunes to give him a chance to get things back on track, but all that seemed to happen was more bad luck.

St Chad's mattered for another reason: Hardman's had produced the fabulous stained glass and been instrumental in the commissioning of Pugin to design the Roman Catholic cathedral twenty-two years earlier. It had Hardman's thumbprints all over the interior, from the ecclesiastical sculptures and pews, to the ornate silverware, much of which had been produced by Old Zac, by commission. John was not the only member of that Catholic community that owed much of his previous success to the patronage of John Hardman; there were many of the same religious denomination in the locality who could find work only there. Despite the supposed religious tolerance of Birmingham as a non-incorporated town attracting masses of religious dissenters, if you were Catholic it was usually synonymous with being Irish, and the Irish were despised by the local people for being perceived to take jobs away from the indigenous community.

Many of the Irish, like John, kept themselves to themselves; it was best not to open your mouth in public or get into discussion, as it usually led to trouble. Past hurts and previous fights, had taught John to stay away. He had the daily battle that everyone had in his position – just to survive. He had often thought had it not been for his mother he would have returned to Ireland – he felt like he did not fit in Birmingham – and he had unfinished business that he had left behind to sort out. But his mother would not return, she was adamant. He had considered that this was due to the pain of her memories of all that she had been through and all that she had lost, but actually she would not return because of John; she had been determined to get away for his sake, and she was determined to stay away at all costs to herself to give him the chance that he deserved. And for a while, despite everything, it had been a very good move; the church had helped to find John an apprenticeship – with a nice old Jewish man of all people, a very kindly old soul who had property in the quarter in which he was more than happy to let John and May live rent-free, while he imparted all of his knowledge and skill of working precious metal and stones to John.

And for the last nine years they had felt safe and secure. For the first time in John's life he was able to lay down some roots and tentatively begin to trust again, but only a few would he let in behind his wall. He really had to have an affinity with a person to communicate on any level, and friendship was something he did not have time for, except with his old master, of course. But that relationship had formed over years, and when the old man had finally passed away nine months previously, he had taken with him more than just the rent-free lodgings that John and May so depended upon. The closeness of master and boy, of skilled artisan and acolyte, had been broken; John had lost the only friend that he had depended upon. Every day since had just been about existence, keeping a roof over their heads, hoping for better things.

Mr Jennings was right, of course, John could work silver like a master – thankfully, Zachariah Jacobs had taken him under his wing and taught him well. All those years producing piece after piece. He was known at Hardman's; all he had to do was walk up the hill and ask for work, but that would mean some loss of face for John. He had thought of himself as more than just a silversmith; he could work gold and gems, and the money for smaller items had been more, but nobody had ever predicted that the death of the Prince Consort would cause such devastation to the industry.

As he gazed through the dirty windowpane, he knew that he must make an approach to Hardman's: he had no other choice. He opened his hand, which had remained clenched since Mr Jennings had departed. The ring had made an indent in his palm because he had been gripping it so tightly. What to do with this? Why had he taken so much time over something that was worth nothing, yet worth everything? Best he just wrap it up and put it away for another time. He took the black felt bag and dropped the ring inside, tying the ribbon tightly.

Vi dragged her feet the last fifty yards of her walk from the factory. She was reluctant to get home too quickly and resume her household existence. Normally Vi could have taken her time chatting to Fanny, but Fanny had been determined to get home to her smaller charges and feed them, and that had meant going to buy the food first, so she had dashed away at the end of work. As the swarm had surged onto Graham Street, Vi had been caught in the forward momentum which had returned her to the courts faster than she would have liked. She had slowed and dropped back behind the crowd, barely shuffling her feet, looking down at her shoes and thinking of that morning's drama of the young jeweller and his beautiful ring; she was just at the spot where it had all happened.

Something caught her eye in the gutter, a long piece of metal, a lot thicker than a needle, and shining. She bent down to pick it up. It was a file, a jewellers file! He must have dropped that too and not realised that he had left it behind. He must have missed it, he probably really needs it! Vi resolved to get the file back to him whatever it took to do so, and maybe... just maybe... he would let her have one last look at that ring!

Chapter 4

Fleeting glimpses

Vi stood at the spot where the previous morning's calamity had happened; she was scanning the horizon for any sight of the young man at the centre of the drama, and had assumed that he might be there at a similar time, not realising that John did everything he could to avoid the crowds and had already passed her court and was even now heading off into the distance towards the factory. She looked up the street and saw the cloth-capped, tall stranger purposefully striding onwards, just as Fanny rounded the corner from her court. Breathlessly, Vi turned her head quickly.

'Sorry, Fanny, I can't wait, I have to do something.' She dashed off down the street. Fanny stood stock-still, somewhat puzzled by her friend's rapid departure and accompanying sense of urgency, and watched as she ran towards the factory. By the time Vi had reached the Gillott's, the cloth-cap was hastily turning the corner at the end of the street, she knew that he would not hear her from where she stood, and she would not know what to shout to attract his attention anyway, so, there was nothing left to do but run after him.

By the time she turned the corner into St Paul's Square she was grasping her side with a stitch pain, as she caught sight of the cap crossing the square and heading for an old doorway on the other side. She drew a deep breath, and clutched her skirts and ran after him, hoping she would reach him before he entered.

'Hello!' she shouted breathlessly. 'Hello, please wait?' But the cloth-cap either did not hear her, or chose not to, and scurried inside the doorway. She reached it, leaning on the doorpost, breathing heavily; she was hot and flustered and she was going to be late for work. She was in a dilemma:

pursue her quarry, or turn around and head back to the factory? She knew that to be late would mean a lockout until lunchtime, but she had been so determined to return what she had found to its owner, that any sense of logical reason and better judgement had escaped her; the consequence of her actions would mean the loss of half a day's wages, but the cloth-cap may not be here for long, he might just be visiting someone? This may be her only chance to return his property. She opened the old door and entered into a very dirty passage which led to a darkened staircase. She had not got a clue where he might be, but she would climb the stairs anyway.

When she reached the top, there was just one very large and wide door. She knocked apprehensively: there was no reply. She knocked again harder, hoping for a welcomed voice from within: still nothing. This time she banged on the door. The door was opened fiercely.

'What do you want?' came an abrupt question, accompanied by a puzzled stare and a vague recollection. 'Oh, it's you... from yesterday. What do you want?' Still anger in his tone. Vi was taken aback by his apparent aggression.

'I... I... followed you. I found something... something that I think belongs to you.' She held out the file to him.

'Oh, right.' Swiftly, he snatched it out of her hand and made to shut the door, but she came back quickly.

'B... but... I thought you might have missed it... I thought—'

'You thought you'd get a reward. Well you're wasting your time, there is no money around here, now if you don't mind—' Again, he made to close the door.

'No. I came to get it back to you... I ran after you all the way. I don't want a reward... I... I...'

'Look, Miss, some of us have work to do... I have to get on.' He made his third attempt to shut the door, and the normally mild and gentle Vi finally snapped.

'You are just so rude! Fanny is absolutely right about you, you're just a stuck-up ignorant jeweller who thinks himself better than us. Well I had work to do too... and now I am late because I wanted to help you by returning the property that I thought you would miss. Now I will get locked out till later and lose half a day's wages on your account. I didn't want a reward, but a thank you would have been nice!' And with that she swung her dress around and began to march down the stairs.

John was suddenly brought to book and gripped with remorse.

'Look, I'm sorry... it just is not a good time. Please come back... I am sorry, and I should have said thank you!'

Vi stopped on the stairs and slowly turned. He continued.

'Look... come in. Maybe I can find you something, just a penny or so—'

'I don't want your money. But...' she thought carefully how to ask. 'Could I please have one more look at that beautiful ring? That's if you haven't sold it, of course?'

John smiled, as much at the pathos of the situation, that a ring that he could not sell for the value of the materials seemed so appreciated by the two women who had held it.

'Yes, I will let you see the ring... and no it is not sold; nobody wants it.'

This statement left Vi shocked and speechless. In her simple world how could something so beautiful not be wanted? She climbed back up the steep stairs and followed John into his attic workshop. She was surprised how small it was inside; with the size of the imposing oak door she had expected a vast space on the interior, but it was quite compact, barely enough room for three or four people to stand in around the few pieces of furniture, the main piece being a big old jewellers bench with a place either side to sit. Both sides had a small gas torch and some assembled tools lying adjacent. There was a crescent curve cut into the front of each side of the bench and a leather skin attached to the crescent, so that sitter could catch any falling tools or off-cuts. Around the wooden arc, more tools were held in holes in the bench so that their handles pointed upwards. Each side of the bench was at a right angle to a small attic window, the only source of light for the worker as he sat.

John passed to his side of the bench; it had always been his side since he was fourteen and, despite Zac's passing, he could not bring himself to take his master's place on the other, even though there was more space and the light was better there. He felt that it would be disrespectful to seat himself where his friend used to work and pass the time in conversation with his eager young apprentice.

She watched him as he took his seat, reaching into the pocket of his leather apron as he did so, bringing out the black felt bag tied with the ribbon. She was suddenly struck by size of his hands, they were so large, she had not expected that in someone who made such fine work. Of course, they were in keeping with the rest of him, for he was very tall, but she had expected finer, smaller hands. As he struggled to undo the ribbon, she glanced around the small workshop. On every surface were small and large pieces of tarnished silver; some petit finished bowls, embossed and chased, some engraved. Other pieces seemed half-finished, as if an apprentice had practised their craft, or experimented with a new idea. Some pieces were almost black with the oxides that had collected on the surface. This blackness made the beautiful, polished gold stand out even more when it was finally exhumed from its cloth place of safekeeping. John handed her the ring.

Carefully, she took into her hands, in total awe of its beauty, she had never held anything quite so remarkable or as valuable in her life, and Fanny was right – she was never likely to again. She stared into the deep purple amethysts, unaware of the attention that she was being given. Attentions that were given to very few because there were very few who managed to connect with him.

Where Vi was standing, the morning sun that shone through the other window had caught the back of her hair, giving it an almost ethereal glow, a halo, of auburn red. He was fascinated by her face, she had very angular and pronounced features, with a refined aquiline nose. But it was her eyes, like the colours of sapphires, and deep, so blue against her flaming hair and white skin. For a moment he was transfixed and lost, such that he had not heard her question, which jolted him back to reality.

'Why is it not sold? It is so amazing. Why does no one buy it?'

John felt his own presence, and was alarmed about his temporary loss of self in another; he locked himself down again and answered in a matter-of-fact tone.

'God bless Queen Vicky, she won't wear jewellery since her beloved Albert died and, because she sets the fashions, every woman has stopped wearing it and now buying it… it has been a complete waste of my time. I should have stuck to doing what I do best: church silver! Now really, I have things to do, you are going to have to go.'

'Oh, yes, I am sorry. Here…' Vi handed the ring back filled with a sense of loss, both for not holding the ring any more, and for this sad stranger; and he was a stranger, she did not even know his name.

'I will go and let you get on. By the way, my name is Violet, Vi to my friends.' She hoped that he would pay the same courtesy, but he was too busy placing the ring back from whence it came. She turned to open the door. As she did so, he softly said:

'I am John… goodbye.'

And with that, Vi knew her brief dialogue and audience had ended with this strange young man. She did not turn around, but closed the door behind her as she stepped out onto the staircase.

An hour later, Vi was still sitting in the churchyard in the middle of the square. She had been reluctant to return home and have to explain her appearance there, yet she knew that she would be wasting her time to arrive at the factory door; she would not gain entry until lunchtime. So, she sat musing, lost in her thoughts of this strange aloof young man, who had angered her with his abruptness and ingratitude, although she sensed that his coldness stemmed from a deep sadness; something had damaged him and made him distrust and internalise his pain. She was fascinated by his contradictions of character: someone who could devote himself to the production of such amazing beauty, yet, showed disdain for everything, and everyone.

Some verse that she had memorised in school kept repeating in her mind, a few lines of Shakespeare's poem, 'The Life without Passion':

> *They that have the power to hurt, and will do none,*
> *That do not do the thing they must do show,*
> *Who, moving others, are themselves as stone,*
> *Unmoved, cold, and to temptation slow:*

He appeared, to her, closed and unapproachable but she had felt a strange connection with him. Maybe it was her romantic, poetic notions that had swept her up into turmoil. She felt in her heart that this would be not the last time that their paths would cross. As she sat, the street door to his garret opened. She panicked, and hoped that he did not see her, just in case he thought it strange that she should still be there. For a moment, he just stood outside on the pavement, fumbling in his pockets, checking for something; he made a move to return inside, but then changed his mind and began to walk out of the square away from her.

She watched him as he strode purposefully on. He was so tall, with dark hair that could just be seen underneath his cap. He had his skin rolled up under his arm and did not look up, keeping his face down, avoiding any eye contact with passers-by. He did not slouch, or stoop and, despite his aversion of his gaze, he walked upright and erect and carried himself well. She wondered what he was about, where he was going in the middle of his working day. That, she was not to know; all she knew about this sad stranger was his occupation and his name, John.

A few hours later she finally gained admittance into the factory, as all the other girls had begun to return to their overcrowded large departments. She entered a huge cavernous workshop that echoed with the many female voices who worked the different presses, and passed the embossers where Fanny was just taking her place.

'Hey, where have you been? Brown's been looking for you, he didn't seem none too impressed. Are you alright?'

'Yes, I just had to deliver—' Vi was cut short in her reply as a large red-faced man had appeared at her shoulder with a face like thunder.

'Right, Miss Foster, and what are you doing 'ere, seeing as you didn't turn up this morning?'

Vi stuttered as she coloured-up with embarrassment.

'S-s… sorry, Mr Brown, I had an important errand to do for my m-m… mother and I was late so I had to wait… I am really sorry.'

'You'll be more than sorry, Miss, you can't just turn up an' expect to carry on working, we have hundreds to take your place, you can collect your wages—'

Fanny stood up indignantly.

'Oi you're not being fair! Vi has told you she's sorry… she never takes time off, she is never sick, she is a good worker, you can't just sack 'er? She's told you it was important, she would not do it deliberately she is not a slacker!'

'I can do what I like, Miss Hoighty-Toighty Tulloch, and you be careful or you'll be getting your wages too. We sack anyone who don't turn up; we have plenty more waiting, one missing is two thousand pens not worked on in a morning. We can't have this!'

'But you let my sister Kitty get away with it? I haven't known 'er do a full month without missing at least one morning. 'Ow come you don't sack 'er, then?'

Mr Brown was suddenly brought to book, and was flustered in his reply.

'She's got friends in packing... if you know what I mean. She never gets the trouble, but I am the gaffer in 'ere and you will do as you are told!'

Fanny was somewhat taken aback by his response.

'No, I don't know what you mean. What do you mean "friends"? Our Kitty ticks everyone off. It's one rule for her and one rule for everyone else.'

'She's got friends in the foreman and his mates down in packing, and they look out for their own... especially one so good with their favours.'

'I 'ope you're not suggestin' my sister 'as got loose morals? You shouldn't be spreadin' gossip like that, I will take you to the manager and I will have a go about you sacking V. We all know you are on the fiddle – more bloody pens are going out in your pocket every day than reach packing!'

Mr Brown slowed his response; he realised that questions might be asked about his own light-fingered conduct, and now was the time to show a little generosity of spirit. If he had just been getting rid of Violet Foster, the little girl who did not say boo-to-a-goose, that would be one thing, but taking Fanny Tulloch on when she was in high dudgeon with a point to prove was something completely different; his tone became smarmy and softer.

'You got me wrong, girls. I'm not sacking Miss Foster, no… just scaring 'er so she thinks twice before she does it again.'

And to make sure that all of the others got the message, he spoke loudly.

'And the lot of you… let this be a warnin'! Miss a half day, and you can find a job elsewhere. I won't take it! Got it?' And with that he marched down the aisle of benches back to the main desks.

Fanny regained her composure.

'Ooh, that was a close one, Vi… you 'ad better get to your work, he's gunnin' for us now. I would like to know what he's insinuating about Kitty, and I would like to know what you've been about, because I know you ain't been doin' jobs for your ma, but it will have to wait; we are in enough trouble now, we'd best crack on.'

Vi nodded and dashed to her bench to cut the pen slits on the other side from Fanny. They both worked like drones for the rest of the day, not daring to stop or chat, as the ever-watchful Mr Brown scrutinised the efforts and their output.

Chapter 5

A meeting of minds

John rose from a deep sleep with a new determination. Today he would find work, he had to, his mother had passed another bad night and seemed to be deteriorating daily, he must get a doctor to her and soon. He had spent the previous afternoon in a fruitless search for work, he knew that Hardman's was his last chance. He stole out into the court and then into the quiet street; he had no desire to be followed or meet any uncalled mishaps today. Although... the thought of her auburn hair and blue eyes had overtaken his dreams and his mind, no matter how hard he tried he could not shake her image away; the way in which she had cherished his work in her hands, and worshipped the ring with her eyes, and those eyes, how they had shone with the reflected colour of the amethysts, almost violet in colour... of course, her name... that was her name.

He jolted himself back to his reality, he must make amends to a friend before he sought help for his plight, before anything else he had to do that. As he walked up Newhall Hill, he felt a nervousness throughout his whole being; he had never had to do this alone, visit other clients or customers, he had always followed his master. That is why working alone had suited him so well, because of this discomfort that he felt whenever he had to enter a place with people. He had always hidden behind Old Zac, who had such a way with words, who had so many contacts and friends. John had always been considered as 'his strange lad', a bit too quiet for everyone's liking. He did not tend to make friends easily, could count very few in his life, and those living, he had failed to keep in contact with when his problems had first begun to manifest themselves with the death of Zac some eighteen months previously. John had been filled with a sense of guilt and remorse for not having taken the time or of making the effort to maintain one particular friendship; today he was going to do something about that.

Even before he had sought the foreman, or spoken to the works manager at Hardman's, John had crossed into the mason's yard and past the large blocks of rough, uncut marble, with the thick white dust that seemed to blanket every surface. There were a few large pieces too, angelic faces and cherubim, imposing decorative slabs and pillars, finished and part finished, too large to be maintained in the interior workshop, or waiting for final assembly as the next piece in the jigsaw was carved by skilled hands, and he knew which hands had carved most. It was an unmistakeable talent that had been obvious to all the day that he had first started as a sculptor. He climbed the wooden exterior staircase into the studio, but he did not have to look far, for he had been seen.

'Johnny boy! How nice to see you!'

He looked upwards to where the voice emanated from. A young man, younger than himself and smaller in stature, but possessing the same dark hair and blue eyes, was balancing on a stepladder above a particularly large monument of the Virgin Mary, with a broad chisel and round mallet in his hand. He wore a leather apron, his face was chalk-white with the dust, and his hair looked prematurely grey.

'Well I'll be… how good to see you!' The voice descended the ladder in haste, practically throwing his tools down in an effort to get to his long-lost friend with speed.

'I was just saying to my Susan that I had not seen you in quite a while… I was going to come into the quarter and look you up. How are you? No, don't answer that… I know how you are.' The voice hardly drew breath, John had to keep opening and closing his mouth in order to attempt an interruption.

'Hello, James. Yes, I am sorry I have not been for a while but—'

'Yes, I know, Zac died, and you have had it a bit tough since. Don't look surprised, word does get round you know. And it is not all bad, a lot of people have lot of time for you.'

'I wish they would have more than time, I—'

'Oh, its work you're after then? Do you want me to put a word in for you then? Oh, how stupid of me, you won't need that, you have been producing work for them longer than I have been here...' James gabbled away nineteen to the dozen, so pleased was he to have been reunited with John Connolly.

'If it hadn't been for you, I don't think I would have stuck those first few months here when I started my apprenticeship, it was your friendship that gave me the strength to keep going... now look at me! Six years later I am practically running the show... well, not the stained glass, but certainly the monumental stuff... anything in marble the, bigger the better!'

John smiled at the eager young man, who did not hold a grudge for their lack of association, but was expressing his happiness to see him again.

'Your work is incredible, James, where is this piece destined for?'

'Australia, would you believe... Sydney, Australia! It is quite incredible that these pieces travel so far, yet I travel so little. One day maybe, I will follow them and see these places but it will have to wait for now. You don't know, do you? I married a few months ago, a lovely young girl, Susan... Susan Emily Fox, a prettier miss you could not meet. I am so happy. And you? Have you anyone special?'

'No, James, just Ma and me... I have no time for that. It has been hard... but it is harder since Ma became ill, that's why I am here. I could manage if it were just me, but since the jewellery market has gone, I have to find some regular work. Ma needs a doctor.'

'John, if you need money, I can lend you some to get you through?'

It was a genuine offer, and kindly meant, but John was not one to take such a liberty with a friend and his pride would not let him. He was slightly offended that this offer should be extended, as it only set to heighten his awareness of his own failings to provide, especially as the offer had come from a younger man, a lad whom he had watched start an apprenticeship, when he himself had become quite a skilled artisan by the time they had first met. He had to measure his reply, and curb his reaction so as not to show ingratitude for the kindness.

'That's very good of you to offer but I cannot take your money. Anyway, you are recently married – congratulations, you will need every penny, a wife is an expensive pastime. No, I will get work, I know that they need the workers here... but thank you.'

'If you are sure? The offer is there any time. Susan is not like many girls, she shares my views and thoughts, you would like her. She often comes to debating meetings and is very forthright, sometimes too forthright. And you, John, have you still got some fire in your belly?'

'I haven't much time for other things; when I am not working I am looking after Ma, and nothing changes, it does not matter what we do.'

'Don't lose your faith, John, there are many that share the strength of feeling that we had. Don't you feel it here? All those ghosts that haunt this hill; Donnelly, O'Connell, the Union, the Monster Meetings? It is all around us here, I am sure this is where I get my inspiration for everything from.'

'Yes, but despite all Mr Bright's feisty speeches, this town still contains the greatest mass of under-represented people in England, it is almost as bad as the home; and what hope have the Irish got here, if the people born and raised here cannot get their voices heard? You are still a dreamer Jimmy, I am just too cynical for all that fighting and blasting the "great" and the "good" to help us. Nothing changes.'

'You really have had the stuffing knocked out of you, Johnny boy; where is that radical that I first met here, who believed that we could make a difference? We still can! I have joined a debating society locally, you ought to come, just hear what they have to say? There are some strong voices there, not everyone holds our views, I grant you, but it is good sparring, and this town is going places. If you feel the fire, you will catch alight! They meet in a few weeks, please come with me, John, if only to give yourself a change of scenery.'

'I don't know, I really don't have the time for such fancies.'

'Just come the once, only the once… just hear them. If it is not for you I will not make you again, but it would be good to spend some time with my old friend, and the next debate is just up your street. It is "Irish Employment: a blessing or a curse?" I bet you have an opinion to share? I certainly have.'

'Let me think on it, James. I really must go now, I have to get some work sorted out. I will be in again and see you then.' John witnessed the disappointment in his friend's face because he had not responded with a positive confirmation of his attendance; he attempted to redeem the situation and sugar the pill.

'I will think about it… if Ma is better… maybe.'

Kitty leant against the gatepost of the factory, enjoying some brief afternoon sunshine before she would have to return to the claustrophobic packing department. She had made up her mind since her experience in the alleyway, that if she were going to seek male company, that she had best aim her sights higher and further away from the tittle-tattle of the place where she worked. She also had a victim in mind, hence her dallying a while longer than she should when the others had returned inside. The factors were due to visit to collect their orders, not a particularly attractive bunch of men, but more successful than the male incumbents with whom she worked. She knew if she waited that the first through the gate would be her prey, as long as he was as punctual as he usually was.

It was not long before a stout chap in his mandatory tweed suit, with matching bowler hat, appeared in the distance, bowling down the street with his empty carpet bag. As he came into closer view, his complexion seemed redder than normal, being a man who enjoyed more than one drink in an evening, and his nose was glowing, probably from overexposure to the afternoon sun. He was not a small man, and could handle himself if he had to, his face bore the scars of more than a few brawls, of which he had obviously been the victor. He approached Kitty, and raised his bowler as he was about to pass by; she stole her chance.

'Well hello, Mr Smith, it is nice to see ya.'

He was slightly taken aback by her open approach, normally Kitty would not have given him the time of day, never mind a cordial welcome; he was slightly suspicious.

'Well hello, Kitty Tulloch, and what are you doing out here? Shouldn't you be inside by now?'

'Yes, but I couldn't drag myself away from the sun, but I will walk in with you, you can tell the foreman you 'eld me up, because you needed some 'elp.'

'Oh, right, going to use me for illegal goings-on are you? Well I suppose for a pretty snippet like you, it is worth the trouble.'

'Ooh, sir, I am worth a bit more than trouble, but maybe when I next see you in the alehouse, we can chat about that?' She used her most flirtatious smile and angled posture to emphasis her double entendre. It was not lost on

Stan Smith, though his caution led him to a reluctance to exchange more than a playful response.

'We'll be seeing about that, Missy, and what 'elp do you think I needed?'

'Ooh, I don't know, directions? Or advice? Or maybe you dropped your bag and lost your stuff outta it? I don't know, we'll think of summit, I'm sure.' And with that, she hooked her arm into his and skipped lightly into the factory.

The foreman was none too happy to see Kitty ten minutes late in arrival, and made his feelings perfectly clear as she entered, accompanied by her sweating factor. Stan Smith jumped to her defence.

'Don't be too hard on her, Mr G, she was helping me, I tripped and lost my footing and my bag, your young lass helped me up, and administered her nursing skills.'

To this admission, two lines of packing girls erupted into whoops and cheers at the thought of Kitty aiding a man: 'That'll be right, Kitty's good with needy blokes,' shouted one. 'Hey, Kitty, have you become a nun? Saint Kitty?'

She responded in kind. 'Well some of us girls are good at extending an 'elping 'and to a fella in need. Ain't we, sir?' She looked at Stan in her impish way, and he responded dutifully.

'Yes, some of you girls can be very caring indeed.'

A furore of noise and catcalls broke out, so much so that the foreman had quite a job of restoring the order in the packing department. Mr Smith passed through to the packing office, throwing a smile back in Kitty's direction. She knew she had hooked the big fish and returned to her place with a contented expression on her face.

John's morning had been more successful than he could have possibly hoped, not only had he rekindled a much-cherished association with James, but he had been welcomed with open arms by the works manager at

Hardman's. The recession had been more detrimental to silver production than he had believed possible; a number of the outworkers had been culled, by death and loss of their benches. John had been a reliable worker of considerable skill and much-needed by the firm to fulfil their burgeoning order books. He came away with a commission for half a dozen alms dishes and a couple of chalices, with more to come if he could complete the work quickly. He also managed to secure an advance on his wages, to enable him to purchase bullion, and a little to spare so that he might get a physician to attend May.

He had returned directly to the back-to-backs, with the express intention of making his mother ready for a doctor's visit, only to be greeted by an anxious Mrs Morris waiting in the court.

'Oh, John, I'm glad you are early, it's yer ma…'

Horror gripped John, he thought that she would be alright to leave this morning, now he wondered if his own good fortune and accompanying self-satisfaction had been at the expense of someone he valued more than anything.

'She's not… dead, is she?'

'No, no, lad, calm yerself. I found her this morning collapsed in the kitchen. I managed to get her into the back, not that she's a great weight mind, but she really needs to be seen… she's breathing terrible bad like.'

John made no delay, he took Mrs Morris's offer to watch his beloved mother while he went in search of a doctor as soon as he could. Not many doctors were willing to visit the courts for fear that they would not get paid, however, he managed to find a young doctor, still enthusiastic to help the needy and, with the enticement of the advance payment of the necessary shillings, he came directly. He was remarkably thorough, and after half an hour came through to see John in the kitchen, while carefully closing the door to the parlour behind him.

'It is not good news I am afraid, Mr Connolly. Your mother has a very bad infection in her lungs, probably not helped by the conditions that you find yourself in here; she is suffering from the damp, cold atmosphere, and I worry that in someone of her age and condition this could lead to pneumonia. I think she should be nursed in a hospital, but she is adamant that she will not go, she seems concerned that she is needed here, and I do not want to worsen her disposition by making her go.'

'If she needs to go, Doctor, then I shall make her. She has to get better, she must get better.'

A darkness covered the young doctor's face, as he held the secret that his diagnosis had led him to, and he knew that he must reveal with care.

'She may well recover from this infection, with good nursing…'

Mrs Morris gripped John's arm, sensing that the doctor's revelation was not going to be what John would want to hear.

'Don't worry, lad, I can 'elp yer. Yer ma's a good soul, she's no trouble.'

John was gripped by a sudden fear, as he realised that he was being handled with care by those around him.

'What are you saying, Doctor, my ma's going to be alright isn't she?'

'As I said, Mr Connolly, with good nursing she may well rally from this infection, which is why I hoped that she would agree to being hospitalised, but… I am afraid you have to prepare yourself for the worst. She has a very weak heart rhythm, and she is very under nourished. I diagnose that she will not live to see this year out, she is too ill to do so.'

John slumped into the kitchen chair, as the cold shock drained from his face down his body into his legs, folding them beneath his large frame. Mrs Morris put her hands on his shoulders in an effort to comfort him.

'But, Doctor, can't you do anything?' He pleaded desperately.

'I am afraid not, Mr Connolly, your mother has suffered many years of difficulty; she probably developed this condition a long time ago, and having spoken to her I have a mind that I know when. But she is weak and her heart is erratic. My advice is to get her well, and restrict her to total bed rest, that is all we can do for her. I am amazed that someone so frail has lasted this long. There must be a fight and fire in her that defies all understanding of anatomy and physiology, certainly mine. For what she has lost in her physical being she makes up for with her mental capacity.'

After offering some bottles of palliative vapours to ease the lungs, and the directions for usage to Mrs Morris, as John, still shocked, sat in silence, the doctor left. Mrs Morris sat facing John, trying to placate his anxiety.

'But, Mrs Morris, she can't die. What am I going to do without her? She is everything to me, we have been through too much. I was just getting things right... just getting things back together. This can't happen?' He looked at her imploringly, like a small child without understanding and lost for answers and explanation.

'Listen, son... sometimes it's our time. You heard the doctor, she could be with us for many months yet. The best you can do is make what money you can, so that we can look after her properly. I will 'elp yer both, yer know that. And, John?'

He stared back sensing a tone of seriousness in her voice.

'You've no need to tell 'er. She already knows... just make 'er happy, son.'

Chapter 6

Atonement and conflict

John had never worked harder than he did over those next few weeks, he knew that her life depended on his diligence. The harder he worked the more orders came from Hardman's, the more money came in, and the medicine and food were purchased to help his ailing mother, with some set aside for the caring and ever-attentive Mrs Morris who barely left her side. It was a great debt of thanks that he owed to the careful devotions of his neighbour, the morning the doctor declared that the danger of her infection had passed for now. Her breathing had eased and some colour had returned to her complexion, but she was restricted to laying in her bed, and was not to put any undue strain onto her weak heart.

He had not forgotten James's request to accompany him to the forthcoming debating society meeting, neither had he been able to remove the auburn-haired vision from his mind. Her looks were evocative of the new art movements that were sweeping the city, for although John had very little time to engage in such ethereal pastimes he was an artist at heart and appreciated the beauty of colour. Edward Burne-Jones had significant connections to the town, having been born there, and through his association with the Pre-Raphaelites, more particularly, 'The Brotherhood', he had inspired a wave of romanticism across the city in the community of artists that existed under the auspices of the art school.

John was familiar with works by Rossetti and Millais depicting historical pageant and legend, and their use of strong colour, and beautiful Titian-haired models. Violet had evoked much of this imagery from his memory, with her striking looks, the red tints in her voluminous hair, with the pale skin and the powerful blue eyes that would not leave his

55

thoughts. He had become fascinated about this young woman, and quite remorseful of his abruptness towards her; he knew he must make amends for his rudeness. He knew roughly where she came from and could remember the time of day that the hapless collision had occurred. He decided that if he chose the same day of the week at approximately the same time of the morning, he would increase his chances of a less unfortunate encounter.

The very next morning, John waited across the street aiming to catch a glimpse of Vi, he hoped without others to witness. Vi's progress leaving her parents' house had been slow that morning, her mother had seemed particularly agitated, and more forgetful than normal. It seemed to be little simple tasks that confused her now: where things were, what they were called and, unusually for this mild-mannered woman, she was becoming prone to outbursts of anger, born of frustration. Vi had needed to take some time to pacify her before she had felt comfortable leaving her on her own. Vi harboured her own concerns of being late for work and the strong possibility that she would lose her job if she was, and dashed out as soon as she could. As she entered the street, she passed Suie, Mouse and Teddy on their way to school, Teddy still as reluctant as ever to make that much-despised journey to the place of torture.

''Ello, V.' Suie beamed as she passed. 'Yum missed our Fanny... she's left already. She waited for yer.'

Violet knew she must run, or she would be in serious trouble. As she hurtled past the end of Fanny's court her progress was yet again impeded.

'Excuse me, Miss...' John tried to catch her attention. She was breathless and could not stop, she raced past him, trying to speak as she did.

'I am ever so sorry... I'm late... I'll catch it.'

John called after her.

'But I need to talk to you!'

'I have to go!' And then, hastily thinking, 'But I can be in your square when I have my lunch… I really must…'

She was such a distance away now, that her words had become indistinct, John was quite crestfallen that his efforts to make amends had been dashed yet again. He was slightly annoyed that he had wasted his time in such a manner, precious time that he could not afford to waste, but there again, her tone had been one of genuine anxiety and worry. He must allow her a chance, she did not know that he would be waiting for her this morning and she had not said what time she would be in the square. Confusion and discomfort irritated him as he made his way to work and then to Hardman's with another consignment of finished silverware, and – as he had on several occasions in the last few weeks – he made a diversion into the mason's yard and up the wooden stairs. His honest intentions to atone with one may have been fruitless but that did not mean that he could not try elsewhere. James was engrossed in his work with his back to the door, unaware of John's presence. John took this opportunity to surprise his friend.

'Jimmy, what day is that meeting happening that you would like me to come to?'

James spun round excitedly.

'Good, John, you will come then? Oh, that is good… so good. I have missed my friend, my intellectual soulmate.' He paused momentarily, and then launched into his enthusiastic self once more. 'It is in three days at a meeting hall the other side of the city. It is a well-attended affair and attracts a lot of the keen businessmen… just the sort of crowd that needs to face up to their social responsibilities. We can meet here after you have finished and walk up together.'

John sat in his garret a little later, impatiently checking his watch, trying to guess when Vi may make an appearance in the square; every now and then he would go down to the street door, taking a look across to St Paul's churchyard, seeing if she had arrived. His concentration was extremely low, and his work rate reflected that. He felt annoyed with himself for his lack of application, but at the same time struck by his own disquiet and the strong impression that this strange creature had made on him.

It was a little after half past one when she had taken a seat on one of the benches, an obvious one to be seen from his vantage point; after all, Vi had been puzzled by his sudden attention towards her, and she was keen to see him again. As soon as John saw her, he raced over to her without closing his door.

'Afternoon, Miss. I… er… I am… I mean… I meant… look, I am sorry for my manners the other day. I just wanted to apologise to you. I really was quite ashamed of myself.'

Violet had risen to her feet to greet him, and now was at a loss for what to do or say. She had expected a conversation, but it seemed that she had undertaken yet another foolish errand to see him, as he gave the distinct impression that he had concluded his entreaties to her.

'Oh… right. Well, I had best get along then… unless there is anything else you wish to say?'

John felt clumsy and embarrassed, he desperately struggled to form articulate sentences, but what? He had no experience of young ladies other than his sisters, and they had long since gone; he had neither the words nor the capabilities to encourage, or woo. He floundered helplessly to reply.

'Well, yes… that was it really. I er… just wanted to put things right.'

For a moment Vi studied more closely this tall, very good-looking man, was he being reticent through shyness? Surely not! He was a man, and much older than herself. Was he just trying to be kind, and show some manners? Of course, and that had to be respected. She knew that there would be no one of his stature and position that could possibly want to associate with her, it was time to diplomatically take her leave of him.

'Well, thank you, John. I am sorry that my friend's sister was so rude, and I am glad you seem more relaxed in yourself than the last time we met. I should best get going… goodbye.' She turned to go, but was stopped in her tracks as John tried once more to regain his powers of speech, he wanted to facilitate a friendship with this girl, not push her away.

'I er… look… erm… I have handled this very badly…Vi, isn't it? Vi, I tend to stay away from people, I mean I am Irish… well, you know that.' His awkwardness was most apparent. 'We are not really wanted around here, so I tend to keep myself to myself, but I would like to get to know you as a friend?'

Violet was now stunned, she could sense his shyness, his attempt to be softer, less guarded; he was trying to offer an olive branch, he was seeking an answer.

'I mean, I would understand if you didn't want to, but if there is a chance that we could be friends, I would like that very much.'

Vi smiled at him with her most gentle manner, her eyes sparkled.

'Of course,' she replied enthusiastically. I would like that very much. 'Shall we sit awhile and enjoy the sunshine? Only, I will have to be back soon… it would be nice to talk.'

John suddenly felt enormously at ease, he sat next to Violet on the bench and they chatted, for so short a time, or it seemed such a short time. Eventually they both realised she had to leave, but they knew this was the start of something, and not the end.

Across the other side of the city, in another rat-infested alleyway, a dishevelled bundle stirred from where it had collapsed earlier that morning in a drunken stupor. Alf rubbed his face, which had suffered from lack of a razor for weeks. The gin had worn off and his head thumped. For a while, he tried to recollect his previous night's exploits, but he could not recall what the day was, never mind the time of day; there was little hope of remembering the previous week. He reached into his trouser pocket as he rose from the pavement, his britches felt damp, and a foul aroma rose up to greet him. He looked down at the darkened stain around the thighs and crotch of his brown corduroys; he had pissed himself again! It barely registered with him, he just needed to know the total of his wealth as it now stood. He pulled out a small collection of loose change. There was still one shilling left, and a handful of pennies and ha'pennies; he had enough for a day, or two, that is all that mattered. Then he would have to seek work and get a change of clothes, but not today. He shook himself into life, belched and farted, and headed off to the nearest public house.

The three days had passed quickly for John, he had a new-found and much wanted distraction during his brief lunch breaks. Each day, Vi had come along and sat and waited for the chance to be together to pass twenty minutes or so in conversation. It seemed to end so quickly and it left both wanting much more; time to spare for either of them was a precious commodity. John had his responsibility to May who, although vastly improved, was still very sick and totally dependent on her son. Vi had her mother's simplicity, which had always been an amusement but was now causing serious concerns for Vi. Her mother appeared confused about little things and incredibly forgetful; Vi feared that she may lose her way if she ventured out shopping, and tried as much as possible to be there. She was in no position to expect more of her new friend in terms of understanding and commitment, she had decided to let fate take its course: if they were meant to be, it would be so. For now, both knew that they must be content with these brief connections that they could make during their working week.

However, John had made a commitment to James which he had secretly admitted to himself that he eagerly looked forward to. James had always been good company, he was strongly intellectual, and highly artistic. He could be prone to lecture others, for he possessed strong radical sympathies. He had always harboured this idea that he was put on this earth to solve some deep political problem; John found this younger man's vigour for the fight a little tiring but humoured his enthusiasms. James had drawn strong affiliations to the Irish problem; although not Irish born, he felt that the manipulations of the English in another country had gone far enough. He had also sensed the enormous inequalities that the Irish community in Birmingham had suffered, not just from his associations with his Irish friend, but the community in general, which comprised almost a quarter of Birmingham's population.

It seemed to James, that the local people, most of whom had been incomers themselves a generation or two ago, were quite happy to exploit the cheap hard-working labour supply that the Irish had given to the town, to enable its enormous transformation through canal and rail construction and general building of houses and roads, but none were willing to recognise these people as part and parcel of the community. Most of the Irish were kept at arm's length and treated with suspicion; there was an atmosphere of distrust of them in general, and as such none of the normal supports and privileges had been granted to them. Yet, only one generation since the Birmingham Political Union had successfully fought for recognition within national government, a cleric of influence from Broad Street, one Father Thomas McDonnell, had sought support for emancipation for the Irish Catholic Community through his association with the Kerry lawyer and Irish Nationalist, Daniel O'Connell. For a while they had been a force for change and had evoked sympathies with many of the like-minded radicals of the city, but then there was an anti-Catholic backlash and once again the Irish were being shunned, being viewed as scroungers and vagrants.

John had witnessed much of this animosity and, although he had met some that were kindly disposed towards him and his mother, they tended to be rare, and were those from different cultures and backgrounds such as Old Zac, who was Jewish, and James, who had arrived from the more ethnically diverse city of London. On the whole, he had found local people to be cold and distant, and he knew of many incidents where Irish families had been ostracised and victimised out of the locally-entrenched courts, to the extent that they had tended to live within close proximity of one another, for mutual protection and support, forming ghettos where only Irish Catholics lived. For these and other reasons, John had kept himself to himself, for fear of reprisals, and since his own problems from lack of work had led to the movement into these courts, he had maintained his distance for safety.

James was a passionate young man, and in his view all things were possible and could be changed. To him, Ireland belonged to the Irish and there had been too much interference from others, with their own self-interests in the accumulation of land. The Irish had had too much bad luck and too many bad harvests, they had suffered greatly under oppressive rule by the government at Westminster. He was not the only voice that felt this strongly, but he was one of very few.

John knew that James was liable to be vocal wherever he was, and as the subject of this debate was so closely connected to his own circumstances, he had best be there to counsel and caution his enthusiastic young advocate, as much for his friend's safety as for any personal self-interest.

They entered the meeting hall quietly that Friday evening. There had been a small and insignificant group of anti-Irish protestors gathered outside, who were vocal in their exclamations against any support for their neighbours. They entered a packed chamber of men, whose attentions were all directed towards a low platform where half a dozen individuals sat, while one led forth from the podium; the debate was well underway. The hall was cloudy with cigar smoke and very warm, they took some vacant seats at the rear, and endeavoured to catch the speech that was issuing forth. The young man standing on the podium was a proud-looking man, well-dressed, with light brown hair, slightly tousled. He wore a black tailcoat, with a high-buttoned collar. He gave a powerful, if a little hesitant, delivery, it became apparent that he was speaking against Irish immigration.

'My friends, one should not forget the good people of this town, who have worked hard generation after generation, to establish their lives and their families here. They depend on us, on all of us for the protection of their status and livelihoods… they have not asked through voice of the mob to rid our streets of this Irish blight… indeed they have welcomed these people and tried to make them feel as comfortable as possible within their communities…'

James bristled and his shoulders became rigid. John sensed his friend's sap rising, as the speaker on the stage continued.

'They have attempted to help these people… but they do not help themselves. Instead, they seem determined to waste their opportunities, and exist in squalid conditions rather than seeking to better their lives…'

'Pah!' James could not contain his disgust any longer, and uttered his feelings, all eyes turned to look, and then turned back to the speaker, who continued haltingly.

'They have chosen to live in squalid conditions... separate from those who have tried to befriend them...'

'Rot!' Once again James could not hold back. John turned to him and whispered:

'Jimmy, this is not the time.'

The speaker threw a look of disgust towards the back row at the heckler, and once again attempted to regain his composure to continue his delivery.

'I do not decry all of the hard work that their fathers and grandfathers undertook in the growth and expansion of this town. After all, had it not been for their devotions to digging, we would not have any transport whatsoever—'

The hall exploded into laughter, James tensed his fists so that his knuckles began to turn white.

'But facts are facts... the majority will not work and lie idle causing problems associated such a drunkenness and debauchery... while those that do work, deliver shoddy workmanship while stealing valuable employment and an income from a respectable artisan of this town!'

At this point, James shot out of his seat and shouted back at the podium.

'I have never heard such a bigoted load of nonsense in my life!'

The hall erupted into pandemonium, the vast majority called for James to be ejected immediately and were raising a party to do just that. John was clutching at his friend's jacket arm, trying to calm him, to get him to take his place quietly once more. James was insisting that it was a debate and that he had a right to reply. It looked as if the strength of opinion against him remaining was such that he would be forcibly removed, had it not been for the speaker himself, who raised his voice above the melee.

'My friends! My Friends! Please calm yourselves! Are we not a society who believes that all opinion should be heard!' The hall began to calm and redirected its collective attentions towards their most valuable speaker. 'We have a young man here with a different view… let us hear what he has to say… it can only add to the argument, not devalue it in any way. Young sir, you were saying?' All heads turned to see the young enthusiast at the back of the hall. James firmly stood his ground, John released his grip.

'You all should be ashamed of yourselves! If it was not for the hard work and diligence of many of these people that you despise, you would not be sitting here in your grand suits and be able to live your grand lives on the broken backs and sweat of these people! You accuse them of idleness! I have never known an idle Irishman! Like my friend here…' He looked down at John, who tried to sink into his seat to seek anonymity. 'Many have not chosen to come, they have been left with little or no choice as their country has been enslaved into ruin over generations of brutal governance at our hands! And when they have arrived, despite all those who chose to hound them out of these so called "communities", they battle to try and make a living and add to the growing economy here. And what help do they get?' He looked at the many angered faces that stared back at him. 'None! For if they fall on hard times, they don't get poor relief! That is why they live in squalor, not because of idleness or lack of diligence… no! Just because they cannot move forward! This town, so proud of itself, so proud of welcoming those that are unwelcome elsewhere…! That encourages those to come, as I did, from other places to make their fortunes and make the fortune of the town! This town has developed an underclass of people, and not because they are from another town, or even another country… no! it is much more than that! It is simply because their faith is despised! All you Quakers and Unitarians sitting here, where would you be now if Birmingham had not opened its arms to you?' John pulled on James's arm, and he sat back hard in his seat.

The man at the podium smiled and let the rumbles of discontent diminish before making his response.

'A very impassioned response from our young friend there… and a worthy comment for our open forum. For as much as he has been allowed to voice his dissent, so he must respect the rights of others to express their views, whether they are mutually shared or not. Now we will continue with our discussions, I hope, without further interruption.'

Another rumble, but this time of approval, rose from the collective audience. John knew that to continue would only lead to trouble, and he made his feelings clear to James by retaining a tight grip on his arm for the next hour. This, James respected, and gritted his teeth until the forum concluded much in the same way as it had been introduced – with complete rejection for the Irish and all that they stood for. The two men waited in their seats for a while longer, as others rose to leave, passing with looks of disapproval in their direction. John glanced at James.

'I think we had best leave quietly now.'

As both left their seats, a familiar voice approached from behind.

'Might I have a word, gentlemen?'

The young leader of the debate was standing behind them. He may not have been as tall as the friends, but for what he lost in height he seemed to exude in charisma and presence.

'Joseph Chamberlain, at your service, I am the Chairman of this society.'

James reached out a reluctant hand to shake the one that was offered, John did likewise.

'I realise that you are not familiar with our society rules of debate here. We are, as you might consider… a more refined group… we do not herald from previous traditions of this town of open forum, we tend to pass all of our requests to speak through the chair. I realise that that may not be of common understanding.'

Chamberlain spoke with a slight sarcasm, and a supercilious air.

'Might I have your acquaintance for future reference, sirs?'

'I am James Pearse, and this is my friend John Connolly. We both work near St Paul's, I am a sculptor in stone and John is a jeweller and silversmith.'

'Ah, both fine occupations! Now I understand your passion to prove your case. Indeed, I can respect the work of fine artisans like yourselves. My grandfather was a cordwainer, and I have built my fortune on screw making... machined, I know, not quite same handcrafted skill that you two gentlemen pride yourselves upon. This may seem very strange, but I am keen to understand more about your point of view.'

James regarded Chamberlain with some puzzlement and suspicion.

'I would like to come to your places of work and talk to you more at length?'

John became very guarded, he found it difficult to allow friends into his working sphere, never mind a man with such negative views of his own heritage.

'I don't know... I... er...' But James was far more enthusiastic; he immediately grasped the significance of this opportunity to illustrate his strength of feeling.

'Certainly, Mr Chamberlain... you are more than welcome. I... we, look forward to sharing opinion with you.'

As John and James stepped out of the hall, they were both lost in the events of their evening. James was caught in curiosity for the strange approach that they had both received from Joseph; he had found the man both abrasive and challenging, yet he had shown a genuine desire to meet both men in a serious capacity. Joseph was an obviously successful and driven man, from a society above their own. He moved in differing social circles and circumstances and possessed some overt magnetic charm that either captivated or repelled in equal measure. On the other hand, John was withdrawn deep into memories that led him to anger and despair, he knew he must shake himself free from his imaginings or it would have dreadful consequences. He scanned the assembled crowd on the pavement from the top of the meeting hall steps. Some of the gentlemen that had been in attendance were still milling around in discussions with their own kind, the odd scathing look was passed in John's direction.

There were still others gathered, a larger crowd than earlier; they were distinct from the society members by their mode of dress, which was rougher and less formal, the tweeds and corduroys, rather than the black tailcoats and button-down collars. These were a ramshackle mob of those that had recently vacated public houses looking for a fight, and those that had anti-Catholic persuasions, some sporting orange sashes. John realised that there were too many of the wrong disposition for it to be safe to remain, and urged James to hurry. As he did so, he caught for an instant a red-faced stout man in the crowd, his nose glowing with the sun or gin, but it was his companion that struck fear into John, a shock of ginger hair under a cap, and a scarred face. John headed off in the opposite direction, hoping that he had not been seen.

Chapter 7

Mountains of memory

John slumped in the kitchen chair. May had been asleep all of the evening and he did not wish to disturb her, he needed to think, he needed to rest his deeply troubled mind. Had he been seen? Oh God, no! He had worked so hard to become anonymous in the last twelve years, he had kept himself to himself, for the sake of his mother, she had had enough to face in her life.

A pain shot through his heart and nausea gripped him as a fleeting thought passed rapidly through his mind; the flash of silver, the shock of red, and the warm wetness on his face. Why? Why? Yet again he had pulled his life back together, he had come many miles to escape his mistake. He had found a way to make it through each day without remembering, and now… had he been seen? If he had, then they would find him, they would never stop looking, he knew that, he had always known that. But all these years… all these years he had lived safely, even openly, and no one, nothing had come for him. And just now, now when he had begun to make his way again, when he had found love…

John stopped and reeled. He was struck by a sudden fear, a real and destructive fear, that was it, that was the reason he could not think and focus. He felt a sudden anger, a sudden stir in his emotions, not fury with the fate that stalked him, but with his own carelessness. He should not have allowed himself to relax, he should not have thought of his own contentment, not for one moment, not for one day! How stupid he had been, he had always kept on his guard, always watched out, always taken care to keep himself to himself. And now… what had he done! Not only had he risked his own safety, but that of his mothers, a sick dying woman, who needed her last few weeks on earth to be peaceful and easy. And why? Because he had allowed himself to think about someone else, to fall in love... love...

For a moment his anger subsided. He loved her... this was first time he had admitted it to himself, allowed himself to admit it. He actually loved her... but it was useless... now completely useless! He could not ruin somebody else's life, drag someone else through this pain of running, never feeling safe... and if he hadn't had these distractions and lapses into careless behaviour, if he had been more observant, more careful, he would have looked out. His ire rose once more... it was all her fault... why did she have to come into his life? Why could he not just have kept away? He must stay away now, he must! It was the only way he could protect and keep safe, it was the only way he could make it through and stay alive, he must stay away!

The warmth of the kitchen range combined with his fatigue. The evening had been highly stressful for him, trying to keep Jimmy from starting a riot, and then his justifiable anxiety about being seen – he was completely exhausted. His eyelids grew heavy and closed, still seated bolt upright, as if on constant watch.

There was the house, and his da again. Ma at the table, clutching a darning needle, and a man's shirt of discoloured calico, which had seen better days in her hands, her feverish fingers making busy, mending it once again, but the sun shone. He knew he was small then, he sat on the floor, his bare bottom on a sack on the earth floor. He could feel the roughness of the hessian against his skin. They were all giants! Ma and Da up at the table, Cara and Niamh bickering over a piece of old rope that had been found on the road, and Patrick sitting by, egging on whoever would be the victor. They were all giants!

The truth to a child not about to walk, but these giants were children themselves: Niamh just turned seven, the eldest and the feistiest of the sisters; Cara a big five, nearly six, 'too big for her boots,' Da would say, but she didn't wear boots?; Patrick four years of age, but he knew his place, he would side with whichever girl would win the scrap.

Just now, Da stood up from the table and snatched the ragged bit of rope away from the scrapping wains, tossing it away out through the open door, sending all three scrabbling after it, the fastest would claim victory. 'Oh, blessed peace,' he said. May smiling. 'It won't be long till that wee lad joins in the fray, will it now, May?' May smiled and nodded.

John shook himself awake. Now is not the time to dream, he could not dream, he had not got the time, he must think…

His head began to nod again, a piece of slag coal hissed and crackled in the range, but barely registered with his conscious self that was slipping away…

Now he was outside his family's wee house in the field, he was in long trousers, Niamh and Cara were practically grown women. It was the smell, the appalling smell. It was harvest time, he was ten years old, Patrick that bit older and more of the man about him. John could see his Da and Ma frantically digging with their hands, and urging their offspring on to do the same, to save what they could, any of what they could. John's hands dug into the sodden smelly soil and felt for the precious crop, the crop that would keep the family alive through another hard winter. But as he found each potato, which should have been plump and hard, and golden in colour, his hands found a mushy, under-sized, very smelly mass that, when brought forth from the soil, was practically black and stank of rot.

What had started as a normal harvest, hard work, but productive – bringing in the crop, some to be sold against other goods, the rest to be consumed in the hundred ways a good Irish woman could make them palatable; from soup, to stew, coddle to mash – had become a nightmare for the family. As each spade had been dug throughout the morning, it had brought forth more rotten potatoes, a huge pile stood at the corner of the field. A frantic search by hands was now being undertaken by all in an effort to find anything worth saving, this whole sorry mess had not been helped by the incessant rain that had fallen steadily for three days. They had tried waiting for a dry spell but the smell had already confirmed to the family their worst fears and that delay was working against retrieving anything of value from the ground.

May's tears rolled down her face as she scrabbled through the earth and the family's blighted crop. She knew she could not make the money last long, that there was very little food in the store and it would be impossible to keep any sort of meal on the table no matter how careful and sparing she was. She just did not know what to do, and cried silently into the soil, praying her rosary as she did.

'Hail Mary, full of grace, our Lord art with thee. Blessed art thou among women, and blessed is the fruit of thy womb, Jesus.'

Patrick leant over his mother with caring compassion.

'Hey, Ma let me help you, we'll look together, so we will.' He hoped to engage her interest, but still unmoved by her son's direct concerns, she continued to pray for intercession from the Virgin Mary.

'Holy Mary, Mother of God, pray for us sinners, now and at the hour of our death, amen.'

Then John's nightmarish vision switched.

He was lying prostrate in pain outside the house on the ground, his innards contorted in agony. With each inhalation of breath, his intestines cramped uncontrollably in violent motions. He had evacuated at both ends simultaneously and uncontrollably for hours, into his britches. He lay in mortal shame, unable to move, unable clean himself, knowing he was not the only one so stricken, that the whole of his family had become the victims of the bad water which had brought the sickness. A violent illness that had come to swollen malnourished bellies that had little or no resistance to bacteria.

He had heard Niamh's cries most of the day from where he lay. She had been the first to succumb to the sickness two days before, at least she had been nursed for a time, what little good May could do to relieve her suffering and make her comfortable. But as the day had gone on those cries had weakened, and he had no conception of how long he had lain there, but he had no sense of hearing her for hours, not that he could have moved, not that he could have helped. If he could have died there and then, if it would stop the pain and the shame, he would have.

Once again, he shook himself awake. These were the dreams he did not want to revisit, that he had tried so hard to escape that – no matter what he did – haunted him night after night. Even when he had worked himself into the ground to bring on total exhaustion to try and sleep without feeling or thinking, even then these memories were there. And every time he would wake, he would feel the same weight of guilt and of sadness. Guilt because he was still alive, sadness for the loss and tragedy.

That first bad famine, had culled the weak from the strong, and even taken the strongest. As the crop had failed, family after family had followed the same route to try to survive. First using any and all stored food and eking all out, portion to portion. Then slaying all livestock that could no longer be fed. But as the weeks turned to months hunger became a way of life, scavenging was the only way to survive. But it was the cholera that finished many off, it was the cholera which had taken Niamh.

And as each other family member had managed to clean their emaciated bodies and consume whatever watery hedgerow stew as could be held down, they had watched the cart take away their beloved daughter and sister, to a lime pit, to be disposed of with the other poor unfortunates. Each feeling the same: why did it not take me? Why did it take her?

His head snatched at his spine as he lolled forward, and once more came the blessing of waking suddenly from troubled sleep. John shook himself awake and rose from the chair. He did not want any more thoughts to pass through his unconscious self, he had to try and work out what to do. In his groggy state, he crept into the darkened parlour, the laboured breathing was still audible, barely hanging onto life. How she had fought to stay alive.

He had witnessed her sacrifices at the extreme parts of the famine, going without anything for days, to give her children whatever she could find. Every rodent or wild bird that could be caught made a soup of sorts, with what hedgerow greens could be made palatable, whatever little nutrition they possessed. Handfuls of corn could make a shared pancake, just to keep the sharp edge off the hunger. But she had gone without longer, eaten less, and always put her family first.

She had never cried or complained and had done her best to absorb everyone else's pain and suffering, being the gentle arms that would hold you when it had all become too much, the gentle now skeletal arms that held. Even when Niamh was taken, she prayed her devotions over her dead first-born and reflected that at least she had a life, how many of the wee bairns had been taken that had failed to thrive at all. But persistent famine takes both the physical and emotional strength of any soul, and May could be the force for everyone but she could not stop the inevitable spectre of death.

Da had never been a very strong man, even if he had been small in stature and slight of frame. Years of hard work and long hours in the rough Irish climate had taken their toll. Patrick and John were just beginning to shoulder much of the manual work of the farm, but Da had been the sole provider and worker for years. He had always had a cough as long as John could remember, but that irritating hack had changed in its intensity, and John had watched as the paroxysms of uncontrollable coughing had laid his father low for the last time. Within a few days of these fits, the spots of blood grew, then one morning he coughed what remained of his tattered lungs away. Cara sat sobbing holding Da's hand, begging him not to die. May watched on from the table impassive, unable to comfort, unable this time to absorb, the fears doubling in her mind, her silence deafening.

Her breathing was still there, she was still living, after all she had witnessed, after all that she had been through. The enormous fight in this woman to defy death, to cope with the most dreadful of times, to suffer the terrible loss that she had, remained. But John knew why she had never given up, and why even now she clung onto life so defiantly: it was for him. Her biological imperative to protect her son from danger and from harm; to save him. She would not rest until she knew that one thing, or until her body simply gave up. John knew now it would be the latter. He stepped back into the kitchen and sat back in the chair. What could he do? Run now? No… he could not leave his mother. What if they got to her? He had to stay. Mrs Morris was right: she had days, maybe weeks left. He owed his life to his Ma, she had done all that she could for him… he could not desert her now. But Vi… he must not see her… he knew in his heart it could not carry on. He felt a gripping pain in his chest, and wished things could be different, but he must stay away, for her sake.

Fanny was awoken by a loud bang and a simultaneous angry roar from the kitchen. She felt the sinking pit in her stomach and grabbed for her shawl and boots. As she made her way down the steep enclosed stairs, the banging and grumbling was growing in intensity from the room beneath. She was gripped with fear but she knew she must not show this; like any wild ferocious animal 'it' fed on fear, 'it' attacked fear and went for those much weaker. She steeled herself and turned the corner stair into the kitchen and empowered her voice.

'So yer back then? And crashing around waking the nippers up!'

Alf stood in shock, brought to book by his eldest daughter! He was too drunk and befuddled to react to the audacity and cheek that she had displayed, but his initial shock only lasted for a short moment. He reached for a cast iron skillet and sent it skimming across the kitchen with all of his force in her general direction. She moved instinctively, as the skillet collided with the wall near her.

'Gercher… where's me dinna! You ugly who-a...! Dain't yer talk to me like that…! Whom da yer think yer are…! Get me dinna …'

Fanny felt her own vulnerability, she knew that neither Kitty nor Tom were home; not that Kitty could have done much good, unless she had wanted something from him. Tom had been spending more and more nights out, sometimes not returning for days. She knew if he had come home this night he would have come through from the parlour by now. She was on her own, she had to protect the little ones from this violently drunken sot, he was capable of anything. She must protect them, particularly Suie, she was about the right age now: he had no moral compass whatsoever. Her initial reaction to fight fire with fire gave way to the common sense of the vulnerable situation. There was very little food in the house, there had been very little money with Tom and Kitty's perpetual absences, but she knew that whatever she had, she must give it to him to placate his anger. She moved with purpose towards him.

The first blow caught her left cheek with a stinging force and, losing her balance, she fell to the floor; the second blow was the connection of a hobnailed boot with her chest, she felt a crack. She knew not to cry out, she knew that if she did it would be worse for her. She contained the searing pain as it ate into her, she clamped her jaw tight and breathed as best she could through it.

'Yer a slovenly tyke! What did I teld you? Hey? What have I teld you before… never… never… never argue with me!'

Each never was, reinforced with another kick. After the full force of the first it was more of a nudge now, but Fanny lay still, no sound and no reaction.

'Now I want sumit to eat and make it quick. I am going for a lay down. Working man needs food when he comes home… and rest!'

With that, Alf stumbled into the parlour and lumbered forward onto Tom's unmade bed. He lay collapsed in his reeking clothes and boots, half on and half off the bed.

Fanny, eased herself to her feet as best she could. As she did so a knife-like pain in her left side caused her to wince and clutch her chest; she muttered under her breath:

'Damn him… another cracked rib. Christ!'

She felt the left side of her face. Her eye felt like it was going to explode, her cheek was double its normal size, she grabbed for a damp rag and dipped it in a pail. Wringing it out, she pressed it lightly on her eye and cheek, the relief of the cold against the burning pain was a blessing. She lifted the lid on the remains of the cobbled stew that was going to last her and the young ones another night. It was just enough for them, but it would not be enough for him. With one hand, she found two more potatoes and a carrot and set about trying to peel them. She rough-chopped them and put them in the steeping pot to boil, and gingerly sat herself down in the chair, trying not to move too suddenly. Every breath that she took was punctuated with the pain from her broken rib, and her face was no longer feeling much relief from the damp cloth.

'Fanny…' A tiny voice whispered low from around the corner on the darkened stair. 'Fanny, can I come in? I'm scared.' Little Teddy sniffed and his little voice cracked. Fanny's initial thoughts were to send him back to bed for his own safety. She knew if Alf was in this sort of mood Teddy did not stand a chance, especially as Alf held Teddy responsible for the loss of his wife; not that he had any great love for her, but she kept the bed warm and food in his belly, and now the loneliness of widowhood had eaten into his soul, and in Alf's mind Teddy's birth had caused her death. Not the last kick that Alf had delivered to her back two days before Teddy had made his bloodied entry into the world.

'Come 'ere, little man… dain't be scared. 'Ee's asleep now. Come 'ere and give me a hug.'

Teddy scurried, barefoot around the corner and across the kitchen and then, catching a glimpse of Fanny's battle-scars, stopped dead in his tracks.

'Ooh… Fanny, are you alright? That looks bad.'

'This is nothing, Teddy… 'ee's done much worse than this.'

He crept towards her, attempting to climb on her knee – which caused her to whimper – and trying to reach out with his little fingers to feel the large, blackening lump on her face.

'Dain't do that, it hurts me.' She turned him around on her knee, and looked meaningfully into his eyes.

'Now listen, Teddy… 'ee's got one on him, so you must stay out of his way until 'ee clears off again.'

Teddy nodded and held his most serious expression.

She continued.

'You know if 'ee catches sight of yer 'ee'll have yer hide… so keep yer head down, right?'

He nodded again.

'It won't be long… I promise yer. As soon as 'ee as some money, 'ee'll bugger off again, and then you'll be safe. Have Maud or Suie heard anything?'

Teddy nodded again, and through glassy eyes stuttered a whispered reply.

'Maudi's still sleeping… but Suie heard it all and sent me down to see if you'm alright.'

'Well you go back up now and tell Suie everything's fine, an' Fanny will sort it all.'

Teddy slid off her lap and headed back towards the stairs. Fanny further qualified all that she had tried to reassure him with.

'An' Teddy…' He swung round and listened attentively.

'I think the best place for yer is school for the next few days, right?' Teddy nodded with no objections, his common sense told him that when it came to the man he called his father, it was best to be in the most public place possible whenever he was around, there was a great deal to be said for safety in numbers.

Chapter 8

A gem with flaws

'My God, Fanny! What's happened to you?'

Vi stood on the corner of the court staring at her bruised and battered friend. Fanny's cheek had turned all shades of dark purple to black, and her left eye matched.

''Ee's back ain't 'ee… fists flying as usual.'

'Oh, no… what are going to do? Is Tom not there…? What about the young 'uns?'

'Not much I can do. There's no money to send him off on another bender, and Tom and Kitty haven't been back in days. Gawd knows where my alleycat of a sister has gone this time, there's rumours about 'er and Stan. I am just trying to keep him away from the little 'uns, especially Teddy… and Suie too.'

Vi looked puzzled.

'Why Suie?'

'Cos she's about the right age. I was that age when 'ee tried it on wif me… but he got a good kick to his tackle and Tom smacked him one. Suie ain't so strong, and 'ee won't try it while I'm around, but she's too scared of him to say no.'

Vi was visibly shocked by this admission, having had such a safe home, where her parents gave normal parental affection. Of course, she knew that some families were not so settled and girls were abused regularly by brothers, sometimes fathers, but she had never associated this with her friend. The violence she had seen before – he always left marks on Fanny when he was drunk, when he had not got any money, when he came back from one of his absences – but she had never revealed that he had tried to commit any sexual act with her.

'But what about Kitty?'

'I dain't know about Kitty… she has always got 'er own way with him. She has always been his favourite.'

'Do you think…?' Vi did not finish her question, she left it unqualified, not wanting to be the one to raise the spectre of Kitty's involvements with her father. Fanny cut back quickly.

'No, course not. She's too quick for that… she'd never…' She paused. But there had been times she had heard Alf upstairs in the children's room in the middle of the day when Fanny had come home unexpectedly. She'd never seen Kitty, but the thought suddenly crossed her mind – it did not mean that she had not been there.

'No, I don't think so…' But there was no certainty in her, and some detectable uncertainty in her response to her best friend, and Vi was too astute not to notice it, but nothing more would be discussed.

Vi was lost in her own thoughts most of the morning. She wanted so much to help her friend, who was obviously in dire need, but she had not got a clue what to do. She could not stand up to Alf, she would probably get worse than Fanny; and Fanny and the others would probably suffer more for the involvement of outsiders. Maybe she could find Tom? But she had not got a clue where to start. He had been sweet on a girl for a long time, she knew that, but she had heard that all had cooled, because Tom had told the young lady that she would have to wait because he had to help his family. Since then all she knew was that he had been hanging around with a rum crowd of other, bachelor types, frequenting the alehouses around the town being seen from time to time, but never engaging in conversation with his old friends. Vi always tried to keep her distance from Kitty, because she usually got a mouthful of abuse any time she tried to be nice; she was perceived as the enemy as she was Fanny's friend. And besides, what Fanny had revealed that morning, and what they now jointly suspected but did not dare to confirm to each other, had made up Vi's mind that Kitty could not be encouraged to help for her own sake.

Other thoughts worried Vi. Her mother had become very difficult the last few weeks and, on at least two occasions during that time, Vi had suffered some very sleepless nights, as she had been woken by her father who had found that his wife had slipped out of bed in her stockinged feet and had disappeared downstairs. The first time, Vi had found her walking aimlessly round and round the kitchen, picking things up and putting them down again, looking puzzled and confused at everyday well-known objects that she had used all of her married life. Vi had managed to guide her gently back to bed after half an hour or so and had dismissed this as an incident of sleepwalking, though she had lain awake half the night worried that it would start again.

The second time it happened had been considerably more disturbing. She had once again been woken by her father, who was visibly distressed at finding his wife missing for a second time. Vi pulled on her shawl and her boots, expecting to be spending another length of time encouraging her mother to return to bed. When she descended the stairs to the kitchen she was alarmed by what she saw. Every cooking pot, knife, fork, spoon, plate and other utensil was laid out in neat lines on the quarry-tile floor, but more alarmingly her mother was nowhere to be seen and the door into the court was open wide. The colour drained from Vi's face and her knees began to buckle; she had run off, in her confused, sleepwalking state, she had run off!

Vi raced across the kitchen and out into the dark court: there was no sign. She raced back into the kitchen and shouted up the stairs to her father to come quick and help to search. Her exclamations set a dog barking and within a short time, because of the paper-thin walls, one or two of the more concerned neighbours appeared in their nightwear and gasped concerns and some offers to help. Vi took to the streets, dark but for hissing gas lamps; there was no moon.

She ran down one street and up another, her worst fears were that her mother had walked to the canal and fallen in. Tears streaked her face, making it difficult to see clearly, but she knew a woman in her nightwear, probably barefoot, was going to be easier to spot than most others. Street after street she ran down, breathlessly calling for her mother, just in case she had taken shelter in a door, or in an alleyway. Finally, she ended up back at her court, where there was consternation. People had been looking for Vi, her mother had been found, much to Vi's relief, but where she had been found and what she had been doing, led to even greater concerns for Vi.

Vi had not searched the court, thinking that her mother would have just wandered and would not be waiting around so close by to be found. Apparently, she was in the pitch-black laundry house, no light with her, in her nightdress, a bar of soap and washboard in hand, washing old hessian sacks in freezing cold water; the copper pot was only lit during certain washdays and had gone cold during the week. There was no sense to any of it, and sleepwalking could not be used as the excuse – her mother appeared to be very much awake, but confused and unaware of where she was, and when she had been taken back to her own kitchen she had reacted angrily, that this was not her house, and she wanted to go home. It had taken some time for her to be convinced and calmed enough to go to bed. But the decision was made that night by Vi and her father, that the last person up would lock the door each night and take the key up to bed with them.

And as if all this was not enough for poor Vi to cope with, she had not seen John or heard from him for days and she was missing him dreadfully. She knew that he had difficulties with work and his mother, and she had left him alone until he was ready and had time to see her. But all these stresses and strains had simply become too much for her to bear alone, and she could not confide in Fanny, that was obvious, Fanny had too much on her own plate to deal with. And she would not really put it all on John either, but just to see him, spend some time with him and have some pleasant moments in his company would be enough to help. She made up her mind to go and see if she could catch him for one of their lunchtime trysts.

Kitty's head was banging, a penalty of what she had to do to avoid being mauled by her Stan. As to be expected, her relationship with this man had developed very quickly; he had no interest in courting her, or indeed any long-term desires towards her. In his eyes she was young and obviously available, and he had one intention and only one intention towards her. Unluckily for Stan, Kitty could take as much drink as he could, in truth, probably more. Several weeks, of standing him drink for drink in the public house, and then stumbling back to his flat, him blind drunk, her still coherent, had found him physically incapable of raising an erection, and most nights not even any interest whatsoever. This had led to many considerable hangovers for both parties, and a great deal of frustration for Stan, not helped by Kitty taking advantage of the situation to further demoralise him by ridiculing his under-performance. To date, he had failed to consummate their relationship at all, and Kitty, although feeling rough physically, was quietly content that she had outwitted the fool and at the same time maintained her ale-ticket, and her bed and board, poor Stan being consigned to a broken couch night after night, as his 'nearly' conquest took over his bed.

He had reached the end of his tether, as much as he was attracted to the young piece of flesh, he knew that she was playing him for an idiot, but he was determined not only to get what he had been paying for over and over, but also some sort of revenge against this heartless young bint. He had made up his mind that he would have one over on her, one way or another, and he was going to do it soon because he had had enough of her constant humiliations and jibes against him. Besides, there were plenty of other young fillies far more accommodating and far more compliant than Kitty Tulloch, who was fast becoming a liability. But he would get the goods he had paid for, definitely.

Kitty, on the other hand, although quietly confident she could play this for all she was worth and get much more out of the situation then she had as yet, was plagued by a prick of conscience; she had a family. She may hate her sister for her constant demands on her time and her pay packet, but at least it was a family and home of sorts, and when things turned bad, as they inevitably would, eventually, she would need that family and home to go back to. It was probably pertinent to make an appearance? Maybe it was time to face another shouting match from her dear darling sister? But the way her head felt this morning trying to pack bloody pens, she would take this afternoon to reflect on it.

Vi sat on their bench, looking over towards John's garret, hoping desperately he might be there, and that he would look out of the window and spot her and dash eagerly to join her. She had been there for ten minutes already and had seen no sign. She did not want to go unannounced, just in case he was too busy, just in case he was trying to do business with a factor; it would be such bad timing and would probably not enamour him to her, so she would sit and wait, and hope.

John peeped nervously out the corner of the window; what he had been fearing would happen, had. She was sitting there waiting for him. In his heart he so desperately wanted to go and join her, he wanted to look deep into those violet eyes and drown in her tenderness. He really needed someone's arms around him right now, and even though their relationship had not advanced to that stage, she was the one: he knew it. If things had been different, she was the only girl he would have married, have curled up with in bed at night, burying his face in her warm back, losing himself in her softness. He really needed that comfort he used to get from his mother's arms when he was wee, but no! He knew he had to stay away from her and to not put her at risk; there were too many perils coalescing, too many dangers.

He had been working, finishing off a piece of silver to take to Hardman's. He had been naturally apprehensive since he had been seen the other night and had been constantly checking out of his window; he had walked faster in the street, pulled his cap further over his eyes leaving just enough eye line to see underneath his peak, to see without being seen. He had to carry on earning a living, he had to carry on living exactly where he was, he could not run, not yet. Until May... until his mother had gone, he had to stay exactly where he was and keep on doing exactly what he had been doing, to pay for the rent, to pay for the food, to pay for the doctor, to pay for the medication. What mattered the most in his thinking was that May did not learn of his discovery.

Just as he had been about to leave, he had caught sight of her. He dropped quickly to his knees and hoped that she had not seen his image through the grimy glass. He knelt near the window and peered out the corner, half of him longing to see her and talk to her, half of him willing her to leave, just go, and not come back. He knew he ought to speak to her, make some lame excuse, tell her it was over, that it was just not going to work. He did not have to explain to her why, he had enough reasons that she knew about. I mean, for God's sake, he was Irish, it never worked marrying out of the community and he was a Catholic of sorts, he was certain she was not. And then there was his mother, she must realise how difficult it all was for him, and as far as she was aware this was going to go on for years; he had not seen her since the doctor had made his terminal diagnosis. He could even say that he simply could not afford to ever take a wife and it would be unfair of him to raise her hopes artificially and keep her on a string; there were plenty more nice chaps out there that would jump at the chance of taking her as their intended. But he could not bring himself to do it. If he didn't do it, he had not lost her forever, not yet anyway. So, he carried on peering out the window, and watched as she stood to leave, and a tear rolled down his cheek as he whispered, 'Bye.'

The unseasonably cool summer had given way to a balmy evening, but the weather that should have lifted spirits did little to generate any happiness in two young women who made their silent and troubled walk together homeward.

Fanny was growing anxious as to what awaited her in the court. She hoped that for once, her younger siblings did drag their heels and made no concerted effort to get home; she had little doubt that Teddy was far too scared to want to confront his father without his big sister around. Every step that she walked caused her to wince in pain. She had found an old blouse, long past its days as a garment to wear. She had ripped it into strips and managed with considerable discomfort to bind her chest under her corset and chemise, it had certainly helped, limiting her to very little movement, but she definitely had a fractured rib and the associated bruising was causing considerable pain. Her face had been the subject of some comment all day. Most had been shocked and then discussed it among themselves, they thought out of her hearing but she had caught more than they had realised. A few had been downright rude, and made some observations in very poor taste: 'The boyfriend not happy with his tea then?' or, 'Hadn't you better just stick to water next time?' She had paid no attention to these ignorant jibes; these people had absolutely no idea.

She dreaded turning the corner into the court and finding him still there; she fumbled for her coin purse, the only pennies she had left. Just enough for another scratch stew, but only enough for her and the nippers. It would have to be for him, and she would have to make it stretch as best she could, she would have to go without, no matter how hungry she was. She returned her coin purse back under jacket inside the waistband of her skirt. As she did so she glanced at Vi who had been more silent than normal. Her whole demeanour said it all, her shoulders were drooping, her face downcast towards the pavement. Something had happened to Vi, she knew in her heart. She just could not deal with it now, she had to think about herself for a change.

Vi already realised that Fanny was carrying the weight of the world on her shoulders, and her small insignificant problem, compared to what Fanny had to face, seemed exactly that: trivial and irrelevant. But Vi, burdened with the problem of her mother on top of John's puzzling absence, felt like everything was coming crashing down on her head. She had waited and waited and he had not come. Had she missed him? Was he sick? Was his mother in a worse state? What had happened to him? And worst of all, she had a real fear that it was none of these, that he had just changed his mind about her. That had sent her spirits descending; that brief few weeks of meetings had given her a real hope for her life, that maybe, just maybe, she had met someone finally and was not going to end up an old spinster having nursed both parents into the grave.

Then there was the other real fear penetrating her soul. What was happening to her mother and was it going to get worse? Her father was not coping at all well, and he was worrying himself into a state where he could not work every day, having barely slept each night with the stress of it all. Vi was growing increasingly concerned that her father would get sick with all this and be unable to work, and no work meant no wages. She could not possibly support all three of them on the paltry salary that she earned, and if he was sick too, he would need a doctor and medicine. The only way they would be able to survive would be to visit the bench and beg for poor relief; she knew that the shame of that would kill her father, who had never asked for charity the whole of his life and prided himself that, 'with a pair of good hands, and a tongue in me head, I never will'. Just then, Fanny muttered 'Bye,' or something, and turned into her court. Vi barely acknowledged it – lost in her thoughts – and just continued to her home.

Fanny turned the handle on the door of the kitchen. A couple of her neighbours stood chatting in the court as she arrived, she knew they had been talking about her, they had probably seen him; they shut up as soon as she had appeared and just stood staring.

'Fan… Fan…' Mouse and Suie ran breathlessly towards her, calling out. She released the handle and swung around to greet them.

''Ello girls. Where's Teddy?'

''Ee's comin',' said Suie. 'Just not rushin', that's all… Is 'ee still 'ere?'

'Probably.'

'Oh,' replied Suie dejectedly. Mouse scraped her foot on the ground nervously.

'Look, you two… we needs some veggies for ours' tea.' She shuffled in her coin purse for a few pennies and halfpennies. 'You'm see what magic you can do, Suie… maybe the butcher will take pity on yer and give a few bits of scrag for free, if you ask nicely. Take Mouse with you.' With that the two girls ran out of the court, passing Teddy without a word who doubled his pace in order to catch his sister before she went in; he just made it in behind her as she entered the kitchen.

Alf had been sleeping off his binge most of the day. He had decided he needed some clean clothes and had taken Tom's best britches and shirt and unceremoniously discarded his old ones, stained with vomit and urine, on the kitchen floor by the door. They reeked, as he still did; Alf considered too much washing to be bad for his health, and he had very little sense of smell or hygiene. The gathering noise from the courtyard and the initial rattle of the door handle had caught his attention from where he had been sitting in the parlour, and he decided to stake his claim as head of the household by sitting expectantly at the head of the kitchen table ready to make his demands known.

'Where, the 'ell have you been till this time? Well? And I see yer got that bloody tyke with you.' Alf stared menacingly at Teddy, who froze to the spot, clutching on to Fanny's skirt for security.

'Gercher! You little menace!' Alf roared. Teddy needed no other word, he let out a small yelp and shot past his father up the stairs to hide under the bed in his room, wetting himself as he ran.

'And don't let me see yer... at all!' The loving comments from a loving father, to his youngest child.

Fanny stood still, no emotion showing on her face; inside she wanted to run him through with a kitchen knife for what he had just said. He could beat hell out of her, and he had done, but to take it out on a little lad, his own son for God's sake, in such a vile and threatening way... she could never forgive him.

'Well? Yer got me tea then?' He continued to bellow.

Fanny answered with care, and without any perceivable edge to her voice.

'The girls have just gone to get it. There's only me 'ere... the only wage. You'll have to wait till they come back.'

'What, our Tom gone off and got sweet on someone then? And our Kitty? Bet she's married... she's got more chance then you'll ever have. What an old bag you've become, you'll never land anyone.'

Fanny decided not to answer his goading, the less he knew about the personal circumstances the better. The last thing she needed was him thinking that he could just swan back into the house and be a permanent black spot on their lives. She knew he could never cope with children of Mouse and Teddy's ages, he would far rather stay away, and if the weight of numbers of young people was greater than that of young adults he was far more likely to make this stay a short one. She turned to the range and filled the copper from the water pail, placing it to boil, making ready to stew up whatever came through the door with the girls.

'Cat gotcher tongue? Yer were always a strange mare. If I didn't know yer ma better, I'd swear yer not mine.'

Fanny bristled at that, but thought on in silence, *And I wish you weren't my father.* Just at that moment the two younger girls crept in the door. They both stood nervously in the half-open doorway with the sunlight streaming through, their eyes fixed with fear on their father's face, their arms offering their elder sister the things they had manage to gather.

'Thank you, girls. Run along outside I'll call yer when it's tea—'

'No!' said Alf firmly.

Being summer, and very warm today, both girls had gone out in their thin pinnies and not a lot else. With the sunlight behind her, Suie, who was standing just ahead of Mouse, was now showing her developing curves through the translucency of her dress. Her pubescent nipples, overly large and sharp, were poking through her sweat-soaked chemise like doorstops. Alf was transfixed and his eyes were full of lechery and lust. Fanny realised, but it was too late.

'No... (a gentler in tone now)... I haven't seen my girls in so long. Come on in, my Suie. Come on in and take a seat next to yer dear Daddy... (more nonchalant)... and you too, Maud... you sit back there. And you come sit near me where I can see you, Suie...'

The girls moved gingerly into the kitchen, Suie felt very uncomfortable with her father's staring, she did not know why, but she knew it was not right. She edged towards the table and tried to take the seat further away, but Alf was too quick for her, grabbing the leg of the chair as she went to sit on it and pulling it and her closer. She dutifully sat, trying to disappear into herself. Mouse sat further back, looking desperately at Fanny, who mouthed at her to get upstairs; she crept away, Alf did not care, his attentions were firmly fixed on Suie.

'Now... now... sit up straight. You have grown, haven't you... and yer quite the young lady ain't yer? But yer got no draws on, a young lady yer age should have 'er draws on.' Alf laughed, Suie felt desperately uncomfortable with this comment. He had looked through her dress, he was her father! She felt disgusted and revolted and desperately scared. Fanny interjected.

'I need Suie to 'elp me make the tea. Yer always 'elp, dain't yer?' Suie nodded, she very rarely helped, but anything to get away from him. Alf was reluctant to let her move, but then thought better of it; he had no view of her sitting, and the one thing he wanted was a good view.

'You heard yer sister, Suie. Yer get up and 'elp, there's my girl, and if you make me sumit nice... I'll gi' yer sumit nice after.'

Suie escaped towards her sister with enormous relief. The nuance of what Alf had just uttered had not been lost on Fanny who knew exactly what his intentions were. Whatever he tried she was going to protect her little sister from his unwanted attentions. But how? She could barely move, let alone stand her ground against him, or fight him. She had only ever caught him by surprise once, and that was the first and last time he had tried it on with her, but it was also the first and last time he had let her surprise him; every time thereafter he had beaten her black and blue as soon as he had seen her, as a reminder to her she would never get the upper hand again. Where the hell was Tom when she needed him? This was one time she really needed him here.

Alf looked covetously on, as his two daughters made busy with the tea. Fanny tried to stand in front of Suie as much as possible, but he would demand that she moved every now and then, or insist that Suie worked at the end of the table peeling and chopping the vegetables. At one point he insisted that she stoop to gather water from the pail, just so as she did and her dress rose ever higher he could get a better look. Fanny felt helpless, unable to do anything. She knew that the longer she could take to make this meal the better, and maybe if she could raise his anger against her it might distract him away from his lecherous intentions to his still small and under-developed daughter.

There came a point where she could string it out no longer, she had to serve. Alf had insisted on Suie sitting right next to him, and kept touching her leg every time he cracked tasteless comments about the family. 'Yer sister is an old bag, ain't she? ... She's not like our Kitty... Kitty's a really good girl, she knows 'ow to be good to her Daddy. ... Do yer know how to be good yet? ... Dain't yer worry, I'll teach yer.'

Mouse had crept back down, but barely ate a thing. Teddy was too scared to even show himself and remained shaking under his bed, sobbing silently, feeling desperately alone. Fanny felt totally helpless. She had to do something, she had to irritate him or make him aggressive, then he would lose the urge for other things, or so she hoped. She plucked up the courage.

'When yer going, then?'

Alf ignored it at first and continued being over-familiar with Suie.

'I mean, we dain't want yer 'ere. Yer an overgrown bully. Dain't yer think it's time to go?'

Suie and Mouse froze, as Alf stood up suddenly, brandishing his knife at Fanny at the other end of the table.

'Who the 'ell da yer think yer are? Yer can't talk to me like that. I am going to gi' yer a damn good sorting out… with this…'

The girls screamed as he made a lunge across the table for Fanny. He overbalanced and fell, which made him furious. Mouse and Suie shot into the furthest corner and clutched each other crying, not knowing what to do. Fanny knew she had said too much, he was going to kill her, she grabbed for something, anything, to defend herself and the lumbering ox tried to pull himself to his feet. Just then the door opened; Fanny felt enormous relief, it had to be Tom.

''Ello, Daddy!'

Alf, halfway to his feet, was left speechless, and so was everyone else. Kitty knew what she had to do, and put on her most flirtatious voice.

'Hasn't me Alfie got a nice word for his little Kitty, then?'

Chapter 9

The course of compromise

How different things were for Vi that evening. All her dread and depression gave way to an enormous sense of relief as she entered the kitchen of her home. Her father was sitting at the table and an air of normality pervaded as her mother went about her business making the tea for the small family. Vi stood somewhat stunned, her expectations of chaos had not been made manifest, and it was as if it had all been a bad dream. Her father, sensing her discomfort with the sudden rationality, broke the tension wanting to ensure that things would remain stable.

'Come on in, love. Your ma's just making tea, aren't you, Ma?'

Vi's mother nodded, and beamed her broad smile at her daughter, a warmth filled Vi from the inside of her being and made her tingle. Perhaps all was going to be fine now, no more sleepless nights and bad times.

Later that evening they all sat in the parlour as normal, her mother mending, her father with his feet in a pail to soak and Vi with her head in a book; more to stop the need for any conversation rather than for any relaxation of her mind. Vi's was still distracted by her lack of contact with John; the same thoughts passed through her mind over and over again. She veered from fearing that he had come to some misfortune or his mother had, in which case she felt he might need her, to wondering and being anxious as to whether he had decided that she was too young and not right for him. She worried herself into circles of self-doubt and anxiety, while feeling a certain amount of comfort that all was now at peace at home. Eventually, after a few hours of personal agonising, she decided that she had to know either way, and not seeing him and actually finding out was a more fearful prospect than finding out that her worse fears had been realised and he no longer actually wanted her. Tomorrow she would go again to St Paul's Square, but she would not just sit there this time, she would go and see if he was there; at least then she would have an answer, at least she would finally know.

Kitty's arrival was perfectly timed, and Alf forgot or decided not to display his aggression towards Fanny, and his focus thankfully shifted away from Suie. Kitty chatted away to all as if she had never been away and as if she had always been the perfect sister. Although totally out of character, the two younger girls found Kitty's friendly demeanour a comfort after what they had witnessed and what they had both feared that Alf was about to do to Fanny. Fanny said nothing, and just stared at the highly animated Kitty with some incredulity. After a short while, Kitty persuaded Alf that he needed a rest and ought to go for a lie down. Alf compliantly agreed, with a certain expectation in his voice which Kitty skilfully ignored.

'Now, Alfie, you go for a rest and we'll clear up.'

The two younger girls were sent to bed. Suie was told to help clean up Teddy and bring his britches down for drying, Mouse, somewhat red-eyed, clung to her big sister.

'Fanny, I'm scared, 'ee's not going to hurt yer is 'ee?'

'No, Mouse, I won't let him, I promise, and 'ee is not going to do anything to you either, I won't let him.'

This placated Mouse, who scuttled off to the safest, warmest place in the world: the bed she shared with Suie and Teddy.

Fanny went out to the yard to clean the pots and plates, Kitty followed her out.

'Seems like I turned up just in time, dain't it?'

Fanny said nothing and carried on rinsing under the court tap.

'Listen, Fan, there's no need to treat me like this, is there? What's beefing you? I have only been gone a short while… (reaching into her belt) …and I got some money for yer.'

Fanny swung round and snapped back.

'And tell me, Kitty, how have you lived for two weeks without using yer money, eh? Or shall I guess? And I really dain't want to, but people keeping tellin' me things!'

'And what yer been teld, yeah? I bet it's wrong… I bet yer thinking is all wrong!'

'I know what I know – that you been shacked up with Stan the man… yeah. And why has 'ee let yer live rent-free, eh? Cos as usual yer been a little too free with yer favours, ain't yer? The shame yer bring on all us. Dain't think about anyone 'sept yerself, always been the same, yer'll neva' change!'

'You are wrong, as usual! Not everything is like that, all simple black and white like Fanny Tulloch likes. Sometimes it is a bit different. But yer'll neva' see it at all. I dain't know why I'd bovvered coming back, you dain't eva' appreciated a fing I do. Well yer can have yer money, yer stuffy cow, and yer can deal with him. Why the 'ell should I? I have had enuf of this bloody family.'

She flung two shillings on the ground, they clattered across the cobbles. Fanny traced their path with her eyes, more concerned with their trajectory than the fact that her sister had swung round on her boot heels and was heading back towards the kitchen to make her goodbyes to her siblings. Fanny placed the pail of kitchen equipment down and scurried to redeem Kitty's contribution; it may be the answer to their prayers, a way of getting rid. If he had money to drink, he would go off again. There was always hope.

Kitty was angry and felt very misjudged by her holier-than-thou sister. She decided that it was best to go now, she could make the alehouse and Stan and have a bed for the night. She swung round to the bottom of the stairs to see if the younger members of the family were still awake. She did not notice the open parlour door, and only looked up the darkened stairs just as she reached them. She stopped suddenly and with alarm. She could make out Alf at the top of the stairs, his shirt open, his braces on his britches down as if he was about to make ready for bed. He had his hand on the door handle and his right ear to the door of the children's room; he was about to go in. He had his back to Kitty and had obviously been so determined to act he hadn't heard her heading in to the kitchen. In a second Kitty reacted, she knew exactly what he was about, and was shocked by his audacity.

'Hey, Alfie… what yer doin'?'

Alf turned, and looked guilty.

'Now, now, I thought this was between us, Alf? Yer dain't want Suie, not really, do ya?'

Like a guilty schoolboy who had been caught stealing he shook his head, not making eye contact.

'Cumon, Alf… why dain't yer go back to bed… we're all tired tonight. Yer neva' know, yer might get lucky tomorrow.'

Because he had been caught, by the one person who really knew, the one person who was not scared of him, he compliantly agreed to her request and descended the stairs in silence and walked into the parlour, shutting the door behind him. Kitty let out the breath that she had been holding, and went to the kitchen table and slumped in a chair. Just then, Fanny came in.

'I thought yer were off? Changed yer mind have ya?'

''Ee's after Suie, aint 'ee?'

'Looks like… but dain't ya worry yerself, I'll die before I let anything happen to 'er.'

'Yeah… 'm sure yer will. Shame no one did for me.'

'What da ya mean? Me and Tom took care of yer. Anything you got inta yer did yerself. Anyway, yer were always playing games, getting yer own way wiv him. We saw yer.'

'Oh, that's right is it? World according to Fan. Yer think I have always done exactly what I wanted, yeah? Well Tom looked after you, but no one gave a damn about me. You two cared about me? Huh, that would be right! Kitty had to look after 'erself and that's what Kitt's done eva' since, Ta! But I won't let Suie get hurt either, Miss High and Mighty. And I think we have to get rid of him as soon as… before he does get his hands on 'er.'

'Think what yer like, Kitty… we always looked after yer. You forget we were kids too, we could only do so much. And 'ee beat me to pieces all the time, jus' like now, not that yer noticed. And yer money will 'elp me send him off again.'

Kitty thought for a moment, she looked purposefully at Fanny.

'But that's not enuf, and yer know it. 'Ee'll be back again, and 'ee'll try again. Yer need him to stay away, and for good this time.'

'Yes, Kitty, of course I do, but have you got any bloody ideas how? Cos I know I haven't. And sooner or lata' 'ee's going to get to Suie. How the 'ell do we stop him? I only have so many bones left 'ee can break.'

The two sisters sat in silence at the table, both aware that a monster lay asleep in the next room. A vile inhuman creature that had blighted both of their lives for too long. But he was strong and powerful, and he controlled everything and everyone with violence; he had always separated each person in the family from the others before inflicting his cruelty in its worst forms. Kitty was the first to break the silence.

'Look, we both know what 'ee's like. We both want to make sure the scraps are kept safe from him, 'ee's done enough damage, ain't 'ee. We have to work together, dain't we.' Fanny nodded, Kitty was speaking sense for a change. 'And we will find a way. We will get rid of him… we just got to work out how. I will stick around for a week or two. Yer do need me, even if yer dain't want to admit it. I'm tired, I'm off to bed. Do what yer like.' And with that, Kitty left the kitchen for their shared bed.

Fanny sat for a while, nursing her side which was aching from all the strenuous movements of the day's activities. She was angry with Kitty, and angry with all that she had heard about her sister's activities. But something that she had said had struck home with Fanny. Maybe she had not seen the truth about Kitty? Maybe she had been so busy trying to survive herself that she had failed to see that Kitty was as vulnerable as she was. And she was right, she was a survivor as much as Fanny was; maybe they both had the same force within them, the only difference being that Fanny had always felt responsible for the others too, whereas Kitty had never really given a damn about anybody else except Kitty. That evening, Fanny had glimpsed a different side to Kitty, a side that she had never witnessed before. Kitty had displayed caring and compassion, and for the first time ever she was going to help protect the ones who had always been Fanny's responsibility.

By the time Fanny climbed wearily into bed, Kitty was sound asleep. From the light of the paraffin lamp, Kitty looked calm, almost angelic, in her features. She had the face of a child, an innocent child, not the hard, calculating expressions that her conscious state displayed all day every day. When she was relaxed, without a care in the world, without the worries of her own personal survival, she portrayed an unsullied innocence, and she looked like her sister, not Fanny or Maud, she looked just like Suie; really, she was just a child.

In the alehouse, a very drunk red-faced man sounded off at the barman, who was not the least bit interested in this drunk's philosophies, but he knew he had to listen anyway because he was a good customer.

'Yer know, Mick… yer know what's wrong with this town… it's the bloody Micks, Mick… (he laughed, drunkenly)… sorry about the pun mate. Bloody Micks, Mick… (he laughed again). The bleedin, lazy fuckin' Irish, they come 'ere and take all the jobs… then they do knuffing and sit on their arses. If we could get rid of the bloody Paddys, then Brum would be a nice little town again. Yer know, all the Micks I have to deal with, all they want is more money… and they dain't work for it so I won't give it to them.'

Mick the barman, from County Longford, shifted uneasily as he realised the drunk in front of him had forgotten he was Irish.

'And the other thing is the bloody Jews… them jus' as bad… they'll rob yer blind as soon as look at yer. I used to get shafted regular like by that bastard, Old Zac, but I got me own back a few times. Then them bloody women at the pen factory… all whores and bags… I wouldn't go near any of 'em… they use people all the time. That bloody Tulloch that's been hanging around thinks she got me round 'er little finger… but I'm going to give 'er one, you just see if I don't. She's a flirty piece of trash that plays games. Well she played wiv the wrong bloke here… she's going to get 'ers.'

Fanny was the last to leave the next morning. She had made sure both Kitty and the others had gone before her, and she had left Alf sleeping and a bowl of solidifying porridge on the table for when he finally woke. Vi was waiting for her as she left the court, a brighter Vi to the one that she had attempted to say goodbye to the previous evening. She stared a little at Fanny's shiner, which now made her look like a bare-knuckle fighter, but said nothing. They walked towards the factory passing idle chit-chat between them, and Vi was surprised (but pleased, knowing the difficulties that Fanny was having) that Kitty had made her return, and even more pleased that Fanny seemed quite relaxed about it.

Vi still did not reveal her concerns about her mother. Although she had passed what appeared to be a normal evening, Vi had noted that she had not seemed to know what to do with her sewing any more; she had repeatedly picked up thimbles, and needles, and threads, and just replaced them in her box, without appearing to do anything at all. Neither did she mention her plan to use her lunch break to go to seek out her male friend again, and this time confront him.

The morning passed slowly, and Vi could not take her eyes off the clock which seemed to take forever to reach that needed lunchtime. Then all of a sudden, she found herself walking into the square and an enormous sense of foreboding had come over her. Was she doing the right thing? Surely, she should just turn around and go back, or just wait for him to see her? Would he not find it wrong of her, an intrusion, to be seeking him out like this? She agonised as she reached the door of his workshop and paused, trying to decide what was the best to do. Finally, she decided she had to know, one way or the other; she had to put herself out of the misery, she had to know. She turned the large handle on the overly large door and climbed the rickety steep stairs once more.

She braced herself outside his door and then knocked with firmness and purpose; there was no answer but she heard someone moving around and heading towards the door. The door opened and John was standing in front of her, it was obvious by his expression that she was the very last person that he had wanted to see standing there. As if to qualify this further, he said dismissively:

'Oh, it's you.'

Vi stood dumbstruck, she had hoped for some warmth even if he was going to tell her that he could not go on, but just to be rude in this way, when he had obviously not bothered to seek her out and let her down gently… she found it very rude and deeply hurtful. The shock of his reaction welled up inside her, and silent tears began to roll down her face.

Inside himself John was mortified. She was last person in the world he would want to hurt or had intended to hurt. He had been mentally desperately trying to extricate himself from this relationship because he knew that he loved her and wanted to protect her from the potential harm that being with him could cause her. In his efforts to strengthen his resolve, he had hardened his manners and his speech, and as a consequence had spoken roughly to her before he had thought of the reaction it might bring. The last thing he had expected was to witness her breakdown in such a way in front of him. He thought she would be angry and hurt, and fight back with words, those words he knew he could face and, if had a strong, hardened exterior, he could maintain the pretence of not caring and she would leave. But she was crying, her beautiful eyes were full of pain, and he had caused it. He had to explain, he had to make her see, but not the whole truth – that was too much for anybody to understand. He softened his tone and moved a little back from the door to allow her entry.

'Look, I'm sorry, Vi… please come in. I need to talk to you. Please?'

In a blur of tears and pent-up emotion Vi stumbled in, wanting to collapse, wanting to run away and hide. He directed her to Zac's empty chair with a guiding hand under her arm. He stood a little way in front of her, then, realising he was too tall to be able to exchange a conversation with her while she was seated, he crouched so he was a little beneath her height. She peered at him through her tear-filled eyes, biting her lip. He began, faltering, trying to find the words.

'I meant to come and see you, Vi, but it's been so difficult. I mean work and Ma and everything… you understand don't you?' She nodded, but she didn't understand really. 'Well, it's all really difficult, you see… I am having to work twice as hard and twice as long now trying to make the same money that I used to. I mean, it is good that Hardman's have given me work, but it is harder work and longer hours… and I…' He stopped, he did not know what to say. Vi studied his agonised expression and she could no longer contain her thoughts.

'It's because you don't want to see me, isn't it? Because I am too young. Isn't it?'

John came back quickly.

'No, Vi… no. You have got that all wrong… that is just not right. That's the last thing I think about you.' Vi wasn't listening, her head hung down and the tears were falling unconfined into small splash-pools on the wooden floor. 'Vi, I wouldn't do anything to hurt you… you've got to believe me… you are the most special person in the world to me. For God's sake, I love you.' He stopped again, suddenly; he had let it out and admitted it. Her head raised and she held him with her gaze, her eyes probing his for proof of his statement. How could he make such a statement, yet be so cold with her?

'Yes, Vi, I know that I love you… but things are not that simple. I cannot love you, don't you see?'

A sudden horror – which had not formed part of the many scenarios which Vi had considered – gripped her with fear.

'You… you… are not m-married, are you?'

He smiled, and tried to assuage her new fears.

'No, Vi, I am not married… I can promise you that… I never dared. But that is just it – I don't dare now. I have to work hard to scrape enough for rent and food, and me ma needs medicines all the time, and you know I must put me ma first, you understand that don't you?' She nodded. 'And it's just that… that… I can't have a wife… I can't take care of a wife. But you are truly beautiful and I know… I know there is bound to be someone out there for you… someone who will take care of you… someone who can look after you.' He stopped again, his heart breaking inside.

Vi could not let him go, not like this. He loved her, and she knew, she had known since she first clapped eyes on him, that she felt exactly the same way. There had to be a solution to this, two people could not be in love like this and feel what they did and let it slip away. They had been brought together through fate, through happenstance, there was a reason for everything, and Vi was not about to walk away from this.

'But, John, you don't have to take me as your wife yet, I can wait. I can wait years if I have to, some things in life are worth waiting for, don't you think so?'

The roles were reversed; now John's eyes were downcast, the futility of it all had got to him, he wanted just to hold her so much, and what she was saying was true: some things could be endured. But she did not know the truth. If she knew the truth she would not want him anyway. It just would never work, he had to try to deter her.

'It's easy to think that now, Vi, but there are things we cannot change that will always work against us. I am Irish, no one in your community will ever accept me properly, you will lose friends. And I am Catholic.' He fixed his look on her. 'And I don't think you are.'

'John, I don't care you are Irish, and those friends who do care are not friends of mine. My real friends will support my choice, not shun me for it. And you are Catholic… I can change. It's easier for me to change to your beliefs. I didn't really have much churching anyway apart from Sunday school. I do believe in something, but maybe this is what I need… a reason to believe and proper teaching. I can wait as long as it takes. I know that you have commitments and things that you must put before me, I understand that and accept that. I will wait as long as it takes for you… I will do whatever is necessary… anything… please? Just give us a chance? Please? Just see if we can make it work, and then if it doesn't I will let you go, but please, John, please, just give us a chance?'

In her eagerness to convince him of her true devotions she had grabbed both of his wrists and was staring purposefully into his eyes. John's heart melted and his resolve fell away. He could not escape what he felt, and she was so determined. Maybe he could keep her out of his troubles? Maybe he had not been seen, or if he had they would leave him alone? She was so lovely, he knew that she meant every word that she said and she obviously cared very deeply for him. He took back his arms from her grip, he smiled his soft smile; she knew, he knew, she leaned forward into his space and he enfolded her to him. They would find a way. Somehow, he would find a way to keep her safe.

The Tullochs sat around a very tense tea table. Fanny sat at the opposite end to Alf, flanked by Suie and Mouse; Kitty sat between Suie and Alf, with an empty unmade space opposite her, as Teddy had once again hidden, and Fanny felt it was for the best for him. Alf carried on with his licentious talk in front of his daughters, making Fanny feel very angry, but she contained it well. Suie was visibly uncomfortable, as much of it seemed directly aimed at her; Mouse just wanted to run and join Teddy.

Kitty was the only one to make light of his bawdiness. Her strategy was simple: humour him, and he was less likely to anger and fly off the handle. At the same time, she tried to draw his attentions away from her younger sister. She was trying to bring his desires back in her direction so he would leave Suie alone. But even Kitty knew – it was all about control, had only ever been about control, and Kitty was far too confident and brazen now to interest Alf. He desired the tension of fear, the excitement of making another completely powerless, and as much as a sexual conquest was needed, it was not his main driving force, and Kitty was only just in his sphere of interest. She knew she could no longer control him through titillation and temptation, or lewd naughtiness; she needed to be more direct in her approach. This prospect revolted her and she was struggling to come to terms with it. Every time she looked at Suie she saw the fear etched into her little sister's face, and she remembered that if she hadn't been on the stairs at that moment the previous night, she would not have stopped him. Kitty knew she had to do something, however much it sickened her, however much it made her feel ashamed. She carried on with her raucous replies and eventually sent Alf to 'rest' in the parlour. As he shut the door, she looked with the utmost seriousness at her two little sisters.

'Right, you two… get yerselves up 'em stairs, shut that door and dain't let me see yer till the morning, right?'

Both girls looked to Fanny for confirmation of what they had to do. Fanny was slightly puzzled by Kitty's urgency but, as with Teddy, it was probably for the best that temptation was removed from Alf's gaze. She nodded at them. Without further comment they both scurried away up the stairs, being as quiet as they could so not to attract any attention from the parlour.

Fanny looked at Kitty across the table still covered with plates and odds and sods of cutlery, unwashed and discarded.

'What's going on, Kitty? Why the sudden need to get the girls out of the way, we really needed help with this lot… well, I did anyway.'

'I'm sorry, Fan, but you saw the way 'ee was looking at our Suie. It can't happen to 'er, Fan, and I won't let it. Look, despite what you think I never wanted it, you know. I had no choice… like I have no choice now. If I dain't, 'ee'll go for 'er, you know that?'

Fanny was shocked. She knew what Kitty was trying to say, trying to tell her, but she did not want to hear it, or believe it. She could not possibly be proposing what Fanny thought she was? It was just too unbelievable to be true. Kitty continued.

'Look, if you can get on wiv this lot… I'll take care of that!' She nodded at the parlour door and practically spat out her comment. Fanny was speechless, she could not believe what she was hearing.

'B-b-but, Kitty, yer can't possibly do this? I mean, think before you do. Surely 'ee'll want more… and maybe he won't go if you do? If 'ee's not lucky then 'ee'll bugger off anyway?'

'Fan, if I dain't do this 'ee'll have Suie. I know this, cos that's what 'ee did to me after you knocked him back. It's not like yer think, but I dain't want to talk about it now otherwise I won't do it. I just want you to go out into the court and wash up. I dain't wanna know yer in 'ere, do you understand me? Just go outside. By the time yer done I'll be done… then I'll talk, but not now. Just go, will yer, or I'll lose my nerve.' She stood up, gripping the chair facing the parlour, about to make the longest walk of her life.

Fanny rose to her feet, numb. She gathered the dishes in the pail and headed towards the outside door to the court, while Kitty headed for the parlour door. Both girls stopped, facing their doors on opposite sides of the kitchen, Fanny waited for the confirmation she needed. Kitty raised her clenched fist and knocked lightly on the parlour door. She steeled herself and coquettishly called through to the man full of anticipation of what he knew was coming to him.

'Alfie… it's your little Kitty. Can I come in for a cuddle… Daddy?'

She opened the door and slid through the smallest space, shutting it behind her.

Chapter 10

The bitter and the sweet

Fanny placed the pail down, pulling the sharpest knife she could from it and walked towards the now firmly closed door. Her anger had reached snapping point, she no longer felt any sense of reality, she just had to stop him from whatever vile act he was about to commit. As she reached the door there was a solid thump against the other side, as if a body had collided with it full force. She heard Alf's voice.

'Cumon, me little Kitty… draws down, skirts up… there's a good girl… yes that's better…'

Fanny recoiled from the door in horror, even if she could snap out of her paralysis, she knew she could not get in. Alf had Kitty against the door, probably for the very same reason: to stop any interference. Fanny backed up to the kitchen wall, dropping the knife as she did, breaking into silent sobs. As she did so, a second hard thump came from the door, which heralded a rhythmic thumping, accompanied by male grunts of pleasure. Fanny tried to put her hands over her ears in her now crouched pathetic state on the floor, back to the wall, watching the door heave slightly with each thump. It made no difference, she could still hear the bang, bang, growing in intensity and speed. She could still hear him and his animalistic grunting, but there was not a sound from Kitty, not a whimper, moan, or any sort of noise or protest. She was just absorbing the abuse as she had done since she was small: completely and silently.

Just then, the crescendo of destruction rose to a pitch of fast thumping and a long groan, then silence. She heard stumbled footsteps, a loud thump accompanied by bedspring squeaks, then nothing, for what seemed like forever. She stayed crouched, not daring to breathe. Was Kitty alright? Had she been hurt? Should she go and see? Then she heard movement and the door opened slightly and a dishevelled

Kitty slid out in silence. Fanny stared at her, full of pity and remorse for having let this terrible thing happen. Kitty glanced back, and her facial expression hardened as she began to march towards the kitchen door.

'I dain't know what yer so cut up about… it weren't yer. I'm goin' to wash. Leave me be.' With that, she slammed the kitchen door as she headed across the court to the laundry.

Fanny felt absolutely useless. Yes, Kitty was right. What had she got to feel so sorry for herself for? She had not just been subjected to the ultimate humiliation and violence, she had just heard it. Yes, he had beaten her many times, left bruises, broken bones and cuts, but he had never managed to strip her of her dignity. What he had just done to her sister was worse, much worse than she had ever experienced. How long had it been going on? Why had she not seen it? Why did she not know? Maybe she and Tom could have stopped him, as they had managed to when he had tried it on with her? All these years, she had treated Kitty as a selfish, self-centred and careless individual, who was just hell-bent on self-gratification at the expense of all else. But now Fanny was beginning to see Kitty as someone very different. She was a poor pathetic creature, whom nobody had protected. Fanny had been so lost in trying to cope with the responsibility of the little children, and Tom trying to earn to keep them fed, that they had both just assumed that Kitty, being that little bit older could just take care of herself. They had been so wrong. She was still a child herself, just like Suie, just as scared. She had lost her mother and the only parent that she had left was Alf. She was open to being mistreated and misused, and as soon as Fanny had taken a stand against Alf's advances, she had laid Kitty wide open for the same maltreatment, but she had been too busy and too blind to see what was under her nose.

Fanny cleared the kitchen as best she could, she should have gone to bed a while ago, but she wanted to wait for Kitty. She did not know what she could say or do. Maybe it was too late for anything? She just wanted to try and show some support for her sister in a way that she had obviously failed to do for all these years. Kitty was obviously taking her time for a reason, and Fanny knew just to leave her be until she was ready. Fanny headed for the parlour door. She turned the handle, holding her breath. The paraffin lamp was burning low from the interior and she opened the door as wide as she dared. The lamp was casting long, dark, sinister shadows on the grimy walls. The smell made her want to gag. Not only was Alf's idea of personal hygiene appalling, but he had also been using the chamber pot for the past days for all his bodily evacuations; it was overflowing with urine and full of faeces.

'Yer pig!' she uttered under her breath, at the comatose body which lay prostrate on Tom's bed, half on half off. He was face down, snoring, his britches and braces still down by his ankles, no shirt on. He looked as disgusting and as vile as he was. He was unshaven and filthy and now she could see that his body was crawling with lice; no wonder Kitty was trying to clean herself so thoroughly. Fanny thought to herself, *I will have to burn this lot when yer go.* She curled her lip and backed towards the door, creeping out, and shutting it as quietly as she could.

Kitty came in from the court, she was ashen in colour, her hair wet. She smelt strongly of laundry soap and was holding her washed underwear and slip, which she proceeded to hang near the range to dry. Fanny attempted to engage her in conversation.

'Kitty, will yer sit awhile… I really need to talk to yer.'

Kitty carried on looking the other way. 'Why?'

'Cos I feel terrible… what just happened and all… what yer did. I think we really need to talk.'

Kitty snapped back.

'No, we dain't. Why bother now? You haven't given a fig for years, dain't get all sorry for me now. Yer neva' cared a toss!'

'That's not fair, Kitty. I swear I dain't know it were happening to ya, really I had no idea. And I know Tom didn't, cos 'ee neva' saw anythin' unless 'ee was told to. Please, Kitty, will yer just sit for a moment, even if it's just to decide what to do. I mean, you can't do this night after night, not even to protect our Suie. It's just not right!'

''Ee won't be able to do anythin' for days now. 'Ee neva' could. But I'll take it next time, like I always have, until yer get rid!'

'But that's just it, Kitty, I can't at the moment, just haven't got enuf money to send him off. And, yer right… we need him to go for good, but I have no idea how.'

For the first time, Kitty heard the futility in her sister's voice. Fanny had always been the strong one, always had the answers. She organised them all and made things work. Now she sounded weak and unable to rationalise any problem, her voice was trembling, and when Kitty turned she saw that Fanny's whole frame was shaking. Kitty sat at the table, Fanny followed her lead and did the same. Kitty took the affirmative position.

'Look, Fanny, I dain't like what I have to do. Part of the reason I stay away so much is I dain't want to be 'ere any more. I hate the place and all that I remember. I hate him. But I'm 'ere now, and I can't see what happened to me happen to Suie. And as long as I can, because it ain't me 'ee wants… 'ee wants young meat, but for as long as I can keep him from 'er, I will do. We'll get enuf money and sumit will happen, I'm sure.' She paused. 'We can always knock him off?'

Fanny stared at her. Was she being serious? Had she really suggested killing Alf? Yes, it would get rid of him, but killing him?

'Kitty, we'll 'ang for that… yer can't just do him in.'

'Fan, yer have no imagination. We live next to the gun quarter, there are more crooks round 'ere than I've had hot dinners. It's amazing how many accidents happen with guns you know.' Kitty half smiled, and a mischievous expression had come over her face.

Fanny thought for a moment. Yes, murderous intent had crossed her own mind, but that was at the height of her anger and disgust for the despicable act he was inflicting on Kitty. Could she really sit down in a cold and calculating fashion and plan to murder her father? Did she have the capacity within her to take another human life, no matter how much she hated him and was scared of what more damage he could do? It went against everything she believed in, her own moral code. Kitty broke her train of thought.

'It's a thought though, ain't it? At least 'ee would be gone for good, and no questions asked. 'Ee'd neva be able to harm anyone again. We wouldn't even have to do it—'

'No, Kitty... I couldn't. And even if we could do it your way, someone else would always know, another man, and 'ee'd have power over us. I just couldn't. There must be another way, I'm sure there's another way.'

Kitty listened with half an ear. Since she was ten years old, the first time that she had been raped by Alf, she had suffered at the hands of this man. She had been unwell one day and had left school early in the morning, sneaking home, not wanting to tell Fanny or Tom. She thought she could sleep the day away, then go out before they got back. Feeling feverish, she had climbed into what had been her mother's bed for comfort, Alf had gone weeks before. She had drifted off and lost herself in blissful dreams of hot summer days and no school. All of a sudden, she had been wakened by someone pulling at her legs and forcing them apart. She opened her eyes to see her father with no clothes on, his face looming over her menacingly. She panicked, but he was too quick for her. He grabbed her small wrists together in one hand and leant with all his weight on them above her head, so that her hands immediately started to tingle and lose feeling. At the same time, with his other hand, he was forcing her legs further and further apart, forcing her right leg to bend up to her belly, and she felt his fist against her wee wee hole. She pleaded and begged him to stop, she'd be a good girl, she'd not tell anyone, honest she wouldn't, if he would just let her go… 'Please, Daddy, please stop!'

It was like a knife! It was the worst pain she had ever felt, and she could do nothing but scream. Alf's hand came firmly down over her mouth, but his hand was so big he was covering part of her nostrils as well; she could barely breathe. All the time he was thrusting and grunting and telling her what a good girl she was. Thrust after thrust was renting her in two, her stifled screams became stifled sobs, her mind began to grow fuzzy as she fought for breath, he was so heavy and it all hurt like hell; finally, she passed out.

When she came to she was alone, she had no idea how much time had passed, she could hear no noises from the house. She was naked from her chest down where her slip had been pulled up to her shoulders. The blanket lay on the floor, and her legs and lower body felt cold and chilled. She tried to lift herself up by her hands, but she got sharp pains in her wrists; she looked at them, they were dark blue. She rolled a little on her side and raised herself up on one elbow, then she got really scared. Her legs and hips felt sore, her bottom felt like it had been beaten, and there was blood all over the bed from near her wee wee hole. She cried out a pathetic little whimper. She had a fear that she was going to bleed to death, that she had been injured, but then she was scared that Fanny and Tom would find her and blame her. She had to get rid of this blood, they mustn't see this blood!

Within ten minutes Kitty had managed to get herself out of the bed, and cover herself the best she could, all the time clamping her lower body as much as she could because she felt like her innards were falling away. She stripped off the dirty and now bloodstained sheet and had made her way to the wash house. Thankfully, it was empty of women, and the copper boiler was still warm. Kitty plunged the sheet into the boiler, and felt the warm water on her hand. Instinctively she began to clean herself, the streaks of bloody water ran down her legs. She scrubbed and scrubbed at herself until she stood in a pool of water. Then the enormity of what had happened to her hit her with full force. In her shocked state she tried to fathom why. Why had her Daddy done this? Why? Maybe she had made him, maybe she had been a really bad girl? And if the others knew they would blame her too. She never ever wanted this to happen again, if she was really good and said nothing then no one would ever know, and she would not be in any trouble.

That had been the day it had started; it had never stopped, except when he was away. Her fear of what he would do and what the others would think of her turned to anger as she realised that they must have known what was going on. As her sexual realisation had developed, she felt certain that the whole family was somehow complicit in his acts, or at the very least complacent in their acceptance of what he was doing to her, because if it was happening to her it was not happening to them. Kitty had nursed a growing resentment and hatred for her siblings, and in her challenged mind, she had decided that at least she could make these abuses pay from time to time; getting money from Alf with flirtatious blackmail, she had made his gratitude pay. She was going to get away from him, and them, no matter what she had to do. She had to, otherwise she would kill him. As Fanny had said no, Kitty knew in her heart that she would have to do this alone; she could not persuade her sister. How and when she was going to act she did not know yet, but she would make an opportunity, and she was not going to swing for ridding the world of this vile abuser.

John sat with his mother, although by now it was quite late and he was feeling very weary. He had to grab

114

these opportunities while he could as she seemed to spend many hours sleeping and her body rhythms had lost the sense of night and day, causing her to be wide awake in the wee small hours. He had been feeling very elated since seeing Vi, and although his better judgement had led him to believe that it was in her best interests that he kept his distance, her convincing arguments to the contrary and their strong mutual attraction had caused a change of heart and change of mind in him. All he wanted now was to find a way to make it work and, if necessary, protect her from any harm. He was quite preoccupied in his mixed emotions as he sat with his mother, and even in the depths of her failing health, May could sense her son's uneasiness.

'Johnny boy... what's troubling you? Tell yer ma. Maybe I'll be able to help you?'

He looked at this frail woman, barely skin and bone, barely enough breath in her lungs to keep her alive. Why burden her with problems which she could not solve for him, that would just cause more anxiety and misery in a person who'd had more than her fair share.

'No, Ma, its nothing. I don't know what you mean.'

'Now, John... you really think you can hide this from me? What is troubling you? Is it money again? I will worry if you don't tell me.'

He knew she would fret, he must tell her something, but he must be careful how much he actually revealed.

'It's always money, Ma, I never seem to have enough these days. I am desperate to make you more comfortable, to give you all the things you want, and need. Every day just is one big struggle to make ends meet. I mean, I am very grateful to Hardman's for their work, but I have to put in the hours to make the pieces and then I never have any time to do anything else.'

'But, John, I don't need anything more than I have already. All I need is to rest and that is the best medicine for me. You don't need to do more and you know that. And it will get easier with work, eventually, it always has. You just have to wait a while, things will pick up I am sure, and once you don't have my mouth to feed—'

John cut her short. 'Ma, don't you dare say that. You are not a burden, you have never been a burden, I won't have you talk like that. I would do anything for you, and without you I would be totally lost. So, don't you go leaving me.'

'No, John, I know. But you have to face facts; I am old, I am ill. I am not stupid, John, I have seen death many times, you know that. I know when he visits, I have seen him in the face too many times to count. He is close by, I feel him. You will have to let me go sooner or later.'

Both sat in silence, reflecting on the power of her words. A huge emptiness had come with her admission. May knew that her words had affected her son, but she also knew that he had to face the prospect of being alone before she died, that it was better for him to begin to adjust now.

'I do worry about you, Johnny boy. You have always kept yourself to yourself... a little too much, maybe? I understand why, I realise all the fears that you have in life. But you cannot live in fear forever, you have to live a life. If trouble will seek you out, it will find you, and all these days of worry won't make it come any sooner and it won't keep it away either. Maybe we have had our lot of bad luck? After all, we have had more than most to deal with in our lives. Maybe your share is done, and only good fortune will seek you from now on? You should give yourself a chance to live, to get out there and meet friends, to let people into your life.'

'But, Ma, I do have friends... well, I do have *a* friend – Jimmy Pearse. And he's married now, so I have two friends, and I am making an effort to see him. He seems very pleased that I am. In fact, I am going to a debating society with him every month now, and seeing him at Hardman's of course. It's just time, finding time... that's what I mean, hours in the day. And even if we hadn't had all of the bad, people round here, apart from Jimmy of course, despise us Irish, they see us as scroungers and ne'er-do-wells. I keep my distance.'

'That's not true, John. Look at Mrs Morris. A nicer person you could not ask for, she has been a tower of strength for me just recently. And the others. I know they are rough diamonds, but they don't mean you ill, they think you are bonny, you make their day. There are many around here like that, John, you have to give people a chance. And as much as I am glad about you and Jimmy, you are far more likely to find trouble with that young man than the people round here. He has a little too much to say at times, and he does not think that his opinions might cause harm.'

'I know, Ma, but at least he thinks; it's nice to share time with someone who wants to care about the real problems in this world. And I am careful, I am careful for him too, I don't want to see him come to harm because he is careless with his tongue.'

'Johnny, you need a girl, you need to settle down and take a wife, someone who will love you and care for you like I have. Nothing would make me happier, nor give me greater rest than to know that you have found some happiness.' May paused, she had suspicions there was a great deal more to her son's uneasiness than he was prepared to admit. Sometimes a more direct approach was necessary in order to get him to admit to his own feelings.

John scrutinised her face. She knew, how did she know? But she always knew. Whenever he tried to hide anything from her, even as a small child, she would know, but she would always expect him to own up to what he had done, or what he was trying to conceal. If this was what would rest her spirits and ease her mind, then maybe it was the right time to tell her. He was certain of his feelings for Vi, and after hearing Vi's appeals to him, he was certain of her feelings for him. Yes, they had to wait for a while, but his mother already understood the issues of time and money. At least if she knew, she could be happy for him and share in his joy.

'Well, Ma, you are a little behind me for once.' He knew she was not, and that she already knew, but she liked his humour when he made light of her profundity. 'I have met someone, but it is very early days and we are taking our time. She understands my situation and is prepared to wait.'

'Wait? What for? If you have found love, Johnny boy, you should act on it before it escapes you... these things are sent when they are sent for a reason. The sooner you act, the sooner all is resolved. Tell me about her. What is she like? Does she deserve my boy?'

'Oh, Ma, she has hair the colour of copper and eyes as blue as evening sunset. Her name is Violet, her father named her after the colour of her eyes. She is truly beautiful, both of looks and heart, a more loving heart I will never find. You will love her.'

May's eyes shone with glee.

'Is she an Irish girl? With that colouring she sounds Irish... and no doubt Catholic too.'

John tempered her enthusiasm.

'No, Ma, she is a local lass, but it proves you are right, there are many a good person round here, I just had to open my heart and my eyes. And no, she is not Catholic, though she has little of anything, and she is happy to convert.'

'Oh, well, no matter... she sounds fine. But she is not young, is she? That's even more reason not to delay John, you need to make a home and a family. You shouldn't worry about me. I am sure if she is as good as you say, she will have no problem with having yer old Ma for a wee while.'

John panicked, she was rushing things he had tried desperately to delay, simply to get things level and protect Vi from any possible reprisals which may be coming his way. He had to slow her gallop down a little, however much disappoint this gave. Things had to move at the right tempo, it was best for all.

'No, Ma, Vi needs time too. I need to earn more to support her. She works at the pen factory and she helps supports her parents. There is only her, she has no brothers and sisters. Don't you see, if she marries her wage will stop, but her parents will still need help. I know she cares for them a great deal, and I must be in a position to support her parents, just as I support you. I just cannot do it for now, so we must wait. Now, if you don't mind, I must go and rest, it is really late and I am very tired. You must rest too, or you will never get well, and you are looking so much better,' this last, a thought John actually believed. May smiled her knowing smile. 'I will come and see you tomorrow and we will talk again. After I have got back from Edgbaston with Jimmy.'

John fell into a fitful sleep that night. His dreams were incoherent and patchy, flashes of memory rather than the long drawn out narratives that most often plagued him. He would remember the days of just Ma, him and Cara, the terrible days. No one knows the gnawing pain of hunger until they have experienced it. Going without food for a day or two is bad for most but is usually alleviated by a good meal on the third or fourth day. But to go without food for weeks, and then only have rotten scraps to ease the suffering is something that most people will never know. The days that the three just lay still, waiting for death, unable to move, unable to fight for survival any more. Then, just at the eleventh hour, some way would be found to put something, however unpalatable, in their stomachs.

John had a vision of May scratching around in the soil for anything green, or even worms, anything. She would always offer to her offspring first, like a mother bird protecting and feeding her young. At first Cara was revolted by raw weeds and insects, but once desperation had taken hold she would eat as much as the other two of anything she could get. Then John remembered checking the mousetraps for any poor unfortunate rodent that had crossed the hearth; baked on a stick in the fire, one mouse every few days gave some sustenance, however limited. This was the time that only the enterprising or those without morals could survive. There was talk of cannibalism in the valley. As homesteads emptied through the death of the inhabitants, and the smell of death drifted on the wind, the scavengers would go looking for anything; in some cases, even human flesh. The Connollys had only heard talk of this, they had neither witnessed it, nor been driven to that point of desperation.

Cara had turned out to be the best of the scavengers in her ravaged family. From being unable to stomach windfall and weeds, she became the one that would enter the deserted homes of rotten-blackened corpses, and search for anything that may provide nourishment, the stench of vile putrefaction all around her. Every time she left to forage she would come back with something. Her gaunt face and black-circled eyes would glow with success as she returned with a handful of corn, or the remnants of a pantry, left like a bequest to any heirs that may chance upon it. Cara seemed to have the luck to find, and May and John became quite dependent on her enterprise; she seemed to be quicker and faster than anyone else. Yes, the local population had been completely decimated, but there were still others left: all had become a war. If you did not get the food, someone else would. Neighbour no longer helped neighbour, desperation had meant that all would do what was necessary to survive, even kill for food.

That was the depths to which society had sunk, that no one trusted or helped anyone else. Even families had destroyed themselves, because the drive to survive was greater than the drive to protect. That was the memory that John could never ignore: the feeling of total isolation and loneliness that was all that was left for the Connollys during the deepest parts of the famine. They cared for each other; they no longer worried about others, and others would see them as enemies. It was a war!

Chapter 11

The enterprise of compromise

Fanny was drowning in her despair for her sister and the predicament which they now found themselves in as a family. Once again, she had been the last to leave, the youngsters could not wait to bolt from the door, and the feeling of relief that emanated from them as they skipped lightly from the court was tangible. Teddy practically ran to school, having eaten every scrap and morsel that had been offered; the poor mite was starving through fear of being in the kitchen with the man that frightened him to death. Other than their natural anxiety and need to escape, nothing of what had passed the previous night had been heard; Fanny hoped that they had slept right through.

Kitty had seemed remarkably unchanged that morning, which on reflection was something that Fanny knew she should have realised would be the case. After all, Kitty had been caught in this cycle of abuse and deceit for a long time, with everyone else blissfully ignorant of these appalling happenings. It was Kitty who had to manage her emotions and appearance on a daily basis. It was not always with the attitude that had been desired, but now in the cold light of day, and with the benefit of the full knowledge, this was completely understandable.

She was as cold and ill-mannered as she had always been, there were no decipherable outward changes which could be witnessed or sensed by anyone, and neither should there have been. The little ones were faced with a sense of normality, and as long as he slept and stayed out of the way everyone could pretend. But as Fanny closed the door behind her and entered the court, she knew that she would feel the deep dread she had felt the previous night when she returned again. At least if Kitty was right, the events of the previous night would not play out again for a few days, and her sister would have a reprieve for now, and Suie would be left alone.

As she met Vi, their journey to work was once again overshadowed by their individual concerns, both lost in their worlds and consumed by their thoughts.

Although Vi had reason for elation – *He loved her!* – she was downcast at having returned to her mother's erratic behaviours once again yesterday evening. This time she had been completely incapable of preparing a simple meal and, just as Vi had witnessed her confused exercise in trying to sew – picking things up, looking at them, and then replacing them unused – she saw her having the same problems with the kitchen equipment.

Vi's mother had seemingly become completely confused by what things were and what they should be used for, and had apparently been going round in circles trying to remember. Vi had no idea how long her mother had been entrapped in this exercise, but normally food preparations had been long since done and the food cooked before she returned from the factory. Her best guess was that two or three hours had passed in these fruitless endeavours. Vi had sat her mother down there and then, and had taken over. With the extra time that was needed making tea – a very late affair – and with everything else she had to do, Vi was completely exhausted.

She worried that if she and John were to marry, what would happen to her parents? In the same way John had thought of her need to support them, she had come to the same conclusions and the prospect of what might happen to them without her support began to distress her greatly. All her natural enthusiasm and optimism that things would somehow work themselves out, that love would find a way – the words that she had stressed to John – were now diminishing with her every breath.

Fanny was the one to break the silence and the reaction that came from Vi took her completely off guard.

'Hey, I've been a bit stuck in me own stuff… what's up?'

Vi looked at her, it was the wrong thing to say at the wrong moment; the tears began to flow, the emotion was unstoppable.

'Hey… hey… I'm sorry. Vi, whatever is the matter? Cumon, stop a moment, talk to me.'

'W-w… we can't stop,' she said through her sobs. 'W-w… we'll… b-be… late… I can't be late… I can't lose my job!' She marched purposefully on, still crying uncontrollably. Fanny froze, and called after her.

'Now listen, Vi… Stop! Five minutes won't make us late. Stop, please!'

Vi stood stock-still. Fanny caught her up, and pulled her around and hugged her. It all came out like a flood, her worries about her mother, her father falling apart and her biggest secret, the young man that was becoming a very special part of her life.

Fanny felt quite overwhelmed by Vi's revelations and, despite her own impossible situation, she wished she could help, at least do something about Vi's mother.

The girls knew they both had to get to the factory, Vi pulled herself together as best she could, Fanny tried to think of words of comfort that may help, but struggled to think of anything that did not sound patronising, or trivial.

'Ya mean ta say, yer having to lock the door? Every night?'

'Yes, we have got no choice. I ran around those streets the other night scared to death she'd walked into the canal. My dad is worried sick and he's making himself ill, this is the only way we sleep at night.'

'But what happens during the day?'

'Well I'm the last out in the morning, so I give the key to a neighbour, who keeps an eye on Ma. If the neighbour goes out, she locks the door.'

'But isn't that a bit dangerous, I mean locking 'er in like that? What if something happens?'

'What else can we do, Fanny? We have no idea what's wrong with her. Sometimes she's fine, totally normal, then other days she is so angry or forgetful, or doesn't seem to know where she is. I am at my wits end. And there was me thinking I could have a happy ever after… it's just impossible.'

'I've heard of this before in a really old person, but never in someone so young like your ma. I mean, she is only just past forty-five, ain't she? Do you think you'd better get a doctor to 'er?'

'Well, I do… but my dad is dead against it. He keeps saying she's fine, and a lot of time she is. But when she is not… I… it's like she's not there any more, and it's a real worry. What am I going to do?'

As they turned into the factory, Fanny tried to raise Vi's spirits as best she could.

'Look, Vi, I really dain't know what to say, but these things do sort themselves out, honestly they do. I'm sure there will be a way. Dain't give up on yer beau, one of us has got to get hitched sooner or later, and I would rather it be you.'

As much as Fanny was doing a fine job trying to lay Vi's spirits to rest, she was not doing such a good job at convincing herself that all of her own problems would magically resolve themselves. As much as she had found Kitty's suggestion abhorrent, it did seem the only way to stop all of the horror that had descended on her family in a matter of days. If only Tom was around, at least she could talk to someone openly. She just could not talk to Vi, despite Vi's revelations to her. She felt unable to be honest and open, she was simply too ashamed to reveal all to even her best friend.

John waited for Jimmy on Bristol Road to walk to the meeting hall. He reflected how quickly time had passed since that day he had failed to sell his last piece and had made up his mind to seek work at Hardman's, thus rekindling this much-needed friendship with Jimmy. It was now early September; how much his life had changed in such a short time, he thought. Not all had gone well – he had been a good jeweller with a trade, supporting his mother and providing a decent roof over their heads, and now he was a struggling silversmith, robbing Peter to pay Paul. And his poor ma, the start of her descent towards her end had been sudden and dramatic, he had never suspected that she would go like this. On the positive side, life had lifted with Jimmy, and he felt elated with Vi, but there was always that silent demon standing on his shoulder. He was reluctant to meet outside the debating hall, fearing that there may be a reception committee for him, led by a scarred man with red hair.

Just then Jimmy appeared in the distance walking quickly towards him, already throwing animated waves and salutations in his direction. John looked nervously about him, it was very hard to be inconspicuous with a friend like James Pearse – always loud, always enthusiastic, bearing strong opinions, but not necessarily those shared by all.

By the time the friends arrived the debate was already underway, and this time, much to John's relief, there were no protestors or agitators picketing the meeting. Mind you, with the topic for this evening's debate it was hard to envisage a collection of businessmen protesting: 'A fair day's wage for a fair day's work'. This debate seemed to be focused very much on the rewards for hard work for the working man. Birmingham had a large collection of non-conformist Unitarians and Quakers; being a city without a charter it offered dignity and shelter to those who would be outcast elsewhere. Hence, a concentration of entrepreneurs and intellectuals from the more enlightened sectors of society.

The likes of the Martineaus and the Cadburys had settled there, bringing their fair work ethics with them. It was considered good practice to look after those that worked for you, a view held by most, but not all; there were still those non-enlightened employers, hell-bent on exploitation and sharp practice. Which was why there was still the need for discussions such as these.

By the time John and Jimmy had taken their seats midway towards the front, the motion had already been introduced by the Chair – Mr Joseph Chamberlain – and the first speaker had taken to the lectern in support. John could not concentrate on the speaker, who seemed lacking in confidence and charisma, unlike Chamberlain who was always self-possessed and outwardly dynamic. Instead, John studied Chamberlain, who sat to one side of the platform. He was, as the last time, extremely well dressed – black tailcoat and waistcoat. His hair was immaculate and slick, he had a cane leant against the chair, more as a statement of position than an aid to walking. He was peering at a small document he had been handed by the gentleman seated to his immediate left, and was sporting a monocle in his eye; John considered how affected he looked, but he could not deny he was stylish. He could also see that he wore a flower in his left buttonhole. John had a fair knowledge of flora for his chasing work, and from where he was sitting he thought that it may be some kind of orchid. Unusual, he thought, that a man like this should have such a fine interest.

He was totally lost in his musing over Chamberlain's appearance that he had completely missed the supporting address. Mind you, on looking around at those with nodding heads and closed eyes, he knew he was not the only one. Then a firecracker of an individual arose to oppose the motion, and all of sudden the hall woke up. The speaker insisted that if you paid the working man too much he would become idle and complacent, that much of the trouble in society was arising from giving too much to the common man. Rather than just considering their needs to survive, they were left with too much time on their hands because they had been afforded the time by over-generous employers who had failed to envisage the damage that could be done by greater rewards. As a consequence of this wealth of time, the common man was 'organising', a vile term in the speaker's opinion, because that meant union involvement and troublemakers coming from other parts of the town, even other towns, to tell good employers how they should run their businesses for the fairness and rights of their workers; with this, he thumped his fist on the lectern causing an eruption of the hall.

John was amazed how this narrow-minded opinion had merited so much support from what he had thought – hoped – were enlightened men. How could they be so blind to changes that were occurring at all levels of society? Why did they persist in such archaic beliefs? He was so taken aback that he had not realised that Jimmy had taken to his feet and was shouting that the speaker was, in his opinion, a narrow-minded bigot. That attracted everyone's attention in their direction, including Chamberlain's, whose monocle had slipped from his eye and who was now sitting stern-faced, staring directly at them. John grabbed for Jimmy's left arm and tried to get him to take his seat. Jimmy shook off the physical protest, at the same time still giving full vent to the speaker, much to the disgust of most who sat in close proximity. John noted that these were far from gentleman sitting here; most he could recognise as factors, middlemen, those who made their livelihoods out of taking their cut, and they would never support the motion because it would make their lives completely impossible. The speaker continued with intensity, now directed against his antagonist, James Pearse.

'You call me a bigot, sir. I am no bigot... I am a realist! There are many here who owe their existence to the status quo.'

A loud 'hear, hear,' rang around the hall.

'Our society is a balanced and a fair one… (hear, hear)… We provide an adequate salary for which the diligent worker can live, and all we ask for is the job that we pay for be done to a satisfactory standard. These do-gooders, Mr Cadbury and the like – I refrain from identifying Mr Chamberlain among them, as I know he thinks with a similar mind and voice to us…' John watched as Chamberlain shifted uneasily in his seat, his facial expression remained unchanged.

The vehement speaker continued.

'The Cadbury family have done more and are doing most to damage this fine balance. By overpaying workers and offering benefits and housing they are making it impossible for the likes of the average employer, who can only employ a modest sized workforce… (hear, hear)… Firstly, we cannot compete to get the best workers as they all gravitate to the Cadbury enterprise, so we end up with the less skilled and the bone idle. Secondly, if we manage to establish a workforce, they measure themselves against the over-indulgences which are given to the Cadbury workers and demand ever more, and we just cannot compete with this. And if we stick to our guns and refuse, outside agitators are brought in to our places of enterprise. These agitators "organise", and make our workers act against their fair employers. It is they who come to make trouble. This motion is an unfair imposition on the reasonable employer… I rest!'

Jimmy shouted raucously that this man was a prehistoric relic from a bygone age, and he did not deserve a good workforce if he was prepared to exploit the worker in such a way and beat the backs of those who had nothing put by, keeping them with nothing.

The surrounding crowd of factors began to shout abuse at Jimmy. John knew that this was too dangerous a place to be shouting any opposition, and was desperately trying to get Jimmy to resume his seat; it looked as if a

129

number of the men close by were about to swing punches in Jimmy's direction when, thankfully, the Chair stood up.

The effect was immediate as Chamberlain took to the floor. Silence came, and all eyes were focused on this man. John pulled Jimmy down at once. Chamberlain paused for effect, he stood scrutinising the audience, walking from one end of the platform to the other and back, all eyes followed him as he did so. He stood to the lectern and began slowly, and in a considered fashion, to address the assembly of men.

'My friends… indeed, I do call you my friends, for I know that many of you do indeed share my views and opinions.'

The previous speaker nodded enthusiastically from his corner.

'Many of you know that I form part of an enterprise called Nettlefolds. We have a state-of-the-art factory which machines mechanical fittings and screws for industry… a new industry… and industry that this growing city is dependent on. Our product has to be reliable, of considerable quality, while at the same time remaining highly competitive, not an easy task I can tell you.'

There were low mumbles of agreement from other factory owners who shared similar concerns.

'It is, and has always been, a problem obtaining the right men to undertake such tasks, and more often than not now we train our own to do the job at considerable cost and time to ourselves… but we know then that we have the best, and although many think that we use machines, so we need no one of skill or with the brains to be able to do the job… they are wrong. Operating machines to the demanding tolerances that we require takes considerable skill and intellect, and our workers are remunerated for that, so that we keep them.'

Again, low mumbles of agreement came from the floor, and the previous speaker nodded so as to appear as in full agreement, although a little confused by what he was now hearing. Chamberlain continued.

'Despite what my colleague and friend has just aired, I do not agree that Mr Cadbury and his family are in some way failing their workforce, or damaging the prospects of other who run modern enterprise. Indeed, I believe strongly that it has driven up the standards among workers, who now work hard and longer in order to qualify for the proper rewards and benefits of my like-minded colleagues.'

The previous speaker's face began to freeze, as he realised that Chamberlain was speaking in opposition to his opinion.

'Further, I know that as much as my workers and those of many of my colleagues are indeed trained, skilled workers – and some would argue that this is a form of education – they are only skilled to a certain level. There are many in this city, and I know of two sitting in this room tonight...'

At that point, Joseph Chamberlain looked in John and Jimmy's direction with admiration, many faces turned to follow his gaze; now John shifted uncomfortably in his chair. Chamberlain went on:

'...who are the real artisans and craftsman... without whose skills and abilities, and those of their predecessors, this city would never have thrived the way that it has, or indeed made such a significant mark on the map of this country. When I reflect on the incredible undertaking of Messers Boulton and Watt at Soho, I admire and celebrate the quite remarkable endeavours that took place there, and all a lifetime ago. It is simply amazing that such an enlightened group of individuals could dream up such a complexity of ideas for society, and create such an effective place of work, knowledge and skill. If ever I or my partners could repeat the same entrepreneurial vision to bring forth such concepts, we would be worthy successors indeed. But we are not... not yet. However, the likes of Cadbury are, and he and his sons should be respected for what they have achieved and what they aim to do for the betterment of the common man. My friends, the artisans, are fine fellows, they produce work of such intrinsic beauty and joy, and not for the money, because they are exploited more than most.'

At this, there were grunts of disapproval and shuffling surrounding John and Jimmy from some very disgruntled factors.

'No, my friends create their work because it is their life, the beat of their heart, it is what they will always desire to do. That, in my mind, friends, is what this motion seeks to address: recognising that those with the real skills which we all value, which we all take great advantage of when we go to a place where there is vast ornamentation, when we place a well-made suit on our backs... (he stroked his lapels for emphasis)... indeed, when we give the woman we love an item to treasure... these are the people who deserve our respect and reward. Gentlemen, I commend this motion to you unreservedly!'

The hall erupted. This time, the voice of dissension had been silenced; everyone was in full support of the startling speech that Joseph Chamberlain had given. There was thunderous applause from all assembled as Chamberlain proceeded to take his seat. John and Jimmy could not help themselves but join in; despite their reservations and obvious distaste for his previous speech regarding Irish workers, there was no doubt this time that he was absolutely and squarely in their camp of opinion. Jimmy clapped so hard his hands were practically red raw.

The rest of the society's business for that evening rather disappeared into the euphoria that the Chair's speech had generated; there were so many private discussions and comments among the audience, that the debate leaders struggled to keep any grip on the rest of the proceedings. John was in the mind to try and leave, as much to extricate Jimmy from any trouble which could arise from their vocal and dissenting neighbours as to simply leave early. But they were stranded in the middle of the row and knew they had no alternative other than to sit it out. Just then a note was passed from the end of the row to Jimmy. He opened and read it and was very surprised by its contents. He smiled and nodded in the direction of the platform, and handed the note onto to John. It read:

> *Dear Sirs,*
>> *I would be most grateful if you would both remain at the end of the debate, as I have much I would like to discuss with you.*
>> *Yours respectfully,*
>> *Joseph Chamberlain Esq.*

Jimmy was obviously quite excited to have a chance to talk to Chamberlain, but although John found him fascinating, he was a naturally suspicious individual who felt uncomfortable with this sudden attention, indeed he had found elements of the speech patronising. He hoped it would just be passing greetings rather than any long drawn out conversation, and as Jimmy was so keen he knew that he would be in a better position to make his apologies and leave if necessary.

The meeting wound down and gradually began to disband, the factors and middlemen that had been seated in close proximity to the pair made a few comments that were hardly audible, but with enough accompanying looks of contempt to unsettle; nothing which could be heard to be disputed. Many in the meeting were passing their comments in a rather more positive fashion to one another regarding the electrifying speech of Chamberlain, and saw John and Jimmy's involvement as a matter on the periphery. Jimmy sat impatiently, trying to catch Chamberlain's eye; he was still caught up in discussions on the platform.

'You'd think if he needed to see us he would come straight away, don't you, John?'

'He is obviously a very popular man, Jimmy, we just have to wait for him, but I cannot wait for long I have Ma to get back for, so I may have to make my apologies and leave earlier. I hope you don't mind?'

'Aye, no of course not. I am sure he won't be much longer, look... see... he has just nodded in our direction, I think he is making his way over.'

Jimmy rose from his seat to make his greetings, John remained seated momentarily. He was not going to go out of his way to show any enthusiasm for a man that he still considered to be on the wrong side of the political argument. Chamberlain strode in a stately fashion up the aisle between the seats, his face showing no emotion whatsoever, and as he drew closer he extended his hand towards Jimmy.

'My dear sir, how good of you to wait,' he said.
John finally rose and put out his hand with slight reluctance to acknowledge the greeting.

'And you, sir... Mr Connolly is it not, the jeweller?' John nodded. 'And Mr Pearse, ornamental sculptor?'

'Yes, sir, perfectly correct and well remembered,' replied Jimmy. 'I am surprised that a man such as yourself with so many dealings with others, should remember small fry such as us.' Jimmy laughed – Chamberlain broke a half smile. 'Anyway, how can we help you, sir?'

Chamberlain paused before answering, possibly sensing John's reticence or maybe because he felt that John had not got the full measure of the situation or the purpose.

'Gentleman, I was very interested by our brief exchange at the previous meeting, and it has had me considering many things in the last month. I do not deny that I have a slightly more privileged situation than most, and I am somewhat sheltered from the realities of living in a city such as Birmingham in these modern times. I feel it is my duty to get a better grasp of the issues that concern many. I am also concerned, as I hope I made clear in tonight's discussion, that those who endeavour to imaginatively create to a high standard of quality and luxury are correctly recognised for their skill and talent. I would like to discuss this with you both as there is no better way of researching the case in hand than actually going to the heart of the matter.' He paused again to gauge their reaction. John remained dispassionate, but Jimmy beamed broadly and nodded.

'I do realise that this needs proper consideration and we need to arrange more opportune circumstances... how do you feel about that, gentlemen?'

Jimmy replied carefully, which for him was quite a challenge.

'Well, Mr Chamberlain, we are more than happy to talk to you, but surely the best way to gauge this problem fairly, is to witness it first-hand? And as you said, we could not do this topic justice in speech, where things are hard to illustrate? Sorry to use the artistic analogy, but I find that an image or a scene can take the place of several thousand words.'

'Absolutely, Mr Pearse. I am glad we are of one accord and it would be a valuable opportunity now to make some arrangements.'

John's impatience finally got the better of him and he decided that this superficial pussyfooting was something he wished to absent himself from. He knew that Jimmy was more than capable of continuing any discussion without him, so he interrupted Chamberlain before he had a chance to continue.

'I am very sorry, sirs, but I have a pressing commitment that I must get back to.' He looked at Jimmy for support. 'I am sure Mr Pearse can do a much better job than me, Mr Chamberlain, at illustrating these problems. I hope you understand, but I really do have to go.' He extended his hand, this time a little more positively, in

Chamberlain's direction in order to take his leave. Chamberlain received it, saying:

'Well, of course. I am very sorry you have to leave, Mr Connolly, I was looking forward to hearing your particular point of view. Maybe we can have an opportunity in the future to resume our discussions?'

John nodded, more of a formality than of any genuine intent to take Chamberlain at his word. He turned to Jimmy and shook him by the hand, and apologised for leaving him. Jimmy accepted John's reasoning, and John turned to leave, heading towards the darkened area at the back of the hall, conscious that Jimmy and Chamberlain had now taken seats and were happily in a more animated mode of discussion, probably both relieved that John had taken his leave of them. He was so caught up in his thoughts, conscious that time had mocked him again and that his mother would be awake and waiting for him, that he failed to notice the lone individual seated in the gloom, two chairs to the right of the aisle at the very back of the hall. As he drew close he heard unexpected words.

'Yer a dead man, Connolly!'

These words chilled John to the bone and, glancing quickly to his right had his worst fears confirmed; the Irish dialect similar to his own, the wiry, red hair, the scarred red face, Sean Rafferty sneered at him and his eyes flashed pure hate.

John did not pause or stop to exchange any conversation. In absolute shock and fear of the implications he marched on purposefully, his mind reeling. He had been seen! Sean knew it was him, he'd used his name! There was no escaping it on this occasion, no fantasising this time; he was after him! What was he going to do? What was he going to do? He could not think straight, his mind was in a complete whirl. The same thought kept repeating in a loop, a continuing cycle of fear without a face, without form, creating an overwhelming need to run and flee, to protect those nearest to him, but no practical solutions as to how either could be achieved. He just had to get home, and now!

Jimmy stood up to leave, very happy that arrangements were made and a purpose had been put into the debate that had been raised.

'Well thank you, Mr Chamberlain.'

'No… please call me Joseph, and you are James?'

'Well, my friends call me Jimmy… but if you are comfortable with James I understand. I look forward to our next meeting. You really do have to witness the conditions and experience the area to have any hope of understanding. And please forgive my friend, he has a lot on his mind at the moment, and most of it stems from what we have just been discussing. I shall see you soon. Goodbye.'

The men parted affably, Chamberlain heading back towards the platform to collect his cane and other possessions, feeling very pleased with himself, and Jimmy to rush home, also quite elated.

Sean threw the first punch, completely calculated. Just as Jimmy reached him, he rose and caught him square on the jaw, sending him stumbling into the opposite row of chairs, causing every face, including Chamberlain's, to turn. Completely dazed and totally shocked and thinking this was some aggrieved factor and he had a corner to stand, Jimmy came back with a slightly weaker right hook. By this stage a number of those left had run to break up this unseemly altercation. Sean took full and calculated advantage.

'I wan' him up before the beak, he thumped me! He threw the first punch… I wan' yers all there to witness!'

Chapter 12

Seeking justice

'Your honour, James Pearse is charged with starting a public affray last evening, in a place of honourable practice. He did attack Mr Sean Rafferty without any encouragement to do so as Mr Rafferty was innocently going about his business.'

The magistrates' court usher read out the charges to a judge of considerable age, who sat somewhat reluctantly to hear the morning's arraignments. Sean Rafferty sat as the picture of innocence in the front row, facing the man he had accused who stood in the dock. James had not slept, shaved or changed his clothes, he looked the image of a ruffian who had been brought to book. He had spent that night detained in the barracks on Livery Street, with the drunks and down-and-outs that had been collected together for weeks; he smelt like he had been drinking with them. The side of his face was purple in colour and very swollen, but despite the fact that his blow had barely made contact with Sean, Sean was sporting a very black eye. Indeed, he looked like *he* had come off worse from the altercation with Jimmy, and not the other way around.

The lack of sleep did not help Jimmy trying to make sense of what had happened. One minute he had been minding his own business mulling over his thoughts, and the requests which Joseph Chamberlain had made of him, the next moment he had found himself sprawled over two rows of chairs in the hall, having made contact with someone's fist. The 'someone' – he had no idea who he was – was sitting impassively in front of him. He had assumed he was one of the aggrieved factors, but now being able to study him more closely he realised that he had no memory of this chap whatsoever. Mind you, there had been many around with a mind that he was speaking out of turn. But then to claim he was responsible for starting the fight? And further, to have him charged and incarcerated for the offence? None of it made sense. The gentleman – Sean hardly had the appearance of a gentleman, but Jimmy was trying to be charitable – sitting in front of him was going to make a claim that would be disproved; he could not bring a legitimate case against Jimmy, so why go to all these lengths, it just did not make sense.

Jimmy's head thumped as the court barrister made a case against Jimmy as claimed by Sean. According to the court official, Sean Rafferty, of Dale End, had been sitting minding his own business at the back of the hall and had got up to leave when this person, unannounced and unprovoked, stuck him causing grievous bodily harm. When Mr Rafferty regained his senses, he recognised Mr Pearse as the man who had led a group of troublemakers who had come to disrupt that evening's discussion. Jimmy was flabbergasted, and let out an involuntary guffaw at this complete pack of lies. This commanded a stern look from the magistrate, and the barrister paused for effect before counsel was directed to continue. Mr Rafferty had only then reacted, in self-defence he said, for he knew that Mr Pearse had a companion and he was not sure if he was about to become the victim of a second attack from his associate. This was too much for Jimmy.

'This is not true!'

The court stopped once again, this time the magistrate's authority was brought to bear on the situation.

'Will the defendant refrain from any comment until the court directs him to speak! Now is the time for the claimant to make his case. If you continue with further disruption I shall detain you without trial for contempt of court! Is that clear?'

Jimmy realised the seriousness of the situation that now faced him, and that he had better find all within him to restrain his commentary. As difficult as it was for him, he would just have to listen with half an ear so that he did not react, until he was allowed to make his defence. The counsel continued with Sean's claim.

'Mr Rafferty requests that the court fine Mr Pearse for the bodily harm caused, and that Mr Pearse is forced to make restitution to Mr Rafferty for the damages done.'

The magistrate cleared his throat, and with a wry smile addressed Sean.

'Mr Rafferty, we conduct criminal prosecution here, we do not judge civil dispute. If indeed we find Mr Pearse guilty of this assault, the court will issue the appropriate punishment to fit that crime.' He looked sternly at Jimmy. 'And assault without provocation is, to my view, a serious crime. However, if it is financial compensation you are seeking, Mr Rafferty, you will not get that here.' The judge paused, and when he continued the assembled were in no doubt of his racial sympathies.

'I have had one too many Irish chancers to contend with here, so let us hope that your case is a sound one?' This statement caused a low ripple of laughter from the rest of the court, and cast doubt over the point of some of the cases waiting to be aired by the twenty or so other witnesses and claimants in the room. The magistrate began to directly address Jimmy.

'Now, Mr Pearse, are you in the habit of making attacks of this nature on others?'

'No, your honour.'

'That's what I believe, so why would Mr Rafferty make such a claim against you?'

Jimmy coughed to clear his throat.

'I have no idea, sir. I have spent the last ten hours trying to make sense of this and the story that he has just relayed to you. This bears no resemblance to what actually happened, your honour.'

'Well perhaps you could recount your side of the tale... Mr... er... Mr Pearse?'

'Well, my friend and I were attending the debating society meeting... and I got a little carried away with the rubbish that one of the speakers was spouting and put my point across—' The judge cut across Jimmy's testimony.

'You mean you were agitating and causing trouble?'

'No, your honour... I just didn't agree with arrogant rubbish about how we are all scroungers and do not deserve a decent day's pay for a decent day's work.' Jimmy's comment caused a positive stir with all of the assembled working people, and prompted the usher to call all to order. The judge continued.

'And your co-agitator – who is he exactly?' Sean appeared to be listening intently.

'He is Mr John Connolly, a respected jeweller. He lives on the junction of Cottage Lane and Garrett Street...'

Sean sat back in his seat, he had got what he had come for. Jimmy continued.

'He can vouch for me, sir, that I was there as a member of the audience to take part in the debate... in fact, there is another who might stand for me, sir—'

Again, the magistrate cut over Jimmy; he already knew the name he was about to give.

'And would this other name be Mr Joseph Chamberlain Esq. sir?'

Jimmy was quite surprised; how would he know? He stuttered his reply.

'Y-y-yes, sir.'

'Yes, indeed, sir. I already have a communiqué from Mr Chamberlain, to the effect that he does vouch for you as a character, and for your story, sir.' The magistrate looked seriously at Sean. 'Mr Rafferty, with all this weight of opinion in support of Mr Pearse, are you as sure of your tale as you claim to be?'

'Well, your honour... now you come to mention it I might have got it slightly the wrong way around.' Sean was now playing a game with the court and would extricate himself as lightly as possible. The assembled waifs and strays began to laugh at the relaxed Irishman.

'I mean, I had dozed off just before... maybe I dreamt I had been thumped... just a mistake on my part perhaps.' Laughter erupted from all around the court. The magistrate was none too impressed.

'Mr Rafferty! Your claim does not hold water! As I have already stated, another idle Irishman trying to make on creating misfortune for others. Mr Pearse has no case to answer and I hereby order that he is discharged from custody and that the case be dismissed. And, Mr Rafferty, do not let me see you in my court again, otherwise I will lock you up immediately for contempt. Now get out!'

As it was mid-morning by this time and Jimmy was in desperate need of a wash and a change of clothes, he decided it was best to head home rather than continue on his way to Newhall Hill and the workshop; he would make his way tomorrow to tell his strange story to John.

John, on the other hand, was not in such a relaxed disposition. He had been unable to sleep at all and had told a barefaced lie to May that he was ill, rather than admitting what had passed on leaving the meeting. He had no one he felt he could confide in or discuss any of this with, he was completely consumed by a terrible anxiety. He had come to the decision that, as the debating society had been where he was spotted he must keep away. At least Sean had no idea where he was living or, he hoped, what his profession may be, so it would be very difficult to scour Birmingham to find him with ease. And he knew he had not been followed, he had run most of the two miles home, and constantly checked behind him; no one had followed him. As long as he stayed away from the debating society at least it would buy him a little more time, until he could work out what to do. It also meant that he had to do his best to stay clear of Jimmy for a short while; there would be too many questions to answer and it would all be too difficult to explain. And as much as he cared for his mother and Vi, he had begun to regard Jimmy like a younger brother; he had become important to him too. He would hate to drag Jimmy into any of this, he knew what the outcome would be, he had been witness to that before. And Jimmy had recently taken a young wife, she may be affected too. The damage that could be caused if John was at all careless did not bear thinking about.

He had made his way to work, simply to try to distract himself and earn the much-needed money for all of the possible plans that may have to be made. Any pieces that he could make for Hardman's now would all add to the possible escape fund for him and Vi. He hoped Vi would not make today one of the days that she may drop by for lunch; he had not seen her for a little while, but he knew that when she could she would come to see him, he just hoped for it not to be this day. He tried to apply himself to the tasks, but he found himself constantly distracted by either his confused thoughts or by the view into St Paul's Square, particularly scanning for any passers-by with red hair. He sensed that Sean would come looking for him, but he could not understand why he felt like this because all the evidence was to the contrary; it was just not possible within the realms of mathematical probability that this man would 'just happen' to turn up here.

By the time he had come to the end of his working day he was completely exhausted and he had only produced two-thirds of what he had planned to do and was actually capable of. With day turning fast to twilight, he was able to pass unnoticed and anonymously back into the court. Mrs Morris was just coming out of the kitchen as he came arrived.

'Oh, John, how are you lad? Are coping alright with things?'

'Aye, Mrs Morris,' he lied. 'Thanks to you I can get on.' That bit was true. But he noted her expression was more serious than usual and, considering she was spending far more time with May than he was, she was a better judge of the progress of May's illness.

'And how is Ma today, do you think? I thought she was looking a little better just recently?'

Mrs Morris looked at him searchingly, had he not seen the steep decline of the last few weeks? Was he really in denial? Her look changed to pity.

'Listen, lad, we all have our span… and no matter what we do we cannot change that. I think your ma is as well as can be expected, and she is such a cheerful soul that her spirits will never dampen. She is a great lady with a lot of heart, she'll hold on to life until she knows she can die.'

'What are saying? That she won't go until I tell her to?' John was quite incredulous at Mrs Morris's implied suggestion.

'Yes, John, that is exactly what I am saying, because I have seen it before in my own mother. She needed me to tell her that she could go… sometimes you have to do this to give those that you love peace, and relieve their suffering.'

John felt quite aggrieved at this suggestion, but he knew not to react because Mrs Morris was such a good woman, and he knew he needed to reflect on what she had said. His initial reaction was to dismiss this statement out of hand, however, he realised that at that particular moment all things were black to him. He thanked her for her help and turned to go in. Just before he left her, she added:

'I have left a little something on the stove for you both… but do not be surprised if she does not take much. Oh, and a gentleman called for you; he said he would come again.'

John froze in his tracks and asked the question which he needed the answer to.

'Did he have red hair?'

'No. He seemed very nice… he said he would call again.'

John was relieved it was not Sean, but who was it that would call? Jimmy? Why did he not come and see him at his workshop? Then through paranoia, the thought crossed his mind that Sean had paid someone to call; he began to sweat profusely, but realised he was still standing in doorway facing Mrs Morris and not communicating at all. She got quite concerned.

'Are you alright, John? You've taken a funny turn.'

'Aye, I am fine… just tired.'

'You must be. Go rest, son, you'll be no good to your ma unless you rest, you look like you have not slept properly in days.'

She was right, of course. In fact, he had not slept properly in weeks. He felt completely exhausted, which for John was always a blessing as he was always then too tired to dream, but not too tired to remember, of course.

John took a bowl of the broth into May. She was lying propped up, and she seemed to be drifting in and out of reality. She perked up as soon as he sat to talk, and he spooned a few mouthfuls of the food into her. As he did so, he remembered the time when any food was eaten quickly out of necessity; now she barely touched a thing, but she smiled, that never-ending warm smile. That cheerful disposition that kept all around her going when everything seemed completely hopeless. Her voice was faltering and frail.

'How… are you… my boy? Have you had… a good… day?'

'Yes, Ma. I finished two alms dishes. I still have another chalice to do… then I must ask for some more work, but I think I'll get it. And you… how are feeling today? You look stronger.'

'Aye, I try, Johnny… you know that. And Vi… have you seen Vi… today? Have… you said… that… I wish you… both well?'

'No, I have not seen Vi for a few days. But she does work you know, and I know she helps her parents with the house, so maybe she has been busy? I don't know. Do you think I should find out? I mean, I am not good with girls, you know that… since Cara, I have not really got close to any women, so I don't know what to do.'

'Johnny, I am sure you are right. Maybe Vi is busy. Just trust and… be gentle. Love… will do the rest. And some are just not meant… to make the journey…with us. Cara travelled as far as she could… as Niamh did.'

'But Cara…' John stopped himself. What he was about to say would open more wounds and do more damage. If his mother had adjusted the way she had, he must leave her be with her memories, at least they were no longer agonies. May seemed very tired and John let her take some rest. He went through to the kitchen and sat with a bowl of broth in front of him, unable to eat. His problems seemed insurmountable: his mother lay dying in the next room, he was barely able to make enough money to keep body and soul together, never mind support a young wife and her family, and now he was being chased by a man he knew would never be satisfied until he had his revenge. Had he not been through enough in his life? When was it all going to stop? He missed Cara, he missed her so much.

Cara had been the one most like their mother. She was always the person who would solve the problem. When everyone else had failed to find food, she had taken it on herself to scavenge for her mother and brothers. She would enter the habitations with the rotting corpses and risk the vileness and the disease to find what scraps she could, and she would never sneak and eat what she could first, and claim that was all that she had. Despite her own famished state and pain, she would bring all of what she found back from however far away, and make sure it was all shared equally. She kept her two loved ones sustained, and each admired her bravery and tenacity.

It was on one of these journeys to seek out scraps that Cara was watched. She travelled six or seven miles from her home; as each place was cleaned out by the scavengers she was having to travel further and further into the wilderness of the hills, to the more far-flung cottages, in the hope that there may be pickings there. But she was not the only scavenger on the trail. She had not as yet encountered any problems with others, as she would always wait and watch from the outside of any seemingly deserted place before entering, just to make sure she was alone and that no others had interests there. If she was not alone she knew she could never fight for food and it was best to wait until they had departed and then see if anything was left.

She had found an old crofters place – an old sheep farmer. The skeletal remains of his paltry stock lay in a small corral outside, with what looked like the remains of a dog. As she entered the small soddy-cum-croft, the aroma was more sick-making than most times. The old man had obviously passed away on the floor some months previously, the flies and blackened putrefaction of the skin had made any human features indistinguishable. At any other time before the famine, she would have vomited ten yards away from the smell alone, but wasted stomachs became strong and saved anything just to survive. She felt herself wretch slightly, but swallowed it back. She approached the small wooden settle, which appeared to be slightly open. There may be some grain left if the mice had not got it; all places must be searched and this was a start. She opened it, but was disappointed to find nothing.

She headed further towards the back of the cottage, obviously the driest of places and where the old man appeared to have slept. There was a straw-filled mattress that had seen better days and an old tartan plaid laid across. She hoped that he may have stored something here for safety. During the height of the famine, before the first large wave of death and disease, many had found themselves the victims of looting by starving neighbours. If they were lucky they lost what they had stored; if they were unlucky, they lost their lives. She began to root through the mattress holes with her hands, exploring for any sacks or bundles. The smell of the straw was musty and old, the noise of the crackling dry mass

147

was very loud and she did not hear the footsteps that had come into the cottage. The first thing she knew was the hand which smothered her mouth from behind her head, while the other large hand pushed her head down into the mattress.

She could not scream, not that there was anyone to hear, as her face was buried in the mattress and plaid and any noises she could make barely made a sound through the large male hand: her frail whimpers were muffled. He had made sure she could not turn to see him either, for what he was about to do to her was his shame as much as hers. He ripped her dress in his desperation to get to her, and tore her clean draws off. She was bent double over the makeshift sleeping area, practically laid flat. He used his strength to kick her legs apart. He freed the hand that was across her mouth but kept the other firmly on the back of her neck, so her face remained buried, and she was practically unable to breathe. With his free hand he fumbled in his crotch and in his clumsy efforts to force her to take him he entered her like a pederast. But this man was not going to stop now, his bestiality had overtaken, he persisted over and over, forcing himself further and further into her. She was resisting through discomfort, the more she clamped her muscles the more painful it became. She was screaming for all she was worth, but it was deadened by the mouthfuls of straw mattress and woollen plaid.

He pushed and pushed as hard as he could and yelled half in pain, half in complete satisfaction as his full body weight fell upon her. Her body, frail and small, was completely trapped by this man. She felt completely violated and petrified. She could not free herself or get away, what was she going to do? She lay for what seemed like an age beneath his weight and then noticed that his breathing had become rhythmical and heavy: he had fallen into a deep sleep on top of her. His grip had relaxed, his penis had shrivelled and her body had mercifully expelled him; he was slipping sideways. She knew if she moved very gently and slowly she could free herself. She held her breath, and began to slip to the side that he had vacated. Just then, he moved as if reclaiming his position. She froze, her heart thumping, he fell into his catatonic coma once more. Again, she edged slowly, little by little. Finally, all that remained under his body was her left arm and hand. She carefully slid it out.

She was free. She rose very slowly to her feet and, as she did so, she caught sight of her attacker. She was expecting to see a man of maturity, but was surprised to see a young man not much older than her brother Patrick. She was horrified that one so young could do such a terrible thing. He had very hollow features and sandy-brown hair; he looked like an angel, yet he had behaved like a complete animal. His perfect face was only marked by one blemish – a pronounced red birthmark on his left cheek, but even that had beauty, it was the size of a halfpenny and shaped like a perfect heart. She committed his face to her memory and despised every inch of him. She backed slowly and quietly to the door and, when she was sure she could run, she bolted as fast as she could. She ran for two miles at least before collapsing in a hedgerow, completely terrified and shocked. Her adrenaline had left her, her fight or flight reflex had brought her here and now her emotions came forth. The tears rolled like rain, she felt so sore, she was too scared to squat or sit and she felt wet and uncomfortable. She felt so ashamed.

After a few hours, she had managed to make her way back to her home. Both the brothers were in the yard. Luck had been on their side that day and they had trapped two rabbits, a feast that they had not had for a long time because there had been too many chasing the same wild quarry; now most of their near neighbours were dead, there was more to go around if you could catch it. Patrick called out to her as she approached, limping.

'Hey, Cara, what you got…? We have rabbit tonight!'

She said nothing, just carried on walking. Patrick saw that she was in distress and her dress was badly torn. He guessed immediately that she had been attacked, he ran to her, and tried to pick her up to carry her; she screamed and pushed him away, she was nearly hysterical. May came rushing out to get her. She instantly realised what had happened by the state of her daughter, and did her best to soothe her and sent the boys to a safe distance. She coaxed her daughter inside, to help her recover and hear her disturbing revelations.

Hours passed. The boys could not cook the rabbits, no one appeared hungry or interested in food. They hung them in the meat store, then sat and waited. What was happening, what was being said, they knew was between women and it was not their place to intrude, but

149

Patrick was angry; he knew something dreadful had been done to Cara, and his instincts were to find the culprit and beat him within an inch of his life. John, though disturbed, was not as great a victim of his surging testosterone as his slightly elder brother.

Finally, May came to them. She had calmed Cara and left her sleeping. May looked completely broken. The woman, who had nursed one daughter who had died of the most terrible sickness, who had lost her beloved man so young, who had borne the worst of the famine with complete grace, was utterly beaten. She told her sons all that had happened, more in an effort to come to terms with it herself than to communicate the extent to which their sister had been violated. She was shocked to her core. They all sat in silence, each lost in their own anger and hatred for this atrocity, but in differing ways and measure. May's fury was of the act. The act of rape, any rape, was repulsive, but this was sodomy, it broke two of God's laws, the culprit would be damned to hell, his spirit would never find rest. John was angry about not being with his sister to protect her; he had just naively assumed that because she had always returned unharmed that she would always, and inevitably. If he had been there to protect her, if he had been there....?

Patrick was angry to the point of destruction. His initial reaction, to beat the living daylights out of the beast, had turned to murderous intent: he was going to kill if he could. May knew that Patrick had reached fever pitch, and this was the one and only time that she was completely grateful that nobody knew the offender; no one could avenge the destruction done. It was more important in her eyes to find forgiveness, only then could they heal this vile wound, only then could they heal Cara's pain.

John shook himself back to reality. Too much remembering, too much pain, and that had been the worst pain of all. Watching Cara day after day destroyed his trust the world. He witnessed her descent into incomprehensible grief; she was grieving for her loss of herself. She would shake uncontrollably and could no longer be left alone anywhere; her fear was real and tangible. No one could comfort her and no one could convince her that it would not happen again, that she was safe. He had lost count of the many times he had been woken up by her screams in the middle of the night as she had yet another nightmare. And all the time Patrick's anger grew perceptibly. His need to find the culprit and make good the wrong to his sister became all-consuming, creating a sickness of his mind: an obsession.

May anguished over her children's pain, each suffering in their own way. It was at this time she felt her faith was tested to the absolute limit. No mattered how much she prayed, she could not find the right words to counsel her offspring, and neither could she find the peace to rest her troubled soul. For the first time in her life she felt that God had left her, that she had offended him so much in such a terrible way that she knew not how – she felt Godless!

Chapter 13

Stealing time

Teddy kicked a stone along the cobbles. He had had a bad morning and now he'd be in for it if Fanny found out he was wagging school. He had struggled with learning his letters that day, and had felt the pain of complete humiliation when he had been subjected to ridicule by the schoolmaster. He had been near to tears all morning, and fearful of the name calling and bullying that would happen if he cried. Finally, he could no longer suppress his pent-up emotion, and ran out of the schoolroom and the school, leaving the schoolmaster standing speechless in front of the class.

Teddy knew that he could not head back to the court, too many would see him there and he had to think what to do. He harboured another more tangible fear that the man who most despised him in the world would be hanging around the house, and God only knew what he would do. Teddy had always known that his father had blamed him for killing his mother. He had felt so guilty from the moment that he understood that his mother had died within moments of his birth; he would agonise over it, despite Fanny's reassurances to the contrary, that 'it was one of those things, bab, yer not to blame.' Somehow, he could never shake off the burden of guilt that he carried.

In his eyes, if he hadn't been born there would still be a family and everyone would be happy; in fact, today he wished that he had never been born at all. What Teddy did not know, and could not know because he had not been there, was that the family were even more pitiful before he was born, simply because Alf was always there and his violent behaviour towards the whole family, in particular Teddy's mother, had just been part of life. His mother dying from her haemorrhage had actually been a blessing for her and her children. Alf could not handle children or the responsibilities of being a father, and had immediately taken off to find solace in a bottle, leaving Fanny and Tom to pick up the pieces.

There had been many more times of prolonged peace and stability that followed, and some degree of normality had been assumed as a result of Alf's absences. Unfortunately, this calm atmosphere was in stark contrast to that created upon his returns, which were punctuated by fear and abuse.

Teddy was scared of Alf. He held no other emotion for him whatsoever, there was no love or admiration as a boy would ordinarily feel for a father, but there was no hate either; Teddy was quite simply petrified. Not that Alf had ever really had a chance to enact any twisted revenge that he was harbouring for the little lad; the ever-watchful Fanny shielded Teddy from any undue interest. She hid him constantly, or sent him off on errands so he was simply never in front of his father.

Alf could not tolerate the sight of Teddy, because he reminded him of the day he had kicked his wife in the back on the floor when she had not got his tea on the table at the time he had expected it. After striking her and sending her flying against the range, he had put the boot in for good measure. Two days later she had bled to death in the exact same spot, giving birth to her little Teddy at the same moment.

Teddy found himself drifting around the streets, heading away from the court towards St Paul's. He knew it was safer to be further away and he thought of where he might sit and pass the time until Fanny had finished work and he could seek her protection, not that she would be happy with him. Teddy would not lie to Fanny, he could not lie to her, he trusted her implicitly and knew that she only had his best interests at heart. He was always honest with her about his problems at school, although she did not always seem to understand that he did really try his hardest; it just all looked so strange, and even if he managed to learn something one day, he would forget it the next. He knew that he needed school, that his big sister was right, if he wanted to get on he must learn his letters and numbers, he just could not get the hang of it.

It was September and felt like the end of summer, the sun was still making its presence felt, the odd bee still droned its way to find any city-locked garden or hedgerow that may still hold a flower treasure to collect from. He looked at his black feet and legs and felt in his ragged pockets for something. He found his prize stone that he always kept with him. He had discovered it a couple of years ago in Warstone Cemetery and was immediately attracted to its colour and smoothness. It was shiny and brown, almost polished, and it had lines of different browns and beige striations through it, but when he turned it over he could see a picture in all the lines – like he used to see pictures in the grain of the wooden planks near his bed, and in the fire – he saw the beautiful face of a woman.

Teddy decided that this was his mother and she was being close to him even though she was dead, although of course he didn't even know what she had looked like. He knew not to show it to anybody or tell anybody about it; Suie or Mouse would nick it and laugh at him. He always kept it with him and it made him feel safe. And when the teacher was shouting at him, telling him he was 'useless and stupid', he would feel for it in his pocket and hold it tightly in the palm of his hand.

He looked at her face, and felt warm inside. He continued on his way with greater purpose, towards his place of sanctuary; then he would sit it out and think of how to tell his sister what he had done. As he passed through St Paul's he noticed Vi sitting on a bench, luckily enough he saw her before she caught sight of him, and he quickly dashed into a side street, deciding not to risk crossing the square directly.

Vi had seen him, but knew that he should be in school and would not want to be discovered truanting, so she pretended to ignore him. She sat waiting for John; she had not been for days and felt that she must make the effort and put on her bravest face so that he would not know of her troubles. She had delayed returning to work awhile and wondered if he was there or away at Hardman's; she hoped he was not hiding from her like last time.

Just then, she saw his tall frame marching into the square from the direction of Fredrick Street. He had obviously been to his new employers at the top of the hill, his folded skin was tucked tightly under his arm. He raised his head slightly to get a better view of their bench from under the brim of his cap. A broad smile filled his face from side to side when he saw Vi waiting; he headed directly to her.

'I am sorry, I had to go to Hardman's… I had no idea that you would be here.'

'It's alright, I was just here on the off-chance… but I do have to go back now.'

'Oh.' He pondered. 'Look, I will finish early and wait for you and we can walk back together?'

'Oh, John, that would be lovely.' She genuinely felt her spirits lift as she knew he was making the effort to see her. She smiled, and her eyes twinkled.

'Good… right… well, I'll see you later then, you'd best get back.'

Both stood for a moment soaking in the other, before turning in their opposite directions to get back to their respective places of work.

Teddy made it to Livery Street and crossed over towards the railway cutting near to Hockley Station. It had steep banks and if you sat on the sides you could lose yourself in the undergrowth and not be seen by passers-by or anyone on the embankment above. Quite often, the Wolverhampton train would pass going towards Hockley or in the other direction to Snow Hill; it was always a big Great Western Railway steam train, a wide locomotive, dark green in colour. He liked to try and see all the different people inside and wonder where they were going and why.

He slid himself gradually under the fence, being careful not to lose his footing on the steep embankment. There was a rocky outcrop about halfway down which he could anchor himself against, to stop sliding down further if he fell asleep which he often did. The embankment was quite overgrown with couch grass and brambles and he caught his britches a few times, but they were already ripped and quite short. It would not be long until another pair would have to be found from somewhere.

He lay his head back against the bank, relieved he could just sit and think and be on his own, if only for a short while. He decided he would try and get back to meet Fanny as she arrived, and then he would tell her what had happened. She would not be happy, but when he explained what the teacher had said and how it had made him feel, he was sure that she would have more sympathy for him than anger, well at least he hoped that she would. He turned his head to the left and saw a little pink sowbread flower; a small bit of joy in all the weeds. It made him smile and he lay there for ages just studying every detail of the pink petals and the luscious dark-green leaves. A train passed, and then another and another, he had no idea of the actual time, but tried to judge it from the late afternoon sky.

He knew Suie and Mouse would not rush to be back either, as Suie had been given the task of going for food again. She always seemed to do that now. But the last thing that Teddy wanted was for Suie to blab and tell the story all her way first, and get him into even more trouble with Fanny, so he would have to go soon and wait somewhere nearby to catch his eldest sister. Reluctantly, he rolled over on his belly, to make ready to scrabble up the bank back onto the road. Before he did, he picked the flower, and without damaging it put it carefully inside the top of his shirt. Then, grabbing handfuls of couch grass and roots for purchase, he pulled himself steadily to the top, posting himself through the dusty gap at the bottom of the fence and onto the cobbled street. He made his way via as many backstreets and rat runs as he could to the corner of Camden Street looking down towards the entrance of his court, to keep a careful watch for the return of Fanny.

Vi made her apologies to Fanny that she had got to dash because John was going to meet her and walk her back. Fanny was obviously a little disappointed; she could have done with the distraction of someone who was not involved in all her problems at the moment. She told Vi that she understood, and that she would hang back a minute or two to let them walk on alone. She did ask if Vi was going to tell him about her mother. Vi looked at her, and thought for a moment;

'Fanny, I can't. If I do, he might change his mind… he might decide that I am too much trouble. I can't risk that, he is my only chance of happiness.'

Fanny tried to insist that she was being silly, that she was sure if he really loved her he would go through anything, and besides, if she shared it with him maybe they could find a solution together. Vi insisted that she could not and would not, and she would deal with it all on her own. Slightly irked by Fanny's nagging, she grabbed her hat and coat and made her way outside.

John was as good as his word and stood waiting for her. He not being one for any outward displays of emotion, and she being naturally shy meant their greeting was slightly awkward, especially in the face of a chorus of cackling women surging out of the factory in their determination to get home. They began to walk side by side towards the courts, just passing pleasantries and making arrangements to meet for a proper lunch in the next day or so. As they turned into Camden Street they could see two figures a little way along: a large, slightly fat man, who had hold of a little waif by the hair and was dragging him along the street. Vi suddenly realised that waif was Teddy and the man must be Alf. Without thinking, or telling John where she was going, she dashed forward, her first reaction to help Teddy. As she ran she saw Alf – who was shouting and raging – punch Teddy, who screamed and collapsed, at which point Alf, in his boots, began to kick Teddy repeatedly while he curled up in the foetal position.

'No!' she shouted.

Alf stopped and looked at this young woman who was sprinting towards him, being hotly pursued by a tall man.

'What der yer want? Keep out!' he shouted back. Just then, Vi arrived breathless and tried to make a grab for his arm. He hurled her like a sack into the street, which caused her to scream.

'Yer keep out of it, you… yer know nothing. I know yer 'er friend, but 'ee's my boy and I can do what I like, yer see—'

But Alf was cut short as John's fist made contact with his chin.

'Don't you ever touch her again!'

Alf's knee's buckled and he collapsed on his bottom, rubbing his chin. Teddy remained tightly curled and Vi had managed to pull herself up with a little help from John. Alf was not impressed.

'And who the 'ell are you, mate?'

'I am not your mate… and my name is John Connolly. You don't touch a woman in front of me. And you don't touch him.' He waved his finger at Teddy, who was still poleaxed on the floor. 'Do you understand?'

Vi rushed to Teddy, and Alf got to his feet; he was not going to take orders from John.

'No Mick tells me what to do with me own kid... and yer know nothing. The wag man's come looking today. 'Ee's in a lot of trouble so yer keep yer big nose out... s'nun of yers.'

He raised his fist to make a retaliatory strike, but John was too quick for him and caught him under his arm and straight into his ribs, sending him flying, winded, halfway across the road.

Fanny could make out Vi and John and guessed that the oaf now sprawled in the middle of the road with a crowd of onlookers was Alf. She hurtled down the street, unaware her little brother was lying battered and bruised on the pavement in Vi's arms; she checking whether he could stand. As always, he did not whimper or moan, and just answered 'yes' or 'no' to Vi's concerns. Fanny got there.

'Oh, my God! Are you all alright?' She caught sight of the graze on the side of Vi's face where she had made contact with the street when Alf had thrown her off. 'What's happened, and what the 'ells happened to Teddy? Are you alright, Teddy? And where's 'ee clearing off to?' She was watching Alf, who was attempting to make his way through the jeering and catcalling crowd and heading off down the street.

A little while later, John had carried the poor little boy back to the Tulloch's home. He was barely conscious, and struggling to breathe. Vi did what she could to pacify Mouse and Suie, who were distraught by the damage that had been inflicted on their little brother. Fanny knew that she must get the doctor to attend him, but how could she pay? She had little enough to keep all fed, never mind clothed, and a doctor needed a fee. It was John who reached into his pocket, it was John who fetched the doctor. As all stood back, the doctor examined the broken body, now black and purple from the kicking that it had received. He turned with a most serious expression and voice.

'He is very damaged. He has severe internal bleeding, I think it is his spleen. The best you can do is keep him comfortable. His is barely in this world. I know that's no comfort, but it is a blessing.'

As the enormity of the situation began to sink in after the doctor had left, Vi stayed to comfort the three sisters. She knew John had to return to his mother, there was little he could do. She asked that he stop by her home and explain to her parents what had transpired. Fanny just sat in silence, holding and stroking Teddy's hand; she would not leave him now.

Vi's father had been taken aback by the visit of this young man. He had no idea that his daughter had found a sweetheart. A very nice young man, he thought. Obviously, he wanted to go immediately to help her, but Vi's mother was having a lost day, she sat impassively in the kitchen staring at nothing. With all else that had gone on in the last few hours, John barely registered the abnormality of the situation. He had his own preoccupations that now consumed his thoughts on his short walk back to May.

Cara, wasting away, losing the fight to want to live. The morning they found her laying still and cold, no drama, just gone, having slipped away in her sleep. The turn of events that had made the mother and two sons decide enough was enough, and they were now to do what many had already done, flee the godforsaken country and find somewhere, anywhere, else. After a difficult journey on handcarts and walking many miles, sleeping in ditches and abandoned crofts, they had made for Dublin and the chance of a boat across.

Then, the night before they were able to sail that chance discovery that would change John's life irrevocably…

He was caught off guard, and the thoughts flowed away as he turned into the court. At his door, about to knock was a frock-coated individual, carrying a cane.

'Ah! Mr Connolly. I was hoping that I might find you here.' Joseph extended his hand.

John was puzzled, he realised that this must have been the man that Mrs Morris had alerted him to.

'Can I help you, Mr Chamberlain?'

'Please, call me Joseph. I can see this is a bad time for you… I was hoping that you may do a piece of work for me? I have tried to see you at your place of work.'

John was flabbergasted. He had been somewhat suspicious of Chamberlain's motives to befriend Jimmy, and he had not for one second considered that he may wish to engage either of their services. He was a man of a considerable income and could walk into any shop on New Street and purchase fine goods without having to meet with the likes of those that worked in the quarter.

Joseph, sensing John's apprehension, endeavoured to explain. 'I am sorry, I have rather caught you on the back foot, I see. Mr Pearse… James… has been explaining what a fine craftsman you are, and you probably know that I have strong connections with the quarter, indeed I lived in Fredrick Street for some years after my arrival in the city. My beloved wife, Harriet, is expecting our second child shortly, and I was wondering if I could commission you to make a special piece for her to commemorate that?' He paused, to allow John to respond without haste. 'I will pay well, I do respect the craft of the real artisan. Here is my card; when you have some time, we could meet to discuss?'

John was completely stunned by the proposal and quite overwhelmed that a man of that stature should even consider him worthy. Of course, he accepted without hesitation, explaining that they could meet in a day or two, and that he would be only too willing to undertake the commission.

Later, John sat next to May, who was for the most part sleeping. She managed to smile and offer a frail hand when he told her about Chamberlain. He refrained from saying anything about the poor little boy dying only a short walk away; he considered that she had been too close to this pain too many times to hear more. He sat to comfort her, just be a presence so that she was not alone; he drifted off.

Patrick and he had managed to find a few days' work loading container ships, and this had helped build a small fund of money to move the blighted family and head for Liverpool, or Manchester, or Birmingham, anywhere a hard-working Irishman may make a future for himself. It was the end of their final day, and they decided to celebrate with beer or two, to toast their new lives and hope. While in the inn on the port, John had passed some time with a very personable young Irishman, another with dreams and plans for a fresh start. Sean, as he introduced himself, came from not too far away from where the Connollys had lived.

'What a coincidence, man! That we are both here on this same night! Me brother is away with some lass right now, let's take another beer?'

It was John that saw the birthmark as Cara had described – the heart shape – across the other side of the packed inn from where he sat with Patrick and Sean. He just caught a side profile, but he knew, he just knew this had been the man responsible. Without thinking, he rose to his feet and made for the offender. Patrick, somewhat bemused by John's action, tracked his path, and as his own realisation grew an insanity gripped him. Confused memories: a roar of anger, an overturned table. A pursuit into a darkened back alleyway. Three men wrestling, a fourth with red hair flew into the fray.

John was brought around from his troubled nightmare with a start. There was a frantic knocking on the kitchen door. His mother lay quietly, her breathing laboured. He hurried to see what it could possibly be so late in the evening and, without considering who it might be on the other side, he opened the door. Vi stood before him, visibly shaking and tearful.

'I-I-I'm… so sorry… I-I-I had to see you.' She sobbed uncontrollably. 'It was so horrible…'

He reached out and pulled her into him, wrapping his arms around her, enfolding her trembling frame as she heaved sobs into his chest.

A little while later, they sat at his small kitchen table, Vi recounting the last few hours. She had felt helpless as she had watched little Teddy fight for his last few minutes of life, barely breathing, never regaining consciousness, just silently leaving. She explained that they were joined by both Tom and Kitty, as the word had gone around the quarter that their little brother had been badly hurt; neither had known the full details until they had made their dash back. Then Vi had done her best to relay the horror of that afternoon, of what she had witnessed and experienced. Kitty was raging and threatening all sorts. Tom merely turned on his heels and shouted back:

'If I find him first, I will sort him!'

All the time, Fanny had sat in silence, in shock and total disbelief, unable to articulate anything or express any sort of emotion; still holding the dead little boy's hand.

'I have to get back to my mum and dad,' said Vi. 'I just couldn't face anyone until I had seen you. I'm sorry, I know you don't need this now.'

Just then, a frail voice called through from the parlour:

'Johnny… bring the lassie in… please?'

Vi didn't think that she should intrude, but John gently ushered her into the dim parlour; he would do anything for his ma. Vi took the bedside seat tentatively, and May reached out a shaking hand for her to take.

'My boy loves you. You make him happy. He has troubles, but I know you will look after him.' With that she loosened a weakened grip and fell once more into her deep sleep.

Vi wasn't sure what to say or do. She was already in a highly-emotional state, everything that was happening around her just seemed so unreal. Firstly, the attack on Teddy and the subsequent attack on her – her face still stung where it had made contact with the cobbles – then witnessing the tragic death of an innocent, and now these unexplained words from someone she did not know. She was too dazed to even consider any of it. She knew that she must return to her parents; however difficult her home life was at present it was the only place that had some air of normality, and would be a welcome refuge from the chaos that had overtaken her whole being since she had left the factory.

Back in the Tullochs' home, two small girls held each other in bed, weeping for the loss of their close sibling. In the parlour, Kitty was trying to coax Fanny to leave go of Teddy's hand, while encouraging her elder sister to engage in some sort of communication.

'There's nothing can be done, Fan, 'ee's gone. You're goin' to have to let go of his 'and, love.' She gently pulled at Fanny's wrist and dragged the holey blanket up over the boy's face. Fanny said nothing, just continued staring at the now shrouded corpse. Kitty continued:

'That man is a bastard. You see what I do if I get hold of him, or Tom for that matter... I bet the shit's run off again. We'll find him! 'Ee's a dead man when we do!'

Fanny got up in silence; she made no eye contact with her sister and walked to parlour. She then proceeded to get a pot and water, and peel vegetables. Kitty was concerned by these actions.

'Listen, love, I dain't think any of us is hungry right now. Come on, Fan, why dain't you jus' sit for a while… You need to say sumit, you know?'

But Fanny didn't, she was locked in her mind and unable to utter a sound. If she said nothing then somehow it all could be undone, it was not real. If she spoke she would acknowledge it and this nightmare would become truth.

Kitty sat with her sister for two hours trying to coax her to talk, not getting one single response. Eventually, in the same silence, Fanny made off to bed. Kitty thought it best to stay around for everyone's sake. Before she joined her sister in their shared bed, she wedged a chair up against the door into the court, and took the large kitchen knife up the stairs and concealed it under her pillow, just in case Alf was stupid enough, or had drunk himself into amnesia, and returned.

Tom scoured the quarter that night looking for any sightings of the man he wanted to kill. He had no care what would happen to himself if he did, he would hang or not. He was incandescent with rage. Alf appeared to have vanished. The last sighting had been towards Livery Street, but from there his trail had gone cold. Finally, Tom made his way to the local; Stan sat at the bar, once more running down the Irish to Mick the landlord, who didn't care just as long as Stan paid. Stan saw Tom enter the bar and shouted over:

'Oi, Tommy Tulloch… what is it with your family? Your old man took off when 'ee was chased outta 'ere earlier. 'Ee was raging about some Connolly fella interfering in family business. Your Kitty been playin' 'er games again?'

Tom rounded on Stan.

'You haven't heard then, you arrogant shite! 'Ee's done for my little brother, I'll kill the bastard when I see him and anyone who 'elps him!' Tom stood over Stan threatening intent, Stan backed down quickly.

'Now listen, mate, I dain't know about any of it. I'm sorry for your loss, like… course I'll 'elp… we all will.'

But Tom was not sticking around for any more, he was already heading out of the door into the night. He had revenge on his mind and a red mist before his eyes.

The last few in the bar rumbled their disapproval at Stan's lack of diplomacy. One man sat in the shadows, a man with red hair and a deep scar on his face. He had heard the anti-Irish sentiment and decided just to sit and listen, but a name had caught his interest, a man he wanted to find, and maybe others would aid and abet his plans.

Chapter 14

A precious thing

The word had gone around the quarter about the awful tragedy that had befallen young Teddy Tulloch, and that was in part why Alf had run; he feared the mob, who at that point had only been aware that the boy had been badly beaten, not that he had died. The community of poor souls who hardly had brass farthing to rub together stood behind the grief-stricken girls left behind. Everyone knew that they were struggling for money, and that paying for the doctor had been the act of donated kindness by one, but to bury the poor mite was quite beyond their means.

A collection went round every court, and every door in each court, every jeweller, every pen factory. A penny here, a ha'penny there, a shilling a half-crown, whatever could be managed. Some of the owners of the bigger places found a larger donation from their wallets, knowing that philanthropy bred content in their embittered workforce. Kitty and Fanny were told not to return for a week or so, to allow them time to arrange all, and grieve a little. Everyone seemed to be affected by the terrible thing that had happened, but none seemed surprised that it had.

Vi had struggled with all of the emotion that had beset her, which seemed to have transpired from a chain of events that she felt she could have in some way stopped. She recollected having seen Teddy trying to make a circuitous dash across the square but, having caught sight of Vi, had decided to change direction. She had pretended not to notice, she now wished she had. If she had stopped him, pulled him up for playing truant, made him stay with her, or got him back to school, maybe he would be alive now? Alf would not have had a visit from the wag man, and then gone off on his rampage to find the child he so vehemently

167

detested. In her mind, she could have stopped this, little Teddy could still be alive. She knew that to tell Fanny would only cause more anger, and that possibly Fanny would hate her. She feared telling John in case he took against her. She wrestled with her conscience and passed a sleepless night.

Her parents had shown obvious agitation for their daughter; her face was badly grazed and bruised. They were angry that she had tried to intervene, she could have been more seriously hurt; they were not concerned for themselves, just their very precious daughter. And more importantly, who was this nice young man who had appeared at their door? He is Irish? He's a jeweller you say? Oh, that's a good occupation, he must be very reliable. There were too many questions for Vi, she was too caught in her maelstrom of grief to have any concern for her personal happiness; it seemed entirely trivial in the light of the terrible events. She was grieving for Teddy and distraught for her best friend, who had too much bad luck for any one person to handle. Having witnessed the pitiful conditions that John and his mother were forced to endure had made her aware that he had more than his fair share of difficulties to deal with right now too, and to burden him further was out of the question. Her only glint of hope was that her mother seemed more lucid and coherent, more herself.

John was caught in his own struggle. His mother clung onto her life. He knew it was as Mrs Morris had stated to him: she was waiting for something, his permission to go, maybe. He was not ready for that, he felt that he had failed her, he had to do something, anything. The only chance he had was that card that he still kept in his pocket; the prospect of a small commission that might help with doctors' bills and food. He put on his best clothes and headed for the home of Joseph Chamberlain Esq. on Harborne Road.

On arriving at the address, he was amazed at the size and the grandeur of the place. To a poor Irishman who had lived in a croft for most of his life and had only achieved reasonable digs prior to the death of Old Zac, the place that he was now confronted with was a palace. He stood at the gate, unsure whether he should even attempt such a foolish undertaking. This gentleman could afford the best of the best, not the work of a jobbing jeweller in a tiny garret in St Paul's Square. Still, he needed every penny he could get, and as long as Mr Chamberlain understood he would have to pay for the metal upfront and for any gemstones he required – and was willing to pay the going rate for John's time – at least he might make a few bob, just enough.

The maid let him in and bid him wait in the hall, while she enquired as to whether Mr Chamberlain was receiving visitors. John could hear muffled voices from behind the study door and, to his surprise, the door was flung open by Joseph himself and the maid hurriedly dispatched.

'Mr Connolly, how nice of you to come… please, come on in.'

Shortly, they were seated either side of Joseph's vast desk, tea on a silver tray being served by the maid. John gazed around in awe. The walls of Joseph's study were practically filled floor to ceiling with bookshelves. Old landscapes hung on the walls that had any space. There was a large ormolu clock, similar to ones that used to be made in the Soho Manufactory, on top of a large marble mantlepiece. Silver photograph frames, slightly at an angle to the viewer, were placed strategically on his desk. One showed a very beautiful woman sat next to a small cut-crystal vase with a single orchid it. John's eyes remained fixed on the posed lady and her gentle expression. Joseph noted his interest.

'Oh, I see you value my vison of loveliness. This is my good lady wife, Harriet. She is in the last stages of her confinement now and is on strict bedrest… doctor's orders. It is for her I would like you to make something special.'

169

With that, Joseph opened a small black leather box that he had sitting in front of him. John nearly fell off his seat. Inside the box was a collection of brilliant cut white diamonds: three of approximately one carat each, and a further six of half a carat each. He had never seen stones of such a size, and so pure. Joseph spoke.

'They are not that grand, but my lady will appreciate anything that I do for her. By the way, she does not know a thing about this, I always like to surprise her. I would like you to fashion these into a brooch for her, and if possible use an orchid as your inspiration? We are both passionate about the beauty of these small, delicate flowers.'

John sat in complete disbelief as Joseph handed the small box over to him. The diamonds were stunning, it would truly be a dream to work with such fine stones as these, but he had not got the skills to produce a piece of the quality that was being expected of him. He tried to phrase his answer with care, somewhat hesitantly.

'Mr Chamberlain—'

'Please, call me Joseph, John… we are colleagues.'

'Joseph… thank you for the offer of such an opportunity, but I do not think that I have the skill for such an undertaking. I do not possess the precision that you are used to, I am a simple jeweller. I am sure you can find someone with greater experience than me, there are many skilled jewellers in the quarter…' He paused, once again taking in the beauty of the items that he now held in his hand, reluctant to close the box and hand it back. Joseph sat for a moment and collected his thoughts.

'John, I pride myself on my abilities to research and understand all aspects of manufacturing. And yes, I do understand the needs of precision… screw making is, after all, about tolerance and accuracy and we have special machines that make all of this possible, with the associated workmanship of men with an engineering skill. I am sure years from now machines will do all, a point not lost on my colleagues or indeed my workforce, as fewer men will be required to make greater quantities. That is mass-manufacturing, that is how enterprises like the one that I am associated with will make the desired profits. But I know that real workmanship, real skill from real artisans is a joy of art.'

He paused again to allow John to reflect.

'If I wanted a piece of value but no consequence I could walk into any jeweller's shop in Birmingham, or indeed London where I come from, and buy a piece. Or I could commission any other jeweller, you are correct. But, I have chosen you because I have learnt a lot about you.'

John looked puzzled; Joseph qualified his statement.

'I have been to Hardman's, John. I have met with James. And do remember I work and socialise with the owners; you are held by all in the highest possible regard. Your artisanal skills come highly praised. They state that some of the best quality work comes from you and that they know that your misfortunes due to the present economic climate are to their benefit. They wish that they could pay you more than they do.'

John felt the colour rise in his cheeks, he had never been one for accepting praise, as he was never satisfied with anything that he had made.

Joseph was determined to press his request. 'I love my dear, dear wife, Harriet. I believe a person of beauty both inside and out deserves things of beauty, and I know a jewel such as the one I propose you produce would be cherished and loved. For something to be so special it needs to be made with love, care and devotion, then the whole composition becomes a work of art, a joy to behold.' He stopped again, and reached for a sealed envelope and handed it to John.

John read the front, written in Joseph's careful copperplate script: 'Mr John Connolly Esq. Advance for commission.' He broke the seal and sat back in the chair in shock. He could see there were several notes of ten pounds each in value. The stones alone were probably worth sixty pounds – more than a year's salary for a skilled jeweller when the market had been strong – and now in addition he held a large sum of money in his hand that was so much more than he would need to buy the gold to make the brooch. He looked at Joseph, stunned by the generosity.

Joseph continued. 'That is an advance, John. I know I am expecting a great deal from you. I would like this gift produced as soon as possible, our expected child is due in October and I would like to give this gift to Harriet then. It means, of course, that you have only a matter of weeks… I have been assured by all that if anyone can manage this urgent commission, you can, and that you will not fail me.'

'But, Joseph, this is too much money and you have overpaid me, I cannot accept this.'

'Nonsense man… what value is love? What value is care? What value is art? I pay for the things that matter, I pay for quality. It is because people are not willing to pay the hours of a man's time that we are losing so many truly gifted and skilled people like yourself. I know about the many problems that you have experienced after your master died. I also know that you are one of many men in the same position struggling with the dip in the market since our good sovereign has taken on the mantle of 'Widow of Windsor'. I want you to understand that this is an advance; when you have delivered the piece to me to my satisfaction I will remunerate you further.'

'This is far too much money, there is no need for further payment. I shall leave the stones with you until I have brought my designs for your approval—'

'No, John, I trust you and I trust your skill as an artisan. I realise that the Irish community suffers greatly from bad opinion circulated by the rabble and thuggery, done in the most part through hatred. I do not share these sentiments. If it had not been for many Irish men and their hard labour, this city would not be standing. Thanks to their efforts we have a network of canals and rail tracks that enable us to transport materials and goods quickly, that is in part why we now have this accolade as the 'workshop of the world'. Many of our buildings have been built off the broken backs and sweat of your countrymen, and I for one wish to show you my wholehearted support and trust. Please, take the stones and the money and return to me as soon as you are satisfied with what you have done, John. I know you are no thief and blaggard, I trust you implicitly.'

John made his way back across the city; firstly, Broad Street, and then back along the canals into the quarter. He had made sure to conceal the small box and the envelope securely inside his clothing before he left. His whole journey back was filled with endless possibilities and thoughts. He had been completely transformed in his thinking towards Joseph. He was not like the others, he truly believed in the rights of those people that had made the city, he knew that without them Birmingham could not be as powerful as it was. John's spirits were lifted, he could do something without struggle to ease May's suffering, he could help Vi and her parents; for once in his life his luck appeared to be changing for the better. Could there possibly be a chance of a normal life for him?

All was quiet in the quarter. The drama of the previous day had given way to a general depression that hung like a shroud over all of the courts and back streets; a shroud of death. Funeral arrangements were being made in the Tulloch house. Kitty had decided that no expense should be spared, they may have more than they imagined possible from the generosity of those that surrounded them, but it would be for Teddy and all about the days that they needed to grieve; they were not going to profit from the death of their little brother. Kitty had to take charge, Fanny still refused to talk, walking around the house keeping busy with meaningless tasks. Suie and Mouse sat in their room, struggling to come to terms with their own loss. Tom had not returned.

Neighbours came to offer condolences, small gifts of food, the loan of clothing for the funeral, anything that they could do; Kitty dealt with it all. The door was rapped again for one of the numerous times that day; it was Vi.

'Can I come in? Can I see Fanny?'

Kitty was relieved, knowing that if anyone could reach her sister, Vi might be able to. Vi and Kitty encouraged Fanny to sit down in the kitchen. Vi began slowly.

'Fanny, it's a terrible, terrible thing that happened. I cannot begin to imagine the pain that you feel... I feel dreadful too, he was like a little brother to me.'

No response.

'Kitty is doing her best, but the younger ones need you, Fanny, they are so lost and scared... we all need you.'

Again, no response.

'You have got to let this pain out, it will do you no good to keep bottling it up like this.'

Vi noticed that tears were now rolling down Fanny's cheeks, and her expression was changing. She reached over to her and put both arms around her neck, as Fanny buried her head into her friend's shoulder, crying pitifully. Vi tried to console her.

'There, there, Fanny, you let it all out.'

Through her sobs, her anguish and troubles began to emerge. 'Oh, Vi! Why little Teddy? Why?'

'I don't know why, Fanny, it's all so painful. The poor little lad didn't deserve any of it.'

'If only I hadn't kept on at him about school. If only 'ee had stayed there... none of this would have happened...'

'There's nothing you can do about it, Fanny... there's nothing to be done.'

'But if I hadn't of forced him to go… I thought it would be the safest place for him. It's all my fault.'

Vi was suddenly brought up short; she was carrying her own guilt silently for not intervening when she saw him making his dash away out of her sight towards the railway. If she had have stopped him, delayed him, taken him home, made him go to school… She couldn't tell Fanny and Kitty, she felt guiltier than anyone; she realised that she had been the last person that he knew – and that cared for him – to see him alive! She should have intervened, and Fanny was in her arms destroying herself in her self-punishment. She had no reason to be guilty, she had done everything within her power to protect the little man; she could not have done more.

'Fanny, please don't cry. We all know you did the best you could. You had taken a beating for Suie, you were having to rob the food out of the others' mouths to keep him placated… Nobody could have done more than you.'

'Yes, they did, someone did.' Fanny lifted her head and looked at Kitty across the table, who kept her eyes downwards and said nothing.

'You see, Vi… I feel guilty because all this time I have been playing at being mum, but really, I were looking after meself. I just put food on the table, let him kick shit out of me when 'ee was around. I thought I was the strong 'un, but really, it's our Kitty. She is a real angel. Me and Tom, we pretended it all… made it up in our heads that she was just out for all she could get, when really we had let her done. I let 'er down… I should have protected 'er better, just like I should have protected Teddy.'

Vi was somewhat dumbstruck by Fanny's confession. She had no idea what she was referring to, and she noted that the normally more-than-vocal Kitty was shuffling uneasily in her seat.

'Sorry, Fanny, I don't understand? It is you that keeps this family together. It's always been you since your ma died—'

'No, that's not true. If Kitty hadn't done what she did the other night Suie would have been next. In fact, if Kitty… she had to… I was 'elpless and I know now, it's always been Kitty that's taken the heat for us all. I'm no good, these girls need Kitty, I'm no good—'

'Now shut up!' came Kitty's violent interjection.

'I won't have you talking this way. Stop feelin' sorry for yourself. We've all had a bellyful of him, and we've all had to take it one way or another. You got the beatins… Tom got a good kickin' every now and then… and me, well… I'm a survivor, I did what I had to do.'

'Yes, but you could have walked away the other night and left us all to it, but you didn't. You stayed. And what you 'ad to take… and I couldn't do anything.'

Kitty could see that Vi felt distinctly uncomfortable, something dreadful had happened but she was caught in the middle, not knowing exactly what the sisters were arguing about.

'Listen, Vi, it dain't concern you, and I've neva' really told no one. Too ashamed, see… I didn't know, I was too young when it started. I'd wagged school too, that day, like our Teddy. I was sick and I thought I could sneak home then pretend later like I'd been at school all day. Problem was, 'ee came back and found me asleep.'

Vi sat there incredulous. She could not believe that a parent, a father could be so cruel and abusive. Although, Kitty had not articulated exactly what had occurred it was becoming obvious now what she meant, and what Fanny was trying to say. Kitty continued.

'And when 'ee'd finished with me, that first time… I thought it was all my fault, that everyone would see it as my fault… so, I kept mum. Problem was 'ee expected it then… often… and more… 'ee's a disgusting pig!' She drew breath

176

as vile, supressed memories of recurrent abuse filled her mind.

'But, I played the game. And I got angry. I thought they knew, both of 'em.' She stared at Fanny. 'I thought that if they were goin' to let it happen I might as well get sumit for it, so I made him pay me a bit 'ere, and bit there. I'm not proud of it… any of it… but what choice did I have?'

Tears began to well up in Vi's eyes; she did her best to stem them, knowing that was the last thing that Kitty needed right now. Fanny sat with a look of admiration for her younger sister, for her strength and her fortitude, and now her surprising honesty. Kitty recounted another terrible memory of being caught by her father in the street one night, and dragged to the railway embankment and forced to preform yet another despicable act. Vi was shocked, Kitty finished:

'I'm not proud… and I would not like the whole world to know, there's already enuf bad stuff being said about me out there. It wouldn't surprise me if it's come out his mouth, the dirty bastard, in his drunken bragging in pubs. But I will tell you now if my bruver don't fuckin' get him, I will! This is the worst! 'Ee don't deserve to breathe any more! 'Ee's killed our mother, now our little Teddy! If there's any fuckin' justice in this world 'ee'll get his, you mark my words!'

A painful quiet fell in the kitchen. Three women sat in their own silent agonies: one who blamed herself for the tragedy that had befallen a young innocent; another for her failings to protect all of her family; and the third because she did know what normal was or even how to be normal any more, and probably never would. It seemed an eternity before Fanny broke the silence, her steel and fortitude returning.

'Whatever happens from now will happen. Tomorra is our Teddy's day. We are goin' to send him off in style… I'm not having my little man forgotten, 'ee had a shit life from start to finish, this is the least we can do for him… ain't that right, Kitty. We make sure 'ee 'as a damn good send off?'

'Absobloodylutely!'

The night-time crawlers made their way through the shadows of the courts and alleys. Stray dogs searching for scraps, female cats screaming in coitus, rats streaming through the middens. On the edge of a court a figure stood concealed in the gloom, he was surveying a door: 'his' door. The figure reached into his heavy jacket pocket, weighed down by metal, a smell of grease and gunpowder wafted gently upwards. He removed a packet from that pocket and a matchbox from the other. As he lit his chosen match and sucked on his fag, the red glow illuminated the deep scar on his face; a scar only a sharp blade could have made. He took three or four draws in quick succession, the smoked coiled upwards and clouded momentarily. He jumped as a cat shot around the corner of the court, being pursued by a mangy dog. He relaxed again and observed the door for any sign of movement. How was he going to do this? This was too public, too many people could see, could witness. With the death of that boy he had noted the sudden pulling together of the community that lived in these parts. He was an outsider, an obvious interloper; he knew they were chasing the drunk who had caused so much harm, and that the abuser was one of their own. He would have to be discreet, choose his moment. The right time and the right place not to be seen. A distraction maybe? A decoy? A fixed meeting? He would need to look around, observe more, see without being seen, watch 'his' movements, 'his' comings and goings. He would get his opportunity. He had hunted for years; a few more weeks would not be any great difficulty. This time he was going to get it right and make sure they he was away and gone before anybody knew.

'I'll get you, Connolly,' he muttered. 'You see if I don't. I owe it to Michael, an eye for an eye. And no blades this time... I'm going to make sure of it.' He clutched the outside of his pocket for confirmation. Yes, it was there, it was safe. Just watch and wait and not be seen.

Chapter 15

Farewell little man

The sun shone with bright clarity the next morning, and although summer was at an end it felt like an August day, the sharp shadows crisply defined, the cool night giving way to an unseasonal warmth. Fanny took heart that this was a good day for her little brother. The undertakers came quite early, they went through to the parlour with all the dignity that might befit someone of much greater wealth and stature, not a poor little waif from the back-to-backs; money will buy dignity in death that could not be afforded in life, it was only going to be the best for Teddy now.

His light little body was placed in an oak coffin with brass handles: a contribution-in-kind from Gillott's. The four pall-bearers lifted the coffin and conveyed it out into the street, where an open funeral cart draped in black stood, with a single black horse bedecked in black feather plumes, his coat groomed and gleaming, his brass freshly polished, black leather blinkers covering his eyes. A chief mourner in a top hat and tails stood slightly to the side waiting to lead the funeral procession. The horse hooved the cobbles in anticipation, snorting slightly in his reins.

The word had gone around the quarter, and at eleven o'clock all fell silent. The normal cacophony of presses and machines, the thump-thump of stampers, the general melee of cat calls and shouts, stopped. Everyone in the court who was not of working age stood in silent contemplation, waiting for the family of bereft sisters. Soon, the four sad souls emerged from the doorway, in borrowed coats and dresses; everyone who could help had pitched in with an offer of this or that.

Fanny looked gaunt, and the large, black, brimmed hit that adorned her head only served to highlight her pale, drawn face.

Kitty held the hand of Mouse, who clutched a small bouquet of wildflowers selected with care from Teddy's favourite bolthole – the railway embankment.

Suie trailed out last, head down and shoulders hunched; if she looked upwards anyone would be able to see that her eyes were red and swollen from the constant tears that had fallen since the tragedy had occurred. The family walked in silence towards the rear of the cart, and one of the neighbours shouted out, 'Gawd bless you, girls and Gawd bless little Teddy.' With that, another female onlooker let out a whimper of grief.

The funeral director raised his silver-topped cane, and started to walk; the cart jolted slightly as the black-suited driver encourage his horse to move forward. This horse had participated in many a solemn occasion, and without false-step or hesitancy he moved gracefully forward in slow, stately gait, step-by-step behind the master. As the girls walked, others began to file in behind; the older members of the community, some young mothers, the few men whose occupations allowed them the freedom to down tools. The cortège moved in silent progress through the narrow roads of the courts, the only sounds the steady march of boots and hooves on the cobbles. Out of Tenby Street, left onto Albion Street, every person who could be was out on the streets, their heads bowed, caps removed as a mark of respect. The procession turned right onto Fredrick Street, normally a hive of activity, with a mass of noise emanating from the pen factories – all was still. The workers had spilled onto the streets and stood in silent observation, watching the little coffin pass by. Some in the crowds genuflected, showing their religious persuasion; others clasped their hands together in silent prayer.

On and on, the sombre walk maintained the same tempo, with more and more joining the tail end as it passed them by. The circular tour they were now making of the quarter led them into St Paul's Square to circumnavigate before heading back out to Warstone Cemetery.

Behind a marked pane of glass, a jeweller looked on in silent vigil, his urgency to commence his commission tempered by his need to show respect in his way, without drawing attention to himself. Among the first few behind the was a handsome young girl with a shock of red hair just visible under a large hat; his heart skipped slightly as he felt her close by. He watched as the long procession of many snaked its way around the square before heading out into Caroline Street. One last look of those at the front of the march, and then his head looked down at his sketch and the open box that burned with fire and brightness; it seemed such a cruel world in which, as one young infant was about to draw breath, one not much older was laying cold in a box; but death he knew only too well.

She had followed her friends. She had watched their stoicism, even the youngest who bit back the tears and walked with the same dignity as her elder siblings. The visible presence of neighbour by neighbour, worker by worker, warmed her heart: this was a community, this was a village. Whatever anybody else had to say about the poor Brummies, they would stand shoulder to shoulder at a time like this, bosses or no bosses, whether the loss of a day's pay was threatened or not; and those employers knew better than to threaten at a time like this. Tools would stay down, presses would remain silent until the procession had moved on. Those self-employed – the artisans and craftsmen – came out in number, she tried to see if he was there, but there were so many, just so many! What a remarkable moment in which the show of mutual grief of the loss of one of their own impelled all to come together.

Eventually, a private party of closer friends and neighbours collected by a freshly dug grave. As Vi stood close by her friend, but not so close as to impose herself on a personal moment, a familiar figure gently pushed his way through those gathered – it was Tom. He said nothing, he nodded in acknowledgement to his sisters as they responded in kind, while the clergyman proceeded with his service. Handfuls of earth dropped down on the lid, hands where extended, greetings and condolences given, and soon just six figures remained close by the graveside, as the digger waited a respectful distance away. The only marker was to be a rough wooden cross; an anonymous mark, for an anonymous soul.

It was Kitty who broke the silent reminiscence.

'Well, at least it stayed nice… I'm glad it stayed…' she paused and stared at Tom before continuing, her voice lightly laced with sarcasm, '…and I'm glad you got here too. Where ya been?'

Tom came back aggressively.

'What do you mean? Of course, I would be 'ere! I was off looking for that bastard!'

'Now, Tom, not over his grave!' Fanny was not happy.

'I'm sorry, but I don't like 'er tone… I was doing what needs to be done.'

'And did you?' Kitty came back hard.

'No. 'Ee's given us the slip… last seen jumping a train at Snow Hill… 'ee could be bloody anywhere by now!'

'Tom! I teld you, not over his grave! You two got problems with each other, sort it at home! Not here! Enuf's gone on! I won't have it 'ere!'

Tom and Kitty acknowledged their sister's admonishments. Fanny turned to Vi.

'Will you come back for a while, jus' a chat like? I'm sure Suie and Mouse could do with yer face around?' Suie looked up at Vi appealingly, the tension of the day and what they had just been through needed some relief.

'Well, if you're sure? I just thought that you would all want to be on your own.'

'No, I could do with a sit down and a chat… please?'

A little later, Fanny and Vi were sitting with a cup of tea in the kitchen, while Tom and Kitty remained in the court talking to the few neighbours and friends who still felt obliged to offer their respects. Suie and Mouse had been persuaded to take themselves off for a walk.

'They needed a bit of normal… whatever normal is. I dain't know any more,' Fanny said.

'It's really hard right now, Fan, but at least Tom is here just in case—'

'Just in case what? Oh! Do yer mean in case that so-and-so comes back? Do yer really think 'ee dares? 'Ee's a dead man, Vi. You saw everybody today. If Tom dain't get him someone will. Actually, I hope it's not our Tom. I'm goin' to try and calm his hot blood down… we dain't need any more trouble at our door. But, I dain't think the shit would dare, unless 'ee's blind drunk and outta his face again.'

The two sat, acknowledging the wisdom of Fanny's words.

'Sayin' that, I'm not sure how long our Tom will be 'ere for now. I mean now there is one less, and less mouths to feed. I know 'ee ain't happy with his life… I know 'ee did have a girl 'ee was sweet on, but…'

Vi nodded, reflecting on her own situation. Yes, she thought, lives do have to move on. Tom cannot be expected just to stay to look after his sisters, and with both Fanny's and Kitty's wages coming in would he have to? It was not the same for her, of course, even if there were some way that John could support her. She felt obliged to continue supporting her parents; she had no other siblings to help, and her father was not a young man. His working life would end one day and then what would her parents do? Yes, her mother had returned to the world again, but was this a temporary reprieve? Would she go home tonight and find her mother, once again, rearranging objects that she had no recognition of, in a state of absolute confusion? Her father could not possibly cope with working a full day and looking after his wife. Vi knew her situation was not as easy to solve as she tried to make John believe; love may not be able to find a way, or find a solution.

Fanny continued.

'Actually, I hope 'ee buggers off soon... I dain't need those two bickering at each other's bloody throats day after day. I have realised that I have been really hard on Kitty, but I dain't think Tom will understand. I mean, 'ee'll be furious like, but 'ee dain't realise it's changed her and she'll neva be any different now, though they seem to be getting on alright out there.' She gazed through the open door into the courtyard, where a shaft of bright afternoon sunlight was pouring in. Tom and Kitty were now standing together a little way over, just out of earshot of all, they were deep in conversation.

'What yer goin' to do if you find him?'

'What da yer bloody think? Buy him a pint? Have a cosy father and son chat? I am going to put his bloody lights out! That's what!'

'I know that, you idiot! But, yer can't just jump him in the street. They'll stretch yer neck for that. I mean how are you goin' to do it...? Have you got a plan?'

'I've got to find him first. It depends where 'ee's bloody gone. I've got mates lookin' out. It also depends if 'ee comes back 'ere or not.' He paused momentarily, opening his workman's jacket slightly, exposing the waistband of his trousers discreetly.

'I got this off a mate in Loveday Street. It's loaded and ready.'

185

Kitty saw the metal handle of a small revolver poking out the top of his trousers, he drew his jacket closed quickly. Kitty smiled.

'Good! At least you can do it from a distance. But I wouldn't go letting any gun off in the street. Yer gotta have a plan, Tom, a proper plan.'

John made a final delivery to Hardman's. He explained that he could not take any more work on for a few weeks. He didn't say why, or more importantly, that he had been given a rather too generous commission in his eyes; he decided the fewer people knew about it the better and safe for him. Carrying a vast sum of diamonds around with him day and night left him wide open to being mugged, or worse. He had no place that he wished to attempt to leave such valuable items. Yes, he had a safe that he usually kept everything in – the silver ingots and small amounts of gold and semi-precious stones that used to pass through the premises in Old Zac's day – but John felt a duty to Joseph for the faith that he had placed in him. He decided the safest place was to have the diamonds with him day and night, and the same applied to the vast sum of money that he had been given as an advance. All was kept in a money belt beneath his shirt. When he had actually looked at the contents of the envelope alone in his kitchen, he had been shocked. On removing the notes, he discovered he had four ten-pound notes and two fivers! It represented a year's income, on a good year, for both master and apprentice! What was Joseph thinking of? And to have offered more besides – why?

The possibilities now for his future were endless; he could marry Vi, he could even see a way to support her parents. He could get better digs for his ma and better doctors. He wished he could do it all today, but this commission would take a few weeks and Joseph had impressed on him the urgency: he could not delay. He could not break even to go and tell Vi of the good fortune that they

186

had. In any case, having witnessed the solemnity of that morning, he did not believe it was the right time to discuss anything. His sensitivity to the horrible misfortunes of Vi's friends made him restrain his enthusiasm and happiness, and to draw attention to himself at this stage would not serve anyone. Plans could only come to reality if he actually made this piece quickly and to the highest quality.

He had spent the day preparing sketches for ideas, which would normally be shown to the customer – most of the time by a factor, who took his cut – for approval. But no, Joseph had insisted that he trusted John's judgement and artistic ability, that he knew that John would produce a piece worthy of investment. Although he had been quite pleased with the results of his thoughts, enormous self-doubt filled him with trepidation; he had decided a discreet second opinion may be in order. Hence, the well-timed delivery to Hardman's would give him a chance to see Jimmy Pearse.

As he entered the mason's yard, the familiar Irish twang of his friend's voice echoed across from his perch.

'Johnny boy! Welcome! Where have you been?' Jimmy raced down his ladder like a young pup, enthusiastically shaking the big man by the hand, a shower of white dust cascading from his arm as he did so.

'How's yer ma? Terrible business I heard down in the quarter... there's talk of a headstone coming from here.'

They sat at his drafting table, while John recounted the dramatic scene from St Paul's Square. Jimmy was amazed.

'What, everyone? The whole quarter? That's incredible! I don't get it, you know, Johnny, how this man can get away like this and none of the authorities do anything? It's as if because they are only working-class poor people no one gives a damn. He's just another dead wee boy! One less to go on poor relief!'

John thought, how typical of Jimmy to see the political rather than the personal, to make the claim for the injustice of the situation rather than the anger and grief of those directly involved. He tried to moderate his friend's thinking.

'This is a big city, Jimmy, it's very easy to lose someone here—'

He stopped himself short from saying what he was actually thinking. He had lost himself here. When his mother and he had made the boat after the dramatic events of their last night in Dublin, they both knew that for safety they had to run, not to somewhere rural or close to a port, but to somewhere big and busy. Liverpool had been too far, as was London. Birmingham had been the obvious choice; to lose themselves in a huge mass of people, to become anonymous – free from their past – was their only hope for a life, for their very survival.

He had tried to distance himself from Jimmy, knowing that he had seen a face in a crowd while with him. The debating society was no longer a place he wished to frequent, despite the good auspices and obvious protection of Joseph. Things had calmed, though.

Jimmy interjected. 'Oh! You don't know what happened to me that night do you? I mean, you haven't really been around much. I have heard that you have a sweetheart, pretty thing I believe. Is it serious?'

John was puzzled by his friend's opening statement about that night, but other questions were being fired at him thick and fast. What did he know, and how did he know?

'Everyone talks around here, you know that Johnny boy! Especially the women – you're a good catch, man! Some hearts were breaking all over when it was realised that you were finally spoken for. Well, are you?'

John blushed when he realised what his friend was hinting at – that he had numerous females that had gazed on him and Vi with envious eyes.

'Her name is Vi… and yes, she is very beautiful both outside and within. She works at the Gillott's. And one day, maybe… if she says yes, of course.'

Jimmy interrupted him, and slapped him on the back, obviously overjoyed by his friend's good fortune.

'Oh! That's a mighty fine thing! I am so happy for you. Susan will be so happy for you! Just name the day and I'll stand up for you, man.'

'Slow down, Jimmy. Things are not quite that simple. I have to earn enough money first, see, there's not just Vi, there's her folks too. She's the only one, and they rather depend on her. I didn't think it was ever going to be possible. That was until the other day, of course.'

He felt in his inside jacket pocket for the sheaf of sketches he was carrying, and he withdrew them slowly. 'I suppose I owe my thanks to you?'

'Ah! You were mentioned in dispatches, John, not just me, you know, others sang your praises here. Joseph came and sought me out after the fracas to make sure that his reference had done its work.'

John looked quizzically at Jimmy.

'Anyway, we passed a very personable afternoon discussing this and that, he then got me invited into the top office, the holy of holies, man. Well, he set about asking for recommendations of a good jeweller, and I am not joking, to a man – and there must have been ten or so assembled – your name was at the top of their list!'

'Maybe for simple stuff, Jimmy. But you have no idea what he expects, and he has been ridiculously extravagant.'

'Oh! John, man! Will you give yourself a break! You're the best damn jeweller around these parts! Everyone knows that! Its only you who doubts himself. There was not a second thought but to suggest you. No doubt you're now checking you have the right idea for him. Let me have a look, then?'

For the second time in their short dialogue, John felt himself flush with the compliments that were being lavished on him; he still did not believe them though. He needed some confirmation that his ideas would be fitting for such an illustrious benefactor, and Jimmy was a real artist; he valued Jimmy's opinions above all others.

Jimmy leafed through few sketches, comparing the size and the ideas carefully.

'Oh, these are mighty fine. It would be difficult to choose one over the other. Your composition is just right...' He looked and looked again. 'I think this one is slightly subtler and reflects the delicacy of the flower. Yes, if I were to choose it would be this one.'

John was satisfied. The chosen sketch was the idea that had resonated with him the most. He had a lot to do now and little time to do it in. He bade his friend farewell and got up to leave, when the question that had remained a puzzle sprung to his mind.

'What do you mean a fracas?'

'Oh, man! It turned out to be something and nothing. I did need you though, but you had gone. Some man thumped me when I was leaving the meeting. I ended up a night in gaol and up before the magistrate the next morning. It was a right to-do. This bloke claimed I had started a scrap and that we had been Irish troublemakers out about a bad business. Of course, the judge asked who the "we" were, so I had to give your name and address, sorry man, it was the beak, I had to say. Anyway, it turned out that Joseph had already spoken up for me. That confused the magistrate even further, as it was in complete conflict with the other man's story that we had started it all. So, it was dismissed... I was free to go.'

John turned to leave.

'It was funny, though... I mean, that man accusing me and you of being Irish troublemakers. For a start, I was

190

born here… but what was weird, and the judge thought it was bizarre too, was that the bloke was Irish himself a… what was his name now? Ramornie…? No, that wasn't it… Rattray…? No… Rafferty! That was it, Sean Rafferty!'

John's step stalled! He didn't dare turn around and show Jimmy that all the colour had drained from his face in an instant, and a thousand thoughts had flashed through his mind. A cold sweat ran down his spine, he managed a feint laugh at his friend's observation and carried on walking with more purpose and urgency to exit.

He stumbled almost blindly down Newhall Hill. Not only had his nemesis seen him, he now had his address! But, why had he not come, it had been days? Why had he not seen him? Why was he so determined to hunt John down? It had not even been him. Yes, there was blood on his hands, but not in that way, he had tried to stop it all! What could he do now? He could not run, his ma was too ill, there was Vi to consider and now he had a chance of making some headway in life because of Joseph's commission. He had been making positive plans not more than two hours before; marriage, his ma, a business that could support everyone. Now his thoughts were once again consumed about how he might flee into the shadows. He tempered his panic, no one had yet come for him; maybe he had decided it wasn't worth it? Maybe, just maybe, Sean had found out that John had so much respect now afforded to him by others, and realised that John was in some way under their protection. Sean was not to know that, like himself, John was still perceived by most as Irish trash. But Joseph Chamberlain – a well-respected entrepreneur – had stood up for Jimmy, and by that effect, for John; maybe that had been enough to deter Sean from further reprisal? All John could do was hope to luck as he found his way home, watching every corner, cap-peak down, eyes hidden. He braced his arms to his side, as the money belt cut into his ribs.

191

Back in the kitchen of the Tullochs, Tom's jacket now hung over the back of the chair, the revolver having been removed from the waistband of his trousers and somewhat casually placed in its pocket, visible to anyone who might glance inside, curious to see what the bulge and the glint of metal might be. The night passed in peace in the house, all was quiet. By the next morning the gun was gone.

Chapter 16

The waiting

Nothing could be normal now. Everything had been changed irrevocably, especially in Fanny's household. Now she made porridge for one less. She would find herself laying out his place at the table, and only realise her mistake when Suie would look apprehensive as food was being served. Fanny missed the little boy who refused to go to school, who always found an excuse to hide. She thought of all the times that she had to reprimand him, grab him by the lughole when he was being reticent about doing as she told him. Making him wash, making him follow the girls off to the nasty schoolmaster who just saw him as a lazy good-for-nothing. And, when he would pitifully run and hide for his life when the cruel beast invaded their home. There was one less voice, one less mouth to feed.

Tom had taken off too. She wasn't surprised, it was as she had predicted to Vi – she had not believed for an instant that he would stick around. She wondered if he would manage to keep his job at Vaughton's; she doubted it. He had seemed fine the night of the funeral, they had all passed the evening amicably. Then the next day she had caught sight of him and Kitty arguing again outside, and just thought things were back to normal between them: the highly aggressive stand-off between brother and sister. She had caught the tail end of their arguments, Tom shouting something like 'you've got it!' incoherently at Kitty, and Kitty always in denial. She had obviously nicked some of his money, Fanny thought; just like Kitty, she will never change. Of course, if that were the case Tom would go, he had always had a big beef about his sister being light-fingered and lazy. Unfortunately, he had always been only too willing to believe the worst, thought Fanny; mind you, she remembered she had too. Things were different now though.

She knew she had to try to help her sister in some way and Tom going was probably for the best.

The only things that remained unchanged were her job and the familiarity of her friendship with Vi. So, as always, they met up before work, and spent the day together before returning to their respective homes.

Vi knew that Fanny needed her and she refrained from trying to see John; she was sure he would understand and, as he would be so busy trying to fulfil the orders for Hardman's to make sure that his mother had all she needed, he really had not got much time. Vi, too, had her own troubles; she had found that once again her mother was drifting off into her other world, and between juggling her bouts of mental disappearances and Fanny's need for support, there simply were not enough hours in the day.

Kitty was torn. Her need to lead her life as she liked – away from the home in which she had known so much abuse, free to do what she wanted and with whom she chose – was now precariously balanced with her desire to protect her younger sisters, in particular Suie. Although Fanny was confident that Alf would never again make an appearance, Kitty was not so sure.

'Yer know a dog always returns to its doings!' she had remarked with some force, at the dismissal of the possibility by Fanny, who believed he would not dare. Too many wanted to see him dead, she argued. But Kitty had insisted that people have short memories, that the fire for revenge would die out eventually, and that he would just come and go as freely as ever. With the inner conflict of her personal freedom as opposed to the protection of her siblings to the fore, Kitty knew she had to stick around. She would do anything to protect them, no matter what the personal cost to herself. Not like Tom, full of testosterone-driven revenge all at that instant but, in her opinion – like any man

– gone when a new interest took his fancy. No, her drive was absolute. She would see Alf in his grave before he ever laid a finger on Suie, and she would go to the rope to prove it if she had to.

John was overwhelmed by all of his problems. He had a dying mother, whose determination to cling on to her life for the sake of her son enforced his belief that she could somehow rally if the best care was acquired. He had paid for a second doctor to attend her, hoping that he would prescribe some more effective medication – now that it was obvious that it could be paid for. His hopes were dashed once more when the new doctor confirmed the opinions of the previous, that May was beyond treatment, qualifying his statement with the assertion that 'I have no idea how your good mother is alive... she should have left us months ago.'

Even the gentle reaffirmations of Mrs Morris had failed to break his resolve to find a cure. He could not bear to think that she was dying, telling himself it was just the poverty that was making her ill, the conditions in which they lived. Once he had completed the commission for Joseph, he would move them back to better rooms, maybe back in the square, then all would be well.

A nagging sensation at the back of his mind kept pecking away, the feeling that he was being stalked, that someone was close by who meant him harm. Everywhere he walked his senses were heightened to every noise and movement, each face that he could see, every set of footsteps that was within earshot. He tried to dismiss it as paranoia; after all, if Sean was going to do something surely it would have happened by now? He must have been deterred by Joseph Chamberlain's name being mentioned; he must consider that John had friends of power and influence. Still, his feelings of being followed and scrutinised persisted. He endeavoured to limit all of his walks outside, moving just to and from his bench and home. He didn't think that being seen out in the open was his best policy. Not that he had seen Vi or had much time to seek her out. The pressure was on him to produce the commission – a piece of work that he knew must be of exceptional finish and quality. He could not afford to make mistakes, he had no time to be able to rectify or – God forbid – start again if he were dissatisfied.

His initial procrastination preyed on his mind, three or four days of wasted time. He had doubted his ideas, and asked for Jimmy's opinion, when all the time he had known which design he had felt most strongly connected to. Now he was up against the wall, every moment was consumed, every hour he could work, he did.

Thankfully for May, the nights were drawing in so his absences were limited by the hours of daylight available; with all of the concentration involved, to work too long after sunset put unbearable strain on his eyes, and gave him a terrible headache.

In her waking moments, that now were few, she would try to reassure him that all would be well, that she had every faith in him. No matter what she said he seemed to dither as if caught in a dilemma; a loss of confidence, perhaps, or something else? Maybe things were not going well with Vi? May knew better than to try and question him. At times like this John's temper would come to the fore. She had experienced his anger when he felt under extreme pressure, which would then give way to extreme melancholia. When things had been better, after he had been working as an apprentice for Old Zac, she had joked to him that it was his artistic temperament. No matter, she could sense his disquiet and she knew he was feeling extreme pressure, best just to say very little until things had calmed.

Anxieties plagued him constantly and sleep was a fleeting occurrence. When he slept he was so exhausted that there was no chance for dreams, just a dead sleep. He would

196

wake early and be out before sunrise, slipping through the dark, deserted streets with stealth. Then he would work feverishly, and return an hour or so after darkness. Mrs Morris took care of May; John had rewarded her handsomely, though in her good nature she tried to refuse, but he insisted. Warmer blankets had been acquired, there was a copious supply of coal to keep the fires and range lit. The house felt warm and began to lose some of the clinging dampness.

Mrs Morris made sure there was always a hot meal of good nourishment waiting for him on his return, though May would take very little of anything. Mrs Morris could see that John was overwhelmed, and that to worry him further, to create more anxiety in the young man at a time when he was struggling to cope was not in his (or May's) best interest. But Mrs Morris could see that it would be a matter of days now, maybe a week or two, then her job of caring would be at an end.

Way to the west of the city, in The Lye, an altercation had broken out in yet another public house – The Bird in Hand.

'Now for the last time, are you'm going to pay for what yow had, or am I goin' to have to get rough with yow?'

Alf was in a dishevelled heap by the wall of a snug bar, where he had been thrown by a collection of burly locals called in by their hospitable local landlord to help with the forced ejection of an unwanted customer. He was already bruised from the last place in which he had tried the same trick: going in, paying for one or two and then taking advantage. He fumbled in his very stained trouser pocket, mumbling as three or four men stood over him ready to do the business if he failed to pay again. The landlord stood expectantly, his open hand before Alf's face.

'Alright, alright, don't get one on ya. Course I was goin' to pay yer. Jus' forgot, that's all.'

He reluctantly parted with the last of his coins, as the men began to back off and the landlord returned to his counter. Of course, Alf had to have the last word.

'Dunno what yer all so cut up about? So much for a warm welcome in yam yam country. You're all a load of miserable fuckers it seems to me.'

That was enough for the assembled Black Country men, ready to stamp *their* mark on *their* territory – they were not going to have anyone run them down. One man's fist connected with Alf's jaw, making his head recoil, and the other two grabbed either side of him and threw him unceremoniously out of the door and into the gutter.

'Get back to where yow come from, yow ignorant Brummie bastard. And don't eva show you'm face around The Lye again! Next time you'm in a box when yow leave!'

He was half in and half out of the world. The jaw-breaker of a punch had done its worst, and in his already drunkenly-befuddled state he lay in the stinking gutter for an hour, unable to rouse himself. In the meantime, a couple of local children had ridiculed him and kicked him where he lay, emulating the older men.

'Yes, yow smelly old tramp… Yow don't belong here… We dain't like people like yow!'

Alf had made a half-hearted getcha at them, unable to even defend the kicks. Then a passing dog came too close and sniffed at the thousands of unsavoury smells that filled the its olfactory senses. Satisfied he had identified them all, the dog cocked his leg and pissed on his face. Alf was brought to his senses by suddenly being aware of the warm wetness.

'Arrgh! Git away! Yer 'orrible mutt! Fuck off!' He flayed his hand wildly in the dog's general direction, but it had already made a speedy retreat.

As the anaesthetic effect of the gin began to wear off, the pain began to descend on him. He got himself unsteadily to his feet and looked around. The door to the bar was firmly shut and he knew better than to try his chances there. It was time to move on, do a bit of thievin', a bit of double-dealin', some gamblin' maybe? Whatever, he couldn't stay here and he couldn't go home, he would have to wait for the quarter to calm down. As he walked aimlessly he mumbled to himself.

'He was an 'orrible little tyke! Should have been drowned at birth. And that bitch of an elder sister too! I did the world a favour and when I see 'er again she'll get it!'

Tom was still in the quarter, his fruitless search had come to nothing. A number of leads had been given, Alf had been seen out Winson Green way, then someone said he was kipping rough in Small Heath park. Another sighted him in Sparkbrook, another Lozells. All had come to naught. When Tom heard that he may have jumped a train to Manchester, he gave up. His dad was long gone. He was sure he would never return, and even if he did, that piece he had picked up in the gun quarter had mysteriously vanished the one and only night he had stayed back at home. He was convinced that Kitty had taken it to flog it for cash; she was always lifting things that didn't belong to her, and always lied even when she had been caught red-handed. He couldn't possibly get hold of another, not that easily. The blood that had run high when Teddy had died had cooled; the quarter was quiet and at peace. People have short memories.

Tom knew he was in danger of losing a good job that had only been kept open because of the tragedy. To continue to search for the bastard was not going to help anyone, especially not himself. He had to try and get his life back together, especially if he wanted to try and court Jenny again. He had to show her he could be reliable and stable. At least with both his sisters working and only two others to keep they should manage; it was not now so essential that he stayed with them, but it was important that he got himself in a better position. Fanny had been right of course, the endless sweeping up and meaningless tasks at Vaughton's would change as they gave him more and more training. He would be a chaser one day – that was a good income!

So, it was the local and a pint, and a chance to chat with his mates. He would find somewhere to crash for a few days or weeks and take it from there. As he sat passing the time, one or two well-wishers came and gave their respects, those that had not done so on the day.

A few seats down sat Stan in his normal spot, his nose glowing. He had made a new friend, much to the surprise of Mick the Irish landlord, for Stan's new acquaintance was none other than Sean Rafferty. Stan was feeling very courteous and at ease with his new companion, simply because this 'rather affable Irish chap' had bought him quite a few nips.

'You know what, mate?' Stan slurred his speech a little. 'You ain't that bad for a Paddy, like… I mean most are a load of lazy good-for-nothing bastards.'

Mick recoiled slightly behind the bar, and threw a glance at Sean, who proceeded to ignore the thinly veiled insult and continue smiling.

'I mean, there's some right thieves and robbers among you lot. I mean, I know that famine thing was not good for you lot, but hey, you've no right taking everything we've all worked hard for.' Stan became reflective, and paused.

Sean sat by, seemingly personable, even nodding in agreement from time to time; inside he was just seething. This was just another Englishman who spouted crap! Someone else that had no idea what they had endured, and their own Queen wouldn't even help and send food when they were all starving to death and killing one another. He blanked his thoughts. He could not let any of his venom show, no matter how much he despised this man; this drunk bigot could be a useful drunk bigot.

Stan continued his racist monologue.

'I mean, like… you were there, weren't you? That night? You know? That night at that meeting when those two blokes from round 'ere kicked off. That one from Hardman's, 'ee's just got a big gob, you know what I mean?'

Sean nodded, very keen to know what Stan was about to say.

'But the other, 'ee's a bloody Irishman. Not like you, of course. 'Ee thinks himself betta than us cause 'ee's a jumped-up little jeweller trained by that old Jew. Talk about airs and graces! 'Ee's no better than the rest of us. 'Ee never speaks to no one, jus' walks around with his hat pulled down. 'Ee thinks 'ee's too good for the likes of us.'

Sean was instantly struck by this tone of conversation. He'd had doubts the day of the fake trial that he had engineered. For a while, he had feared that he couldn't pull this off. Maybe Connolly had too many mates and they would look after him, but from what this bigot was saying, he was neither liked nor respected. This would change the whole situation! He could choose his moment now without fear of much reaction or reprisal. But let the drunk speak; maybe he could give more help to this, maybe Sean could help him in some way?

Stan gushed on.

'Yer know, this is a fantastic town. I mean, look at this place when the Tulloch boy died. Everyone, I'm not joking mate, everyone stopped to show their respects. Not that I would give that family the fucking time of day, but that's another story. But the whole bloody lot came out to show respects, that's sumit special don't yer think? I do, you know.' Stan took another swig from his glass of whisky, which now was empty.

Sean nodded to Mick to pour again.

'Good lad, that's very 'ospitable of you, fella. What did yer say yer name was again? Ah! Sean, that's right. I am very 'ospitable too, Sean, don't yer know… I am. That little lad's sister, right piece of work she is. I give her everything, fed her, boozed her up… she really took advantage, yer get what I am saying? You might know 'em all. She's got a hard cow of an older sister, her that hangs around with that strange red-haired bint that the Irish jeweller's sweet on…'

More information for Sean to hold till he could figure out his plan.

'Anyhow, there's a couple of sprogs in the family, and this one little slapper…' Stan began to whisper, knowing Tom might overhear and he didn't want trouble from a young hothead, '…her name's Kitty. She's been givin' out since she were a nipper… da yer know what I mean, like? Stan gave a furtive wink. 'A bit of how's your father, like.'

His laughter rose above the load volume of noise in the pub. Then he whispered again.

'By all accounts she's had him, too… frequently, like.' Stan took another slug of whisky. 'Well that little mare has taken me for a real mug, but she's goin' to pay, mate… yer get my meanin'?'

Sean certainly did, he knew exactly what Stan wanted. Still Stan continued with his diabolical talk.

'One dark night, I'm goin' to jump her and give her what for. That'll teach her to mess with the likes of me.' Stan paused. 'What did yer say yer did for work? I mean no one gets a scar like that and walks away, yer can obviously handle yerself?'

Sean took a nip and gauged his response carefully.

'Aye I can. Why ya looking for muscle?'

'In my game, mate… factor, see… it's always good to have a bit a muscle around. Times is hard round here and the little runts that I pay they don't think they get enuf. They will try and get it back, so to have someone like you watching me back could be useful.'

202

Sean looked thoughtful. Indeed, he could use the work and it would get his face in front of a few. Maybe his opportunity would grant itself a lot sooner than he first thought. If he could get Sean to turn a blind eye, maybe? If in some way he could get Sean to be obliged to him…? Again, Sean took his time.

'Well maybe I could help you out while I'm here.'

Stan nodded appreciatively.

'In more ways than one.'

Stan looked a little confused.

'I mean, if she's as good as you say she is, I could do with a little entertainment, maybe we could help each other?'

Stan was quite happy with this proposition, having no idea what Sean's ulterior motives were. Stan just thought that his offer to sort out Kitty was just payment in kind for his offer of employment. Hands were shaken, the deal was done.

Vi sat alone in her bedroom. A sudden chill ran down her spine. She had this feeling of impending doom, yet she could not fathom why. There had been so much trouble in a matter of weeks. As if all that had happened with Teddy was not enough, there was also the pitiful state of Fanny after her beating, then the revolting revelations of what Kitty had endured from her own father. Vi thought that it could be assumed everyone was much better off now that Alf was gone. Yet she could not shake this sense of foreboding no matter how much she tried. She needed to see John, and soon. Perhaps something had happened… maybe May had passed? Surely, he would have come and seen her if that had been the case? But she had not caught any sight of him anywhere. Then a real fear gripped her – maybe something had happened to him? No one in his court would think of letting her know, no one really knew their situation.

She tried to dismiss all of her black thoughts. She was tired, she had been shouldering her daytime employment with the additional burden of all she had to do at home with the cooking and the cleaning; her mother was in her own world again, unreachable. Vi knew she was exhausted from the stress of it all: the worry each night that something would happen, that the door wasn't locked properly, that her mother may go for one of her night-time walks around the house. There were so many dangers and hazards around the home that were a constant cause for concern for Vi. Her mother might fall in the dark, even take a tumble down the very steep staircase. She could burn herself on the range, or even start a fire with a lamp.

Each night Vi barely slept, constantly listening for any noise, any bang, creak or thump around the house, other than the snores of her father; he seemed to sleep through everything. Her constant vigilance was taking its toll on her, she had found herself more and more fatigued during the day; very dangerous when operating a press that could mash your fingers. Her work rate was down – that had not gone unnoticed – and the foreman had been very clear if she did not pick up the pace again her pay would be docked; she could not afford to lose money as well. She felt so completely finished; she had barely had strength for the normal banter and conversation that she and Fanny would exchange, never mind a mad dash in her short lunch break to try and see John.

She would give it a little more time, a few days or so, maybe her mother would improve and she would be able to get some proper sleep and be rested and recovered. Yes, it was obvious to her: she was just too tired. Once all calmed down again she would be as right as rain.

Chapter 17

All things come…

And so it was that another week passed and nothing really changed. Fanny held the ship together at home, aided by the helping hands of the younger two. Although Kitty stayed and was for the most part affable, she had taken once more to having the odd night out, 'just to have a bit of a laugh.' She told Fanny she just needed a break from it all, to 'be like others my age'. Fanny knew it was too late to play the big sister with her; the stable door was bolted and the horse had definitely gone. It was too late to try and rein in her wayward sister, and to attempt to explain that good girls – like Vi – did not frequent public houses alone before marriage. It was simply not going to work. She had been free to do what she had wanted for far too long, and nothing was going to change her sister now, as she had insisted to Vi. It was one of the conversations when she had felt that her friend was not really paying attention.

Kitty just wanted a bit of space. She had to come to terms with an awful lot and she didn't want to be constantly reminded of her own problems. She could tell by the way that her sister was being careful around her, treating her a bit like a china doll – when they normally argued like cat and dog – that things were far from normal. She felt that she was being pitied all the time – which of course she was – but it only served to remind her of all those horrible memories she had tried so hard all of her young life to suppress. By 'going down the pub', as she put it, she was trying to distance herself from this endless round of tolerance that was quite out of character for her elder sibling. It was just a drink, after all, with one or two mates; she had no intention of trying to get money or board out of anyone – meaning the men; she felt that everyone knew too much anyway. Or at least, they thought they knew too much, when in fact, they had no idea of what her life had been like. Kitty was quite intelligent and astute – although she played it down. She knew exactly what these people were like, and their holier-than-thou judgemental attitudes used to really get her goat.

Sometimes she would catch sight of Tom, but if he had seen her coming or realised she was there, he would generally leave; he had no time for her, and nor she for him. So, for the most part, she would find herself with one or maybe two others with slightly loose morals, passing an hour or so, laughing at the men, sometimes with the men. Then she would make her way home alone, thankfully at a less antisocial hour for Fanny than she used to experience from her miscreant sister.

Two men sat at the bar viewing Kitty from their vantage point. One whispered to the other.

'That's her… the little flighty madam.'

The other looked on and gave her a crafty wink as she looked in his direction.

Not bad, she thought. Good-looking fella… ginger… but never mind.

Sean just saw her as one thing and one thing only: a way to get Stan to back him, and a way to get Stan to stay silent.

Every morning, Kitty would still dash away, leaving Fanny to make sure the two girls got off to school after their breakfast chores had been completed. The three would then walk in the same direction until she and Vi met, Suie always shouting back to Fanny, as she and Mouse then made their way off to school.

'See you later, big sis… Love you!'

Fanny could see the tiredness etched in Vi's face. She was looking very drawn, and painfully thin. She was obviously not eating properly, which was strange as there had always been just enough in their house. She wondered if Vi had broken with her man friend.

'Are yer alright, Vi? You've not been right for a week or more. I'm getting a bit worried about you?'

At first, Vi did not register that she had been questioned directly; she had spent most days lost in her thoughts, pretending to listen.

'Hey, Vi… I'm talking ta yer.'

'I'm sorry… just a bit tired. I think I'm getting a cold.'

'No, Vi, I can tell when sumit's up. Now tell yer auntie Fanny, love.'

Not for the first time, Vi could feel her eyes begin to well up. She had been bottling everything up inside her, carrying the weight of the world on her shoulders. She had been reluctant to discuss anything with Fanny, seeing her problems as small by comparison to all that the poor Tulloch's had been through.

Fanny pressed her, and then it all came out in a rush. Fanny did her best to comfort her, trying to mop up the tears and hold her at the same time.

'Now listen, you, yer can't go on doin' all this, there has got to be a way this can all get sorted. Have you tried the doctor?'

'My dad doesn't hold with doctors… he says the best medicine Ma needs is rest. I just think he is hiding from the truth.' She blew her nose and continued.

'I've heard of old people losing their minds, doing all sorts of the same stuff as Ma; it all sounds the same. Oh, Fanny, I don't think she is ever going to get well. I just don't know what to do? John can't afford to marry me, never mind take on my ma and da. But what if Da gets sick? What if I get sick?'

'Now listen… these things can all come good. Yer dain't know what's goin' to happen… nobody does. It will all work out, Vi, one way or another. And stop making yerself a stranger. Come round to ours. You just need to sit and rest. After work I expect yer to come back, jus' for a little bit… right?'

That morning, John had finally finished his work. He had been so intensely involved in making it, he knew every join, every fold, every setting intimately. He had carefully bent and shaped the gold with delicate repoussé work, taking great care to anneal each section so as not to overwork the metal and cause it to fracture. Then, after crafting the base of the brooch, he had applied the settings for the diamonds. Each time more had been added he had filed and polished and examined all in intricate detail, before finally setting the beautiful stones and closing the mounts so that they were secure. Finally, he was able to look, really see the piece in its finished state.

It sat diminutively in the palm of his hand. The petals of the orchid curling, the fine edges almost paper-thin, displaying an outward fragility that belied the rigidity of the gold. Every corner and crease, every subtle join, the gentlest touch of intaglio, in perfect balance and harmony because of the care and attention to detail that he had lavished on this work. This piece of metal now shone with a richness of warm glory, the diamonds brought to life with a breath of fire in every gem that sparkled enticingly in the noonday sunshine. He was satisfied: it was ready.

He did not want to wait another moment, he must get this jewel to the purchaser with haste. He had lived on his nerves ever since he had received the stones, which he had kept about his person day and night. Now he carefully wrapped the orchid in a piece of black velvet cloth, and then placed it into a small leather box for protection. Securing it once again within his shirt he made his way out of the room, closing the great door behind him.

Outside in the street two men were about to pay a call on another struggling jeweller, to offer a pittance for another fine piece, quoting hard times to the poor unfortunate fellow who had spent a week in the vain hope of making his rent. Stan was about the quarter with Sean as the muscle as he went from place to place doing the same, tensions rising among all those who struggled to turn a living wage. As John descended the stairs, he heard an Irish accent that struck fear into him just outside. He dashed back up the stairs and, swiftly as he could, he unlocked the door and then once in, bolted it hurriedly from the inside. It was Sean, what was he doing here? Had he found him? Was he coming now to get him? A cold sensation ran down the entire length of his body, he stood shaking, uncertain of what to do. He could still hear Sean talking to another recognisable voice: Stan the factor. Why? Cautiously he moved to window, ducking down in case they were far enough way to look up and catch a glimpse of him. As he got to the window he began to rise upwards to look over the sill, he could see the tops of both of their heads just below the door. His heart thumped. They entered the door he moved away from the window and stood facing the bolted door. He could hear two set of footsteps ascending the wooden staircase. He knew they could not get in, the door was firmly looked and secure; it was a very solid and large oak door, suitable for a jeweller needing to secure his work-in-progress, bullion and gems. However, the panic that now gripped him caused him to lose his sense of rationality momentarily, and he remained stock-still facing the door, waiting for it to be broken down in front of him.

The footsteps stopped on his landing, his heart was beating so loud now he thought it would jump out of his chest. Then came a loud knock… but not on his door! It was on the door of his neighbour across the way. But still, an immediate threat remained, he didn't dare leave, not while they were even in the vicinity of St Paul's Square. He crept to his bench and decided to wait it out. Muffled male voices could be heard from the other side of the door; Stan was being as cut-throat as ever and was driving a hard deal, much to the chagrin of John's neighbour. Money was exchanged and accepted with reluctance as goods were handed over. Soon he could hear the two men descending the stairs. Once more he crept to the window, peering over the sill. Stan and Sean were now heading away across the square to another doorway. Time was moving on, yet John must wait it out until the coast was clear. The two disappeared into the interior of another set of workshops, and twenty minutes later emerged with satisfied looks. Two or three more visits were made to various places until finally, he could see that they were making their way towards Caroline Street, comfortably enough away from where John would have to walk, and thankfully in the opposite direction.

Now he had to act, to delay much more would mean that he would be unable to deliver the commission to Joseph today, and he feared that remaining in such a perilous position in the quarter may be his final undoing. He had to stay away from his bench, he had to stay out of sight as much as possible. It was obvious now that Sean was after him. No matter how much he had tried to dismiss the sudden discovery of his whereabouts and think optimistically that things would not – could not – escalate further, he knew that Sean would not be satisfied until blood had been shed: John's blood. He moved swiftly out of the square, all the time turning back just to be certain he had not been followed. He practically ran down the side of the canal, all the time aware of his vulnerability. He could be mugged at any time and he would lose everything, and if Sean found him he would lose his life, of that he was now certain.

By the time he had made it to the house of Joseph Chamberlain he was physically exhausted and beads of sweat speckled his forehead. He pulled out a cloth from his jacket pocket and mopped his brow, he had no desire to be quizzed and cross-examined about his harried state. Calming himself as best he could, he waited in the hallway as the maid announced his arrival. Enormous self-doubt now raised its ugly head. All of a sudden, he feared that his work was not a worthy piece, and that he would be found out to be inept and all of that investment would be lost; it may well be demanded back.

Joseph was thrilled with the piece. It was not a casual, passing appreciation, or a valuing of technical skill – he was genuinely quite overcome.

'My, John! I have never in all my days seen such a beautiful work.' He turned it around and around, viewing through his monocle, scrutinising every detail. He had stood as close the window as he could to allow the late afternoon sun to play on the surface of the gold and diamonds. He caressed each petal gently.

'It is such fine and delicate workmanship… Harriet will be overcome, as I am. You have excelled yourself. No, really, I knew you were a fine worker – all your referees testified to the same – but I never expected such a piece as this.' Again, he turned it around and around in his hand. You could not have impressed me more… it is a fine work of art. I shall give it to my wife this evening, she will be heartened greatly. She has been confined to her bed for some weeks now waiting for our child's arrival. This will cheer her spirits no end. I shall write to you with her comments, I know she will be deeply touched.'

John sat with Joseph for a while, as he continued to praise the fine jewel. He began to question John on how the quarter was coping with the recession in the industry. He made John aware that he had a special consideration for the area, it having been the first placed that he had lived in on arriving from London. John was amazed at the connection that Joseph felt with the place and the people, and the obvious affinity he had with the position of the working man.

'This town of Birmingham is a fine place, John. It lacks the respect that it deserves, of course. I am a unitarian and am welcome here because of its non-incorporated status. That position has brought a wealth of minds and experience into quite a small area, because other places – incorporated cities – do not welcome those of diverse beliefs. It is because of that concentrated wealth of minds and talents such as yours that I believe the only thing that this city now needs is a charter. If we achieve a charter for Birmingham, we could become a great city! I say we, because I feel more at home here than in London, although that was my place of birth. It is the people, John, the hard-working people who keep this whole town thriving. It pains me to hear that this place of greatest artisanal skill and craft is suffering so terribly. It is a special place to me. I am aspiring to political office within the city, and one day I hope to change things for the people. If we had a municipal vision, if we had clean water and power to every home, office and place of work, we could revolutionise the whole town! It would lead to better health, better education and more investment, that in turn would improve conditions for all and increase wages.'

John listened intently as Joseph described all of the possibilities that could be made real with political vision and will. He became engrossed in Joseph's ideas. He was so inspired and empowered that he failed to notice the sky had darkened; night was falling. He would have liked to have spent more time listening to this dynamic young thinker and fine orator; his passion and real admiration for all of the working people was plain to see. He was almost evangelical when he spoke of advances in engineering, and how it could drive up revenues and improve the city if wholescale use of mass production were to be adopted. At the same time, he stressed the fine craft of the individual, whether that be a jeweller, a silversmith, or a gunmaker. In Joseph's opinion all had to be in balance.

It was as the gas lamp was lit in Harborne Road outside the study window that John realised he had overstayed, and that he had been away far too long. He explained to Joseph that he had to leave, that his infirm mother needed him.

Joseph apologised profusely, reiterating that it had been a great pleasure to take soundings from a man like John, whose opinion he valued greatly and who obviously shared his own all-consuming passion to improve things. But he would not allow John to leave before he had pressed another envelope into his hand.

John knew only too well what the contents were, and he estimated that he had been vastly overpaid by Joseph's generosity and made an effort to return it.

'I cannot accept this… I have not earned this.'

Joseph would not hear of it, and insisted he take it.

'You have, John… believe you me, you have. And if your income had not been so devalued and been outstripped by the cost of living, this is the sum that you would have earned. Money is my business. And this is a fair rate, not what the factors steal. This is yours by rights.'

Vi sat in Fanny's kitchen, her relief palpable. Just to be away from the worry and the strain of her home life, if only for a short while, had brought some respite. Fanny had counselled her just to take each day as it came, that her mother may get better, or at least better than she was right now. She tried to get Vi to be positive.

'At least yer got a bloke who's sweet on yer, love. Look at me, Vi, I'll be an old maid at this rate. Even our Kitty said as much. I can't say anything to 'er. What right have I to tell her what to do? I wish she wasn't so free and easy going, like… she dain't realise that she's not 'elping her reputation at all.'

Vi knew that Fanny had given wise counsel regarding her relationship with John; indeed, she was very lucky. Although, she had not seen him at all for weeks and feared that it may have changed things, but she didn't think it was the best time to see him. She explained to Fanny that, as her time was so limited and her tiredness so extreme, she was scared that her depression might be apparent to him and he would think the worst of her or believe that she had lost interest. She hoped for better days ahead. Then, when she was feeling in a more positive frame of mind, she would seek him out.

Kitty was out on one of her evenings. No longer did she sit with her girlfriends, she had a new interest: something that had grown from flirtatious winks and innuendo casually thrown across a packed bar. It had progressed to a more intimate chat as he came over to where she sat, with his pint in hand. Kitty had not been used to the attentions of younger men, although he was not as young as her by any means, but he was not as old as Stan; she had more experience with older men, for obvious reasons. She felt slightly awkward and unable to judge the situation; she was suffering some self-doubt, but flattered all at the same time. He was a younger man, and not bad looking; he could have the pick of any in that bar, yet he had chosen to centre his attentions upon her. It must surely mean that he liked her above all others.

So, his hair was ginger – not her favourite colour – but his eyes sparkled aquamarine. He had so much charm, Irish charm; he could charm the birds from the trees with the soft Irish lilt in his voice. And there something about him... something she couldn't quite put her finger on; an air of darkness, of menace, maybe? But that didn't faze Kitty. She had always been drawn to the stronger men, those that seemed able to handle themselves in a fight, and he could, judging by the scar that he bore on his face – four inches long – a deep knife wound perhaps, from many years ago, slicing his right cheek diagonally.

She had taken a shine to Sean, and to all outward appearances he also had to her. Only one person knew that Sean's motives were far from honourable, and he sat a way to one side of the bar, in his normal place – Stan.

John raced through the city streets staying as much as he could in the shadows, at the same time avoiding darkened alleys and railway viaducts. He just had one intention: to get home to safety, avoiding trouble, and to tell May the good news and show her how all the hard work that he had put in had finally paid off. He was so taken with Joseph's commitment to the town that it had changed his mind regarding some Englishmen, and Joseph in particular; in John's opinion he had the power and the passion to do great things. It gave him hope that, with his patronage and favour and his prime position within the local society, John would finally be able to make proper plans for his life and to marry Vi.

At last, he made it to the sanctuary of the court; the only place he now felt truly safe. It was late and dark, but to his surprise Mrs Morris had taken a chair from the kitchen and was sitting outside. As soon as she saw him she rose to her feet. He approached her full of enthusiasm, but as he got closer he sensed something was not quite as it should be.

'Mrs Morris, are you alright? Is ma alright?'

'John, I am afraid she has gone—'

She could not say any more, as he made for the back parlour before she could finish her sentence.

'Ma! Ma!' John was beside himself as he approached where she was lying. A paraffin lamp was guttering in the room, the fire no longer burned in the hearth. He knelt by her and took her hand. She was still slightly warm, but chilling fast. Her face had an expression of peace and contentment, a slight smile that made her look younger. The tears fell like rain as he rested his head on the hand that he had placed over her now lifeless one.

'Oh, Ma! Why did you go… why? Why wasn't I here for you? What am I going to do without you?'

Mrs Morris bent low next him, her whole frame creaking as she did so, the flickering light casting unearthly shadows around and about, on the walls and the ceiling.

'John… there was nothing you could have done. She took ill suddenly. She knew.' She paused, John still sobbed, remaining with his head down, his hand and the hand of May saturated in the wetness of his tears.

'She wouldn't have the doctor. She asked for a priest and said it was 'er time. She told me not to get you, that you had important things to do, but of course I sent a boy around to your place.'

John knew that all this must have occurred when he had gone to see Joseph. Mrs Morris continued.

'The priest came… lovely man. He was so gentle and did the last rites for her. By then she was barely conscious…' she paused again. 'It was so quick… I doubt you would have got back in time.'

John raised his head to look at Mrs Morris, his agony etched on his face. She gave one last assurance:

'I know it's no consolation now, but she went peacefully and in no pain… it was a blessing.'

Chapter 18

The reckoning

John stayed with his mother the whole night. He could not leave her. He felt that he had failed her terribly, especially by not being there in her last moments. Despite the assurances of Mrs Morris, he worried that she had suffered and struggled; she had fought so hard to stay alive, he could not quite believe that her final battle for life had passed so quickly and without suffering. She had always been there for him, she had always stood by him despite everything.

He fell into a fitful sleep, mentally and emotionally exhausted, still in place next to his mother in the cold, darkened parlour.

He was back there in the madness. Patrick had his hands around the throat of the young man with the heart-shaped birthmark. John tried in vain to struggle and reason with his brother; they had to go, this was not going to solve anything, Cara was gone!

Sean had come after them both and was shouting irately. 'Get your hands off my brother!'

A sudden realisation had come over John – his drinking companion of the evening was related to this man, the one his older brother was tumbling around the floor with. The same man that had raped his sister!

Just then there was a flash of shining metal from either side of him, it all happened so quickly. Sean tried to lunge at Patrick with a knife. John acted to stop him, grabbing his wrists, struggling as Sean tried to raise his arm to break free. The knife ground into Sean's face, there was a scream of pain as Sean lost his balance, falling against the wall and sending himself unconscious. The knife fell to the floor, and for an instant John thought to grab it. All was shouts and grunts behind him.

He turned, Patrick had his hands around the throat of the other man and was throttling the life out of him. Then all fell silent, another knife lay just to the right. Patrick slumped on the other man, a pool of blood was forming fast next to the two. John tried to get Patrick to his feet, the large dark-red stain growing on his brother's shirt. John was alarmed as Patrick struggled to stand, obviously too weak. The stain growing and growing. John applied his hand on his brother's side.

'Pat! Pat! We have to get out of here! You must try and stand… come on, man!'

Patrick was now too weak to make it and collapsed as the life drained from him. John's hands were covered in the blood of his brother. Patrick struggled to speak.

'Leave me, Johnny… just leave me… there is nothing you can do.' The pain was clearly intense as his life force trickled away. 'Take Ma and go!' With that, he fell into unconsciousness and lay dying, half spread over the man he had slain.

John was gripped by fear. One was dead, one lay dying and the other could regain consciousness at any moment. The instinct to survive was strong, he needed to flee or be caught and hanged for murder. How could he explain any of this? His mother needed him, there was no one else left. He ran.

John awoke in a state of panic; his whole body was covered in sweat. He reached up to the bed to touch his mother. Her hand was now stone cold and rigid. The nightmare that he had just endured had been a real memory. In front of him lay his beautiful mother, who had lived a life of pain and suffering, losing all but one of her children. How strong she had been. How much sacrifice she had made. He remembered how she had taken the news of Patrick's demise with such stoicism when John had returned to the squat where they had waited till they could all take a boat to England. She had not cried or wailed, she had merely uttered: 'God bless my boy… violence begets violence.'

Then she had calmed her remaining child, clear in her plan that they must go, and quickly. Now she lay still and cold, her job was done, she could do no more.

John was so consumed in his grief the next day that he would not allow Mrs Morris to come in. He would not eat, he just sat in a chair in the kitchen, staring aimlessly. He was so lost. He had not even looked inside that final envelope from Joseph that was still secured around his body in the belt. He felt its bulk pinching, but he had no care for the contents; it had all been for his mother and to make a new life, and for now his sense of purpose had left him.

By the second day, Mrs Morris had sought out the priest, fearing for John's mental disposition and being aware that arrangements had to be made. John was like a lost soul. He accepted that his mother must make that final journey, but they knew no one really, and with their need to stay anonymous he had to respect her wishes for a cremation and privacy.

A few days later he clutched a small urn, uncertain what to do next. He felt it was not a befitting end for such a great lady, but she had insisted to him in those final weeks before her death that he was just to find somewhere green and let her go. That was all she wanted for her peace, a feeling of the land and the soil: a greenness rather than any formality. To her, the nearest she could be to God was by being with the soil. He wanted to say words as he stood in Warstone Cemetery, just him and the metal urn. He wanted to have a priest say words, but his mother had insisted not. It was just to be him and her; she had done her best to protect her last precious child to the very end, and now even in death.

No matter how he tried the words would not come, just tears that fell like rain, mirroring the dark grey weather and the inclement drizzle. At that moment, in that place, he felt so exposed and alone. Sean could come and take his revenge, it no longer mattered. He could die there that day and none of it would matter. He knew that whether or not Sean was uncertain which of the two brothers – John or Patrick – had taken the life of his own, he had a vendetta against John. It would be blood for blood. He was never going to rest until he had taken the life of John Connolly. To John's mind, Sean was probably completely unaware of the circumstances that had led to his own brother's demise. Cara had said there had only been one that day in the deserted croft; he may have absolutely no understanding as to why a Connolly had killed his own brother, Michael, in such a brutal fashion. Right at that moment, John had no wish to live or breathe; for him, all was done. Then a voice came from behind him.

'John…' It was a soft and gentle voice, a soul full of care. Vi was there. 'John… Mrs Morris told me where I might find you.' Without saying another word, she stood next to him.

He turned to her, his face pale, his eyes bloodshot, he had manged to shave out of respect for what he was about to do. He opened the urn, paused for a moment, then let the gentle breeze take her ashes as they fell.

He stood for what seemed like an eternity in deep contemplation, Vi standing by, saying nothing, just waiting. He placed the urn on the ground, and took Vi's hand. They made their way out of the cemetery, and passed a fresh headstone on the way; as Jimmy had said, Hardman had had a stone placed on Teddy's grave. It was simple and small, in white marble:

Edward Tulloch
1856 – 1863
Sleep well little man.

They sat in his kitchen, the parlour door now firmly shut. Mrs Morris had prepared some soup, although John's appetite was still limited. He had made a half-hearted attempt to eat, Vi had done her best to encourage him. He had said very little, she knew not to press him, that when he was ready he would talk. Eventually, he began to rifle through this shirt, withdrawing the two envelopes of money and a small black velvet bag. Both envelopes were creased, one was older and had been opened a week or two ago, the other had remained sealed shut. He silently took the contents from both envelopes and handed them to Vi. She was somewhat confused by suddenly having a pile of bank notes, that even without counting she could see was a considerable sum. She stared at the pile, uncertain of what to do, amazed by the amount? What was it for, and where had John got it from?

He reached his hand across the table to take hers: she complied. His face was still drawn and pained, but his eyes were intent as they searched her face.

'Vi… you know my life has not been an easy one. I have never told a living soul the whole story, but I want you to know all. And then I want to ask you something.'

And then he began. He went way back to the happy days, the beautiful land on which he had be born, the loving family that had surrounded him. Vi sat and listened intently, she'd had no idea that he had a brother and two sisters, he had never said a thing about any of it. Then she watched as a darkness descended over his face. Now he talked about the times of the famine. The day they had scrabbled through the dirt when the potato crop had failed, his mother's desperation when she had known in her heart what that had meant for all those that she loved. He moved on to his father's failing health due to the starvation that was descending on them all. Then Niamh's passing, and the terrible agonising pains of the disease that had swept through those that remained. He paused and drew breath.

221

Vi could not imagine the horror of life for this family. The tragedy was overwhelming for her.

Then, he wistfully remembered how Cara had been the strong one; the one who had done the most foraging for them all. Never scared, just driven to survive. He stopped again. He wasn't quite sure how to tell Vi about what had befallen Cara, or if he should; she was a woman, and more delicate in her manners than most. He carefully alluded to what had happened without detailing the terrible assault. How he had watched his sister lose the will to live, and then there were just the three.

'What I am going to tell you now, you may hate me for... I fear I may lose you. I have never told another living soul other than my ma.' The thought of May on her deathbed poleaxed him momentarily, leaving him unable to utter a sound. Then he resumed his retelling of all that had occurred: being in Dublin, finding work to make their passage, Patrick and him looking after May as best they could, living in a squat. Then the terrible evening before they left, that had started so well; a celebration together by two brothers and their new-found friend Sean...

His voiced began to crack with emotion as he described having seen Cara's attacker across the bar, and how a moment of insanity – a red mist – had overcome him, how he had instantly sought revenge. And how he held the deepest of regrets that he acted as he did.

'Vi, if I had not been so hot-headed... if I had just let it rest... none of this would ever have happened.'

By the time he had recounted the bloody fight to the death, and having to leave his brother laying in a back alley dying, the tears were once again rolling down his face, and Vi was equally overcome.

He stopped, and sat waiting for her response, waiting for her to tell him he was a bad man that she wanted nothing more to do with, waiting for her to walk away without uttering another word. She looked at him through

222

her tear-filled eyes, her compassion visibly apparent on her face.

'I had no idea that you and your mother had suffered so terribly. She must have been a very strong woman indeed to have gone through so much and lived as she did. I cannot imagine how anyone is able to withstand so much, with such fortitude.' She paused.

'John, you did nothing wrong! This man, you say he is here, in the quarter?'

He nodded.

'Surely someone can protect you? Could we not ask for help? You know that everyone looks after one another here.'

'Vi, I am Irish. There is so much bad feeling towards my countrymen around these parts, I doubt anyone would care. I have had to keep myself to myself all these years to keep Ma from harm. I haven't been social with anyone, no one knows me… apart from Jimmy Pearse that is, and he does not know the full story. I do not want to get Jimmy involved, he is recently married, he does not need my trouble too. I am not sure what to do, but I know one thing, and that is…' He looked into her eyes, lost in their colour, the fire of her hair, her pale complexion.

'I love you, Violet… that I do. And on this table lies a considerable amount of money, honestly gained – if highly overpaid – from a very generous man. I am saying to you this is what I have, and it's yours… yours, and for your parents too. I will aim to support all of us, that is.' He fumbled in the black velvet bag for the beautiful ring, the one that had brought them together in the first place, he held it in his big hands.

'I thought this ring would earn me money to pay the rent, to get a good doctor to my ma… but that was not how it was meant to be, obviously. Everything happens for a reason, as she used to say, and I made this for a reason. I know now.' He stopped again, offering the ring towards Vi.

'Vi, would you marry me? I will always look after you and yours, as long as you will have me, of course?'

Vi was completely dumbstruck. She had thought that with all that had happened that he had in some way lost interest. Her heart was full. She could not quite believe it all. Not in her wildest dreams could she have considered the possibility that their situation may come good. She had gone in the rain to meet the man that she loved who was grief-stricken, with no idea that she would be confronted with a tale so sad and frightening. It was hard to even begin to appreciate all of the pain and anguish that he had been through in his life, and all of a sudden, he was asking her to marry him! There was nothing she wanted more, the only reservations she held were not for the act of marrying, it was the safety of his skin. She feared for his life. Of course, she would marry him! She took the ring and tried it on, and it fitted perfectly, like it had been made just for her. Her elation was obvious, the smile on her face, the tears now of joy not of sadness. John's spirits lifted slightly, just for a short while, and for the first time in many years he felt happy.

Kitty thought she had found the love of her life. This sweet-talking Irishman had found the way to her heart. Of course, Kitty remained aloof, always suspicious of any male advances. In her experience, men only wanted one thing and she had played the game for so long she knew exactly how to keep them at arm's length, but at the same time, get exactly what she wanted or needed. There was something different about this man, though, he appeared to be quite genuine, and continued to pour flattery upon her and flirt unmercifully.

'Hey, Kitty, with those eyes you could sink ships.'

'How is the most beautiful colleen in the world today?'

'With a figure like yours, you'll never be short of admirers, I bet?'

And his final parry, that final took her completely off guard: 'If I found a lass like you, I would never let her go.'

He would buy her drinks, immediately coming over to her when she entered the bar. He would sit and chat openly, not seemly concerned about her reputation. He would laugh raucously when she made some outrageous statement – which she was always inclined to do for the sake of getting attention. In her perception, it was as if he was becoming fond and proud of her.

All the time, Stan kept a discreet watch over the proceedings, knowing that Sean was using his charm to exploit a situation to their advantage.

Sean, on the other hand, was playing a long game. He knew that one way or another Kitty was the key to him seeking out the man he was going to make pay for the loss of his brother.

In his reflection of that night in Dublin, he acknowledged that he had spent a passable evening with a nice bloke; they had shared a jar or two and planned their future away from the trouble and pain that they both wanted to put firmly behind them. But then, for no apparent reason, this man whom he had shared time with had pursued Sean's brother into a back alley, and the last thing that Sean remembered was being knocked out by John. When he had awoken, he was lying in blood, his brother close by with the life throttled out of him, while another was dead from a fatal knife wound. Only one man was no longer there – John Connolly! Sean had run, for fear that he would be accused of the two murders. He had lost everything he had in the world, even fearing to return to collect any personal things: family mementoes, his coat, even his work boots. He had managed to stow away on a boat bound for Cardiff. He'd struggled to find proper food for some days, tramping across the Welsh countryside, uncertain of his direction, or what on earth he should do next.

Eventually, he had found himself in the Bristol harbour. He did as many labouring jobs as he could: loading and unloading cargo, mending roads, working on the navigations around there, digging like every other Irish native who'd found themselves down on their luck in England. He had been in a few scrapes, had a few fights. He learnt quickly how to handle himself and got quite a reputation as a scrapper, not one to be messed with. Finally, he had worked the cargo barges on the Kennet and Avon Canal, the sixty tonners carrying stone and coal to London. He didn't like London at all; a man could get lost there and never be found, he thought. It was not for him, too big and too much trouble. He had speculated that Connolly may be there, but he dismissed it; if he found the metropolis unfriendly then his nemesis would too. He had made his mind up that Connolly would be in one of the cities to the north.

Sean had switched to working the Grand Union main line from London up to Brum; he got himself a reputation as a hard worker; a good bargee. He was very savvy and able to be quite threatening if anyone thought to rob the cargo. He spent a good few years on that stretch, mainly because he had met a woman. She had seemed nice enough, Irish like himself and working the cut on a small barge that had been her dead father's. She was more of a tinker than anything, she would do odd jobs and make enough for food. She had been nice enough, and they would meet up from time to time, she had even travelled two runs with him; he had enjoyed that – a wifey cooking, and a warm body in the bed. He had considered making it a more permanent arrangement until he learnt that she had been doing a little more than selling pegs and cleaning to pay her way. He had not bothered to catch up with her after that.

Eventually, he had found himself with no work up in Gas Street Basin in Birmingham. Some fellow travellers who were in the same boat – so to speak – said that there was always building work going on, 'with all them big houses going up in Edgbaston.' So, there he was, living up Green Lane with the rest of the Paddys, and working on the sites. By then he was hitting his thirties, he had no wife or kids, no responsibilities. He was a lead hand after a while, and earning good money.

Boredom set in, and he was thinking of make the move up to Liverpool, maybe travelling the world if he could get a passage. In his heart, he knew that one day he would cross paths with the man who had ruined his life; he didn't know how or where, he just knew he would.

It was purely by chance that evening that he had walked passed the debating hall. Seeing a rabble outside, and not reading well, he asked one of those gathering what it was about. He was lucky he spoke to the right man, another from the Emerald Isle, like himself; that man had obviously been the worse for wear and was spoiling for a fight.

'They're talking against Irish, so they are… all them gaffers… the working-class this, the working-class that… I am sick to me stomach! We built this feckin' town for them!'

So, Sean had stood waiting to see what sort of men were running his people down again. If he was off on his travels he might as well leave in style, see a jaw or two broken or even join in: it was good for the craic.

It was then that he had seen him. He couldn't believe his luck. His rage grew inside him and his first instinct, with his blood running high, was to follow him and do him then and there. He looked around and about for cover; but there were too many people, he couldn't get caught. He had to be a little bit canny and find a way, a quiet place with no witnesses. And he wanted Connolly to know why. He didn't just want to kill him, he wanted him to suffer and beg for his life.

Now, after rigging the trial, after having to wait and bide his time, and work for a complete arse, he was that close. Kitty was the key. He knew her sister and the red-head were mates. He could either ingratiate himself with another loose woman to get to Connolly, or he could use that relationship to get a hold over Stan that he couldn't wriggle out of, and together they could finish his brother's killer off. One way or another, he was going to do it. Then he would make for Liverpool and get himself the hell out of this rat-infested country of Irish-haters!

So, he took to walking Kitty back to her court on her evening sojourns in the pub. Always being honourable, never expecting anything other than a kiss.

Kitty was secretly smitten and hoped that this admirations and attentions were leading somewhere for her. She could see herself as Mrs Rafferty.

Chapter 19

There comes a time…

Two women were walking on air as they went to and from the factory. Kitty, because she had found some hope for a future, with a lovely and charming man. Vi, because she knew that she and John were going to be married. Neither, revealed their story to anyone else.

Kitty did not want to jinx her prospects; she was very superstitious and felt that if she were to mention it, then it would never become a reality.

Vi had a more serious reason. She knew that John feared a man who was determined to take a revenge for a crime that John had not committed; to say too much at this stage could put them all in even greater jeopardy. She knew she could confide in Fanny, and she would take a secret to the grave if she had to, but not now, at work. Fanny was liable to explode with joy. She would crow about how she had been right and things had finally come good for Vi. Vi tried to contain her happiness, which was beyond imaginable. She would go and see her friend this evening, and when it was safer to do so discuss all with her parents. Today she had to keep tight-lipped, though it was so hard.

She had counselled John that by not revealing the truth to Jimmy, he put his friend at risk. Although what she said made sense, he agonised most of that morning whether he should or not. By the time he had resolved to do so, the streets were far too quiet, and would leave him too exposed to danger; he knew he must wait until the factories emptied-out at the end of the day, and find safety in numbers.

As Kitty made her way to the pub, Fanny and Vi headed for Fanny's kitchen, and John to Jimmy's yard at Hardman's.

Sean had got wind that the Irishman had got troubles; his ma had passed, there was some talk that now he had no responsibilities he may well leave. A sense of urgency overtook Sean; to wait much longer could be too late, he would have to act, and act soon. He was mightily relieved to see Kitty enter the bar, and having liberally plied Stan with alcohol, he set about doing the same with Kitty; her expectations grew that tonight he was going make his move and ask her. Stan had no idea what was going on, having succumbed to a fog of whisky.

John was glad he had waited till Jimmy had finished his work, as he could be easily distracted and fly off on a tangent; he needed his full concentration for all that he was about to reveal to him.

Jimmy sensed this was more than a social call, having noted John's unusual absence for some weeks and knowing he needed the work. Jimmy had his suspicions that it was sombre news that his friend brought with him, and this was confirmed when he learnt of May's passing.

'Oh, man! I wish I had been there for you,' came Jimmy's impassioned response.

John then set about telling him about Vi, about the large amount of money he had come into, tapping his chest where he still had it all secured. He explained it was enough to begin to make a life again – a life for them both, and her folks too, of course. Jimmy listened intently as John continued.

'There are things I have never told you, Jimmy… things I really need to tell you now. Vi is right, I must make sure I do not put you or Susan in danger.'

Vi and Fanny sat together, it was obvious that Vi was fit to burst with excitement and could no longer contain herself.

'Come on, Violet… what's goin' on with yer then?'

'I'm getting married!'

With that, the two girls screamed with delight. Then Violet began to recount the whole tale, and why she now had to be discreet, fearing for John's safety until they could find a way through.

'Vi, you know how this place works. If we put the word around in the right ears this Irish fella will be chased out. John's one of ours now… especially because yer two are together. We always look after our own.'

Fanny's reasoning sounded perfectly sensible. If John could not get protection from the justice system, then the people of the quarter would provide their own: they always had, and they always would. She felt in some way calmed by the logic, and hopeful that she and John would soon be able to live in her place and look after her mum and dad. She knew that he wanted a better life for them out of the back-to-backs, but it would depend on what work he could get. Although he had been generously rewarded this time, that money would not last forever.

It was Jimmy who was solving the Sean problem.

'John, why the hell didn't you tell me all this, man? You could have trusted me… I could have looked out for you a bit. And it was bloody Rafferty that got me locked up, you say?'

John nodded.

'Well, that's simple enough: we go to Joseph and we tell him all this. Then we will get this bastard. At least he will get a good sorting out and sent packing. I wish you had told me all this before.'

John listened intently. Maybe Jimmy was right, they could ask Joseph for help; he trusted them both, and he was bound to believe them above a man who had rigged a court case. It all sounded like common sense. Doubts still plagued him, though. If Sean had been hunting him for years, was he ever going to stop? And, what if Joseph did not believe them? What if he ended up being tried for two murders?

Jimmy sensed John's fear and uncertainty.

'Listen, my friend. Have you thought about moving back, maybe? I mean, to Ireland?'

John was somewhat confused by this question, and no, it had not come into his mind. Why go back to a place where he had suffered so much?

Jimmy explained his thinking.

'We – Susan and I – have decided that Birmingham is not the place we want to bring up our family, and we plan to have a large one.' He laughed. 'I have enough now to go out on my own, as an architectural sculptor and stonemason. Well, we have talked about where, and I quite fancy Dublin. I am sure a versatile man like myself can make a go of it there. Why do you have to stay here? Why can't we work together? I don't know, maybe be business partners in some way? Your money would go a lot further there, and I am sure you'd have better life.'

John was completely taken by surprise at the suggestion, but not averse to it. He hadn't really thought about going anywhere, but Jimmy was right: to be among his own people, to not feel like a second-class citizen, to be free in his heart. He could take Vi to see the old place… maybe not though… too many painful memories.

John and Jimmy chatted away, the plan had caught fire. Of course, he would have to discuss this with Vi and her parents. Jimmy agreed.

'Well, there is no time like the present. I think I ought to go with you, so she knows it's a sensible plan… and because I fear for you, my friend. At least if there's two of us walking through those streets, there is someone watching over you. Your ma would never forgive me if something happened to you, Johnny boy.'

While the two men discussed how to proceed with breaking their news, Vi had realised that she had completely lost track of the hour: it was late! She did have responsibilities at home and her parents would be fretting.

Fanny was worried too.

'I'm not havin' you walk back alone! If this man is as bad as John claims, 'ee could be watching out for you... have you thought of that?'

No, Vi had not. Of course! She made John even more vulnerable. She accepted Fanny's very kind offer to accompany her back home.

'And don't yer worry about me... I'm a Tulloch and I can take care of meself!'

Fanny gave Suie strict instructions to sit tight in the kitchen with the door bolted until she came home; Mouse had been sent to bed, and Fanny had to be let in. Suie nodded enthusiastically.

'I'll be alright, Fan, and I will sit right here, like you tells me to.'

Off the two girls trotted, back to Vi's court. Upon arriving, Fanny popped her head around the door to say hello, and to apologise for keeping Vi talking too long.

'Well, it's the polite thing to do ain't it?' she had said to Vi beforehand. 'It keeps you out of bovver and stops the questions that you can't answer right now.'

Pleasantries over with, Fanny made her way back. She was halfway along Tenby Street, when a fella she knew from packing stopped her.

'Hi, Fan. Did you know yer old man's been seen...?'

Fanny froze in panic, then she got angry: very angry. How dare he have the audacity to show his face around these parts again! Why was she being made to feel scared and afraid all over again? This had got to stop! Within five minutes she was back at home banging on the door for admittance from Suie. Suie was quite alarmed as Fanny flew into the kitchen and started to turn the place upside down.

Suie asked, slightly worried, 'What's up, Fan? What yer doing that for?'

Still Fanny frantically searched, through buckets and pans, even jars, though she knew it couldn't possibly fit into them. She answered Suie without really thinking it through.

'Alf's back! Up on the bloody railway embankment sleeping rough! Dain't yer worry about it… I'm goin' to put an end to this… once and for bloody all!'

By this point she was halfway up the stairs and heading for the bedroom. She checked under Kitty's pillow. She recalled the big knife having been there, but she hadn't seen it for a while. It was not there! Where else could it be?

She belted back down the stairs and into the parlour, she rifled through everything, she still couldn't find it. Back up the stairs. In the bedroom again, under one pillow, under the other: nothing! Then she saw a slight glint from between the mattress and the wall. There it is! It had slipped down almost to back of the bedstead and got caught in the mattress as it had cut its way in. She snatched it out, and held it in her hand, her knuckles turning white. She had absolutely no doubt what she was going to do. She concealed the knife in her waistband under her jacket and headed out the door. Suie had gone off to bed, Fanny wasn't worried – *He* was not coming back here again. *He* would not be breathing again. She hurried her way through the streets, and as she turned one corner, Jimmy and John turned another in a different direction; she was not seen by anyone.

As Jimmy and John made their way to Vi's, Jimmy noticed a cat, injured in the gutter and yammering.

'Oh, man! I can't leave the poor creature!'

'Jimmy, it's a mangy old moggy, just leave it be.'

'I can't, man.' Jimmy tried to attend to the cat, who did not take very kindly to his approach and growled and hissed, lashing out with his front paws.

Kitty was completely drunk. Sean had plied her with alcohol and thrown compliments at her all evening. He looked at her, and said in his sweetest voice:

'Come on, Kitty my love… let's get you home.'

She almost swooned with delight when he said 'my love.' He helped her unsteadily to her feet and towards the door, casually nodding towards the bar as he did so. Once outside, the fresh air made her condition ten times worse. She was quite oblivious to her direction of travel and commented vaguely, her speech very slurred and playful:

'And where m-m-m-ight y-o-o-o-u be taking me… Seany bo-oy? She laughed raucously as she blindly followed his lead. A little way along, he stopped and looked at her, and said:

'And, Miss Kitty, if I were to ask you to marry me, what would you say?' confidently knowing what her reply would be.

'Oooo… y-e-e-sh pleashe!' With that, she grasped her arms around his neck and tried to kiss him passionately, in a very ungainly way. He gently pushed her from him.

'Let's find somewhere a little more private.' He giggled. Kitty staggered with him to a quieter part of the quarter – a back alley where no courts were close by, only businesses, all shut for the night. Footsteps followed at a discreet distance.

The alley was dark, no gas lamps around. It smelt strongly of urine where people had relived themselves. Sean persuaded Kitty to lean against the wall. He was gently kissing her, telling her he loved her. Then… all of a sudden, his voice took on a hard tone and he had her hands above her head, pinched against the rough brickwork, and he was fumbling with his fly. Kitty was incapable of reacting. She felt that things were just happening around her and she was too slow to make any sense of it. She thought Sean was just being playful. His voice became more aggressive.

'Right you… you owe a friend of mine… and he wants paid.' He called over his shoulder to the man waiting in the shadows. 'Come here and hold her wrists.'

Kitty didn't understand, she was lost. Before she knew what was happening, Stan was there standing next to her, he too was unbuttoning his fly.

'No, you don't… it's me first. You can go second, right?' Stan reluctantly agreed, he had by far the greatest need, and was uncertain if he could contain himself while he watched someone else. But he was not going to argue with Sean.

By now, Sean had her skirt hitched up and he had forced her legs apart. At first, she had not understood, she thought he loved her, she thought that he was just being passionate. She couldn't understand why Stan was holding her wrists. He didn't need to be there. She loved Sean, of course she wanted to marry him, of course she wanted him… As all these thoughts whizzed round in her confused mind, she felt a pain like she had never felt in her life. Sean rammed himself inside her so hard, she screamed; his right hand came up over her mouth, and he snarled at her:

'Shut up, you bitch, and take what's coming to you! And if I get the clap from you, I will kill you!' Kitty was suddenly brought to her senses. He didn't love her! He was raping her, and Stan was helping him. Stan was holding her wrists, desperate to have a go himself:

'Hurry up, mate, it's my turn ain't it?'

'You can have her when I have finished, now shut up!' He kept his hand over her mouth to stifle her screams that had now turned to sobs. Harder and harder he banged her against the wall.

A few streets away, Jimmy had lifted the injured cat, which had screamed at the same time Kitty had. John had heard something, but Jimmy had said it was only the cat, which had continued to rumble and complain. John stopped Jimmy, and strained to hear.

'No, Jimmy, there's something going on…' He tried to make out the distant sounds.

'It's just cats rutting, John.'

Then, more clearly, he could hear a woman's muffled sobs and the low rumble of male voices. His heart stopped.

'It's a girl! Put the damn cat down!' He was running now towards the direction of the noise… it could be Vi! Fear and panic had completely overtaken him, fear that the woman that he loved had been singled out for treatment by Sean.

At that moment, Kitty's chance came. Stan had been so desperate and felt he couldn't wait any longer, he had let go of her right wrist to masturbate. Sean was still thrusting and thrusting, and biting her neck, still with his right hand pressed so hard over her mouth she thought she might suffocate. At first, she tried to push him away with her free right arm, then Stan, realising that he had let her wrist go, tried to crush the flailing limb against the wall with his body weight. Kitty was desperate and, able just to move her lower arm and wrist, she felt the weight of Sean's jacket pocket and reached inside…

Two gunshots rang out in the night… one close by, another further away.

As Jimmy and John rounded the corner into the alleyway, they witnessed a man fall to the ground, as another stood by, completely stunned, his trousers around his ankles. Kitty was sliding down the wall, crying, dishevelled and bruised.

Vi heard the noise a few streets away; she tore out of her kitchen, gripped by a mortal fear – John!

Stan was crying and stammering.

'I-i-t wa-s-s-n't me… i-it was 'er!'

Jimmy stared at the man on the ground, at the fatal gunshot wound to his chest, delivered at close range, and his shrivelled manhood on display to the world. He looked at Stan, in a similar state of dishevelment, and then at Kitty, her hair everywhere, her neck bitten, her wrists blue with bruises. Jimmy could see the slain man was Rafferty. He looked at Stan, and he shouted in very angry tones:

'I know what you were about! You evil man. And your friend here! Unless you want to swing, I suggest you get your despicable self out of the road, now!'

Stan was bending, desperately tugging at his trousers, trying to get them up. Jimmy used the opportunity to kick him really hard in the bare backside, which sent him flying.

'And I know who you are, Stan! Your dirty, dirty man! Don't you ever breathe a word to a living soul about any of this or I swear I will damn you to hell… you got that? By now, Stan was trying to get to his feet, still trying to pull his trousers up, apologising, swearing that he would never speak to anyone. He saw nothing. No one would ever know. He sheepishly looked at John, he knew John Connolly had him marked out, too.

Just at that moment, Vi appeared, very relieved to see John. She could make out Kitty and went to run forward, but John held her fast.

'Wait, Vi… just while we get her away… there's things you shouldn't see. You need to get her home and fast! You never saw a thing, you were never here.'

Over on the railway embankment, Fanny was standing with her knife still in her hand. She was in shock. A

238

man lay on the track. A foul, stinking man, a drunk. He had been shot in the head. A little way from him, on the grass, stood Suie with her back to her sister. Fanny could see she was holding a gun and just standing there, staring; then she dropped the gun, but remained motionless. Fanny put the knife back into her belt and made her way down the embankment. Suie didn't turn around, just stared, looking at the red oozing fluid and all else that had flown from his skull. Fanny placed her arm around her younger sister's shoulders.

'Are yer alright, love?'

'Yeah...' came the quiet reply. 'He dain't touch me... I dain't let him touch me... I knew not to, like...'

'It's over, Suie. We gotta get out of here. But first...' Fanny picked up the gun and lobbed it as hard as she could into the thick undergrowth of the railway embankment. It disappeared into a mass of brambles, as the clouds parted and the full moon shone down on Alf's corpse, face down on the tracks.

'Come on, Suie, the night train will see to him... That's justice!'

The next day, two dead men were found, one who had obviously been in the act of rape. An Irishman, so some people said.

'No... no one knows of him in the quarter... he was new to these parts...'

Even Mick the Irish landlord – who had taken a dislike to Sean and his close association with Stan – denied all knowledge; hardly seen him, didn't even know his name.

Word had gone around the streets that he had raped Kitty, and someone else might have been involved; there was speculation as to the identity of the second man, and Stan found himself ostracised in the quarter within days, and ended up heading off to Cradley Heath.

But when talking to all those in charge, the authorities and the magistrates, no one had any information; justice had been done!

The second corpse, they all knew. He was a well-known drunk, a very violent man.

'Killed his wife, don't you know, so I have been told... and did for his little lad a month or so ago. Should you ask the family about it? No, I wouldn't if I were you, he put them through enough. He's just a drunk wandered onto the line, got hit by a train. I heard his head was so mangled, they couldn't really tell whose ugly mug it was, we all just knew from the stink of him – Alf Tulloch – he won't be missed, mate, I wouldn't bother.'

Epilogue

The circle

It was 21 November, 1863. It was a Saturday morning, with an unusually bright-blue sky. A few gathered on the steps of St Chad's Cathedral, after a personal service of marriage. Two small groups had formed: one with the radiant bride, in her new indigo dress, every inch the lady; the other with the dashingly handsome John Connolly – no workman's clothes for him on this glorious day, he had invested in a suit for the first time in his life. As Jimmy had insisted, they were going to do business now and he must look the part, besides which, he was marrying the most beautiful girl in the world; he had to do her proud.

Fanny was almost tearful.

'I ain't half going to miss yer, Vi… what am I goin' to do without me old mate?'

'Oh, please don't, Fanny, I already feel terrible… it's just such a good opportunity.'

'I'm only messin' with you, Vi. Yer know, there are such good people round 'ere. I dain't know how we'd have got through the last few months since Teddy passed without them… dain't yer eva' forget your roots.'

'You make it sound like I will never see you again! Just give us a few months to sort out somewhere to live, then you come over. Susan and Jimmy are going next week and they are going to help us out. It will be so much easier with Ma now.' She paused. 'Will you thank Kitty for walking them back. Ma got a bit confused, she gets scared. How is Kitty… with everything?'

'Oh, you know our Kitty, as tough as old boots. I dain't think she'll ever trust another bloke again though. Sometimes I think I will have more chance of gettin' hitched than 'er. She says she wants nothing to do with 'em. It will take her some time, I'm sure, before she gets it all sorted in

241

'er head.' She looked around at the street, and then turned back to Vi.

'Yer know, every day our Suie goes and picks flowers off the railway. Well, now it's more grass and brambles cos its winter, like. Every day, the two of 'em, Kitty and Suie, go to our Teddy's grave. I think it's some sort a healin' thing. I dain't understand it meself, but if it helps them... Suie still won't talk about any of it. She won't say, so I dain't ask.'

Jimmy pulled John slightly to one side.

'Oh! she looks stunning, Johnny boy! You came up with a real gem there! Susan has really taken to her.'

'Yes, she's my angel.' He paused. 'Sometimes, with the way it all worked out so quickly, I wonder if my ma had to pass to make it all possible... like she's my guardian angel, making it all right up in heaven. The only thing that happened when she was still alive was that commission from Joseph. I really have to go and thank him, you know, before we leave.'

'Now, John, you know I don't hold with all that stuff. I am a rationalist, though Susan keeps pressing me to take the religion. Seems Vi took to it like a duck to water.' They both laughed. Jimmy continued:

'You obviously haven't heard about Joseph, have you?' John looked confused. Jimmy explained what he knew.

'Of course, you wouldn't have, not with all the goings on. His good lady, she had a little boy – they called him Joseph. Anyway, she took the childbirth fever and died a week later.'

'Oh, my goodness! We must go and see him.'

'By all accounts, John, he is so grief-stricken he has cut himself off from the world and is refusing to see anyone except close family. It will do you no good trying. Once we are over the water write him a letter, see what comes of it.'

'I'm no good at writing and reading, Jimmy, you know that.'

'Well, you tell Susan what you want to say and let her write it… I am sure he would be touched. But not now. Leave it all be.'

They both stood in deep reflection. Jimmy with thoughts of Joseph and his sadness, and John wishing his ma could have lived to see this day. It was John who broke the silent melancholia.

'I have got a man for the bench here, he is going to pay reasonable money. He likes it because he has an apprentice. I am sure Zac would be happy to know that both benches will be put to good use again. It will give us a little more, too.' He nodded in Vi's direction, and she smiled back at him. 'We will probably be over just before Christmas. We will all be able to see the new year in and have a fresh start together.'

'Aye, that will be a party alright… me with me Irish friend John Connolly, I'm sure we'll have a right good craic.'

The small party strolled back through the quarter, the memories of the procession for Teddy's funeral still uppermost in John's mind; for Vi, it was their first meetings. The grumpy offhand Irishman that stole her heart away. She had linked her left arm through his right arm, and her beautiful wedding ring sparkled in the afternoon sunlight; the purple amethysts almost burned with a red heat in their hearts, the peridots were an intense green and yellow. For a moment she was extremely wistful. She was very excited about a new start and a new life, but she knew she would miss this place so much. Despite all of the trauma and tragedy of recent times, and the terrible, terrible things that had occurred, it was still her home; the only home that she had ever known. She wouldn't miss the unremitting day-to-day grind of the factory, or that bully of a foreman, but she would miss the banter and chatter of her work mates, and Fanny, her closest friend: she was almost a sister to her.

As they walked back through the quarter people came out of their houses to wish them well and make their congratulations. John hardly knew anybody and was taken by complete surprise that these people knew him! Vi was known to many, and not just nodding acquaintances. It was just the way it was; it was a village in the middle of a busy city, right in the middle of it all but completely distinct from all else around it. Vi thought to herself how much it was the people that made this place so special; without those hard-working inhabitants – some had been there for three generations – the place would not be the same. She stopped momentarily outside the court where Fanny lived – a small party had been organised. She stood looking up at John, questioningly, he was concerned by her sudden change of mood.

'Are you alright, Violet?' he asked compassionately.

'John… we will come back to visit won't we? Not all the time… just sometimes.'

'Of course we will, my love… after all this will always be your home.'

With that, they turned into the court to join the others.

13275417R00143

Printed in Great Britain
by Amazon